# A Treasure Conspiracy

### A Will and Betsy Black Adventure

**ABSOLUTELY AMAZING eBOOKS**

Habent Sua Fata Libelli

**ABSOLUTELY AMAZING eBOOKS**

Manhanset House
Shelter Island Hts., New York 11965-0342

bricktower@aol.com • tech@absolutelyamazingebooks.com
• absolutelyamazingebooks.com

**Library of Congress Cataloging-in-Publication Data**
Beckwith, David
A Treasure Conspiracy
p. cm.

1. FICTION / Mystery & Detective / Cozy / General. 2. FICTION / Mystery
& Detective / Amateur Sleuth.
3. FICTION / Mystery & Detective / Women Sleuths.
Fiction, I. Title.
ISBN: 978-1-955036-30-6, Trade Paper

December 2021

# A Treasure Conspiracy

A Will and Betsy Black Adventure

## DAVID BECKWITH

ABSOLUTELY AMAZING eBOOKS

# Acknowledgments

Once more, my eternal thanks to my wife, Laura, for her tireless and tough editing. And a special thanks to my friend and publisher, Shirrel Rhoades, for taking a chance with me.

```
JAMAICAN
SINE PAITING
```

# Chapter 1

It was a lazy spring day in Accompong, Jamaica. Colonel Ferron Winter, the longtime elected leader of Jamaica's Accompong Maroon people, sat alone in his mountain yard drinking his morning tea as he listened to the sounds of nature. The air still smelled fresh from a rain earlier in the morning.

Despite being the most powerful man in Accompong, The Colonel's home was simple and unpretentious – a small, shotgun, concrete structure with a rusted tin roof. The multi-colored flowerbeds featuring native plants were neat and had been recently weeded. He sat in his front yard under a massive blooming Poinciana tree on a semi-circular concrete bench with his elbows propped on the round, chipped concrete table before him, lost in thought as he reexamined the photos in the funeral program in front of him.

The Maroons, formerly escaped British slaves, had been an almost invisible, self-governing nation-within-a-nation in Jamaica since 1739 when the frustrated British admitted defeat by signing the Kindah Treaty. This landmark treaty granted the Maroons autonomy and freedom after British efforts to defeat these fierce guerrilla warriors continuously failed during an eighty-year war.

Colonel Winter was an unpretentious, dark-skinned, older, slender, balding man. His physique was not one cultivated in a gymnasium but one which nevertheless gave him a fit, healthy look. When he walked, his posture was erect and confident without being swaggering or outwardly boastful. He was always clean-shaven, and his wife kept his hair neatly cut. While he did not seem well-heeled by any means, even as he sat he had a rigid, military-like presence that sent a silent message that he was very comfortable with being who he was and was a person who was accustomed to being a decision maker and running things. His tasteful, clean clothing being well-worn but not shabby. While Colonel Winter spoke patois fluently and would do so if a situation dictated its use, he preferred using proper, precise English whenever possible.

A barefoot man who was wearing a faded t-shirt and worn checked shorts trudged slowly by The Colonel's house.

"Gud mawnin," he said respectfully.

"Mawnin to yu too," The Colonel said. "Yu gud, Leonard?"

"Everything criss (okay). Mi hat a back mi this mawning (my back's hurting this morning). Arthritis," the man said and kept walking.

As he looked at her smiling portrait picture on the green-tinted funeral program, The Colonel's thoughts turned back to the memorial service he had attended yesterday for longtime Accompong resident Ruby Drain. Ruby had lived a long, full life and had always been an asset to their community. He had been sure her lineage went back to the days of the Maroon wars. The speaker at her funeral service the day before had confirmed this fact.

Accompong, Jamaica is a historical Maroon village located in the Cockpit Country hills of St. Elizabeth Parish. Its name had resulted from the British bastardization of the Akan word Acheampong. The area's rugged terrain had enabled the runaway slaves, who were known as Maroons, and the indigenous Taino to establish a fortified stronghold during the seventeenth century. They defended this home to maintain their independence, first from the Spanish and then later the British once the Jamaican colony changed hands. After a protracted war, the people won their freedom and the right to self-government. In 1739 these rights were codified when the Maroons signed a treaty with the British known as the Kindah Treaty, awarding them 1,500 acres between their strongholds of Trelawny Town and Accompong. Since Jamaica had gained its independence in 1962, it had continued to recognize the Maroons' indigenous turf rights. Accompong's "mayor" and the leader of the Maroon Council is called the "Colonel-in-Chief." For many years, the aging Ferron Winter had served as Accompong's Colonel.

As Colonel Winter contemplated going back in his house for a second cup of tea, he heard a familiar voice behind him.

"Howdeedo."

Colonel Winter looked up and saw the dreadlocked Mikey Mo Mullens stride in from the main street.

"Mi nice and yu, Chicken?" The Colonel responded, calling Mikey Mo by his street name.

"Just came from an interesting meeting," Mikey Mo said, switching to flawless English. "Ruby Drain's daughter, Isabel, asked me to pick up something her mother had left for you."

He handed Colonel Winter an old, dark, calabash gourd and an ancient-looking book. The cover was scuffed, and the pages were old and fragile.

Calabash bottle gourds are common in Jamaica. They originated in Africa and were one of the earliest plants cultivated in the tropical new world. One variety grows on a vine and when young is often used as a vegetable. Another variety grows from a tree. Mature gourds are dried and can be used as a bottle, a utensil, or a pipe for smoking ganja or tobacco. They are known for their durability. Many locals carve designs on dried, hollowed-out calabashes and sell them to tourists as souvenirs. The green gourds turn a golden brown and become very durable as they harden with age.

Mikey Mo was a tall, thin, dark man with dreadlocks. He was now in his early thirties. Some people thought he looked like a black Ichabod Crane. He had an endearing toothy, infectious smile and playful, twinkling eyes. Many locals called him by his street name "Chicken." It had been awarded to him as a child because of his long, skinny neck.

To the world, Mikey Mo was a carefree Rasta DJ and always-ready-to-party-animal. To a smaller group of people, Mikey Mo was reputedly the person who The Colonel had let Maroon movers and shakers know he was supporting to succeed him as the next Colonel whenever he chose to retire. Mikey Mo had been surreptitiously handling sensitive affairs for The Colonel for some time, and The Colonel had been teaching him what he would need to know if he were to be effective as the incoming Colonel.

"What's this?" The Colonel asked.

Mikey Mo shrugged. "She just said Ruby had insisted it was important to give it to you."

The Colonel held the calabash and rotated it so he could examine all sides. On one side he saw a crude carving which almost looked like a prehistoric face. The other side contained an etched inscription of seemingly meaningless numbers.

"Have you examined this gourd?" he asked Mikey Mo and then read the numbers aloud. "1 - 6 – 38."

"Yes. It didn't mean anything to me," Mikey Mo said.

"January 6, 1738, was the date Captain Cudjoe first negotiated the peace treaty with the British," Winter reminded him.

"It really *is* old."

The Colonel then looked at the worn, faded book. It appeared to be written in Spanish. It was handwritten. In it was a bookmark with "comb 1 - 6 - 38" written on it.

"Here are those same numbers again," Colonel Winter commented.

Mikey Mo shrugged. The Colonel opened the cover on the book.

"There's a date in the front – 1740."

"That's shortly after the end of the First Maroon War. Do you think the book has some historical significance?"

"I need to find out. Part of my responsibility as The Colonel is to preserve documents and artifacts pertinent to Maroon history. I'll need help translating this book," The Colonel said. "Do we have anyone in Accompong fluent in Spanish?"

"I'm told there's a school-teacher in Mona who is part Cuban – her great grandmother was from Trelawny Town."

"Get her contact information and bring it back to me."

"Will do."

"Did you pass on our respects to Ruby Drain's daughter?" Colonel Winter asked.

"Of course. I didn't stay long though since it was obvious she was still in mourning for her mother. She's not local. I'm told she lives in England. I'm sure she's got her plate full putting her mother's affairs in order while she's here. Isabel said Ruby had made her promise that you would be given these items as soon as possible after her death and had told her you would know the appropriate way to deal with them."

"Whatever that means," said The Colonel.

"Yep, whatever that means," Mikey Mo said. "The book's probably just a stale historical document – interesting to an academic but otherwise of little importance. But you never know."

Mikey Mo rose to leave.

"Likkle more (see you later)," he said as he left.

"Walk good (take care)," The Colonel answered.

```
+---------------------------------+
|                                 |
|      The  CASBA                 |
|                                 |
|      CLOTHES CLINC              |
|                                 |
|      RENOVATING DUN            |
|                                 |
|      TO ALL GARMINTS            |
|                                 |
+---------------------------------+
```

# Chapter 2

Within a few hours, Mikey Mo brought The Colonel the contact information for a Juanita Halliburton-James. The doctor was an assistant professor at the University of the West Indies campus in Mona, a community in the Kingston area. The Colonel contacted her and arranged for her to read the Spanish diary. She called him after studying it and arranged a meeting at his home in Accompong to report her findings.

Colonel Winter was waiting when she arrived. Juanita Halliburton-James appeared to be in her thirties. With her short, curly hair, The Colonel could definitely see the Cuban portion of her heritage in both her light skin tone and in her features. Her oval face had large, expressive brown eyes and naturally bushy eyebrows. She wore hoop earrings that almost reached her shoulders, paired with an above-the-knee print dress. Strappy sandals completed her look. A simple gold wedding band was on her ring finger. Brightly painted beaded African bracelets in alternating colors adorned each arm.

After a brief introduction, Colonel Winter invited her to sit at the concrete table in his front yard and went into the house to get his wife to brew tea for both of them. Within minutes, he returned with a pen and pad so he could take notes on their meeting. Before they began, Juanita asked if she could use his toilet. Colonel Winter got his wife to show the professor to the house's simple bathroom. The professor used this as an opportunity to place in Colonel Winter's house the listening devices that drug kingpin Dudus Coke had provided her with. Having accomplished this mission, she returned to the yard to make small talk, sip tea, and begin their business meeting.

"Colonel Winter, this is a very interesting diary. May I ask where you obtained it?"

"It was given to me by the daughter of a local citizen who recently died," The Colonel explained. "She told an associate of mine that her mother wished me to have it. She did not say why. I was hoping your translation would shed some light on this matter."

"This is the diary of Francisco Guiral," Juanita began. "He was the captain of a Spanish galleon named the Genovesa that was at the time he wrote it carrying several tons of gold and silver back to Spain. It sank in 1740 off Jamaica and has never been found. It is thought that it sank in the Pedro Banks about 100 miles southwest of Kingston."

"I'm familiar with the Pedro Banks," The Colonel said. "Some people call them 'La Vibora' or 'The Viper' because they are a fang-like reef which has been extremely treacherous for shipping."

"That is correct. Some archaeologists estimate as many as 300 ships have sunk there."

"Sounds like another Bermuda Triangle."

"A good comparison," Juanita said. "Let me continue. Much of this diary is concerned with routine day-to-day shipboard affairs. In fact, it paints a stunning picture of what it was like to serve aboard a seventeenth century galleon, but I'm sure this is not the part that will be of primary interest to you. Indulge me while I give you some historical background information on this period."

She paused to sip her tea.

"In 1740, the Spanish and the British were at war. This war has been called the War of Jenkins' Ear. The Royal Navy Commander of Britain's Jamaica Station was Vice Admiral Edward Vernon. In 1740 he was successful in capturing Porto Bello, one of Spain's colonial possessions. According to the diary, Guiral was uneasy about the possibility that his ship would have a confrontation with Vernon."

"Why is his name familiar to me?" The Colonel asked.

"If you are a history buff, there could be two reasons. One reason is that his nickname was 'Old Grog'. He instituted the policy of giving each British seaman a daily ration of watered-down rum which came to be known as grog. The name came from the fact that Admiral Vernon always wore coats made from grogram cloth."

"The rum tradition persisted until modern times," Winter commented.

Juanita nodded and said, "Yes, it did. The second reason he is remembered is that the American President George Washington named his home Mount Vernon as a tribute to the Admiral after his brother served under Vernon."

"Interesting," Winter said. "So, if the Genovesa sank, how did Guirel's diary come to be in the hands of a modern Maroon towns-person?"

"That I don't know. But one explanation for it had to be that a few days before the ship sank, Guirel had a second concern arise – a possible pending tropical storm. To hedge his bets, according to his diary he offloaded part of his cargo in Jamaica with the intention of recovering it later. And also, according to his diary, he commandeered some local slaves as forced labor to hide the treasure somewhere in Jamaica."

"Those were turbulent times in Jamaica," Colonel Winter said. "In 1838 and 1839 the Maroons outlasted the British and convinced them to finalize treaties recognizing the Maroons as a sovereign free nation and freeing them from slavery, thus ending the First Maroon War. Despite the cessation of fighting, it was an uneasy peace."

"Especially since slavery in other parts of Jamaica continued to exist," Juanita said. "We all remember Tacky's Revolt in 1760."

"Definitely," The Colonel agreed. "Maroons weren't supposed to recruit slaves and were required to aid the slave masters in capturing runaway slaves."

"It may have been a short conflict, but it was extremely bloody. The British almost couldn't re-establish order afterwards. Some say it was the biggest shock that the British colonial empire suffered until the American Revolution."

"So, I repeat. How did the diary remain in Jamaica?" The Colonel asked. Why didn't it go down with the ship? And why did it end up in the hands of Ruby Drain's family?"

"I do not know and can't tell from this document," Juanita said. "Guirel obviously left it here while he was ashore hiding his cargo."

"Does the diary tell us where Guirel hid the treasure?"

"No. It doesn't tell us that either."

"It's a big country," Colonel Winter observed. "And there's a lot of limestone caves in the Cockpit Country. That's why the Maroons' guerilla warfare tactics succeeded in defeating the British. Do we know what the treasure is worth?"

"The entire ship's cargo has been estimated to be about $600 million in today's dollars," Juanita said. "What percentage Guirel removed and hid on shore we have no way of knowing. His diary is not that specific, but it seems to imply that it was somewhere in the Cockpit Country."

"My people would certainly benefit from a windfall of even a fraction of that amount," The Colonel said. "I need to give this matter some thought. Thank you for translating it for me. What do I owe you for your work?"

"The academic pursuit was reward enough."

"Then may I invite you to stay for lunch?"

"That would be delightful," Juanita said.

```
PIGS AND POULTRY
FEEDS. FERTILIZER
CEMENT AND NAILS
ETC.
SOLD HERE
```

# Chapter 3

Academic pursuit may have been one motivating factor in Juanita Halliburton-James' generosity with Colonel Winter, but she was not immune from the lure of possibly gaining a share of $600 million, even if it was only a small share. Even 1% was $6 million. A $6 million finder's fee would certainly set her up for life, and if she didn't get it because no treasure was ever found, she'd be no worse off than she was right now. After all, she reasoned, a girl's got to look after herself. Juanita had distanced herself from some of the more unsavory members of her family, but she decided maybe now was the time to reestablish some neglected family ties who could help her get her share of this windfall. She knew her second cousin, Harry McLeon, aka Harry Dog, was well connected. She decided to give him a call.

Even though Harry Dog did not have an official title, he was considered by members of the Shower Posse to be one of Dudus Coke's inner circle. He was a naturally violent, unforgiving man with a long memory who few posse members would risk opposing. The legend enhancing Harry's reputation was that he had reputedly once executed some family members who had crossed him. He did nothing to dispel that myth. Harry Dog was often Dudus' go-to man when he wanted to be sure something got done precisely.

After securing Harry's verbal promise for a finder's fee, Juanita shared the story of the Genovesa with him. Harry Dog contained his excitement on the surface but in reality, he saw Dr. Halliburton-James' disclosure to be a godsend. He had not hesitated to over-exceeded his authority by making this promise because he was so sure Dudus Coke would later ratify his decision. But if Dudus decided otherwise, he knew he could always easily dispose of Halliburton-James if she became a thorn in his side.

*If this works out, I will secure my position of being Dudus' most trusted adviser*, he thought.

The "Dudus" Harry was referring to was Dudus Coke, the notorious cocaine trafficking kingpin of the Shower Posse. Christopher "Dudus" Coke, a second-generation gang leader, was a Jamaican legend. He was considered almost a "Robin Hood" by many locals and called "The President". He was a vicious and merciless extortionist whose future had been launched when his father, street name "Jim Brown", had contracted the posse's talents to the Jamaica Labour Party to kill or maim its enemies to insure election results. Upon his father's death in prison, the then 23-year-old Dudus had assumed command of the posse. He had evolved into a community benefactor who paid school fees for and helped single mothers raise their children, promoted young entertainers' careers, and resolved disputes to keep peace in local communities.

Wise leaders of other gangs often catered to and answered to him if they wanted to insure their own safety. Coke's poisonous tentacles extended into many levels of Jamaican government, and he had frequently received many millions of dollars of rigged contract awards over the years.

Jamaican gangs are called posses because of Jamaicans' enamorment with American western movies. The Shower Posse's home has always been the slum project Tivoli Gardens in Kingston, but its tentacles have reached to such far-flung areas as New York, New Orleans, New Jersey, Pennsylvania, and Florida. The Shower Posse's name came from its reputation of showering its enemies with bullets. Whereas in the early 1970's, posses' primary revenue came from helping political parties get the "right" vote in elections, modern posses had now diversified into such crimes as drug and arms trafficking, bribery, racketeering, and murder.

Harry Dog was no great innovator. His latest scheme had been derived from one that his personal accountant, Wesley "Weasely" Lineitem, had told him about. It had already been quite successfully implemented by El Chapo Guzman of the Mexican Sinoloa Cartel. Lineitem was not a Shower Posse member, but he had told Harry on multiple occasions he would like to meet Dudus and forge a possible business relationship. Lineitem was also a certified tax attorney. Harry didn't trust himself to adequately explain a plan of this complexity to Dudus. He decided instead to set up a confidential three-way meeting and include Weasely. Then he could let Weasely do the bulk of the explaining.

Harry Dog met with Dudus at his Tivoli Gardens office. He first gave Dudus an overview of Genovesa treasure legend. As he expected, Dudus showed some interest.

"I have a plan that will make a potentially sweet situation much sweeter. It will be a worthwhile investment of your time to meet my own personal accountant and attorney."

After briefing Weasely on his objectives, Harry set up a meeting at Weasely's office in Kingston.

Harry and Dudus arrived and were immediately shown to Weasely's conference room. Dudus could immediately see why this man's street name was Weasely. He reminded Dudus of a rodent or a mongoose. His short-haired head perched on the top of a long neck that protruded from an elongated, tubular, yet still muscular-looking body mounted atop short, squatty legs. Despite his attempts to smile behind wire-rimmed glasses, his intelligent, piercing eyes had a devious look, like he was a born, accomplished liar and a definite carnivore. Dudus got the immediate impression that Weasely was not one to muse very often about moral dilemmas.

*My kind of man - but a person I will definitely keep on a short leash — if I climb in bed with him.*

During a brief period of small talk designed to penetrate Dudus's defenses, Weasely showed himself very adept at handling himself on his feet.

With no further delays, the meeting got formally underway.

"Mr. Coke …," Weasely began.

"Mr. Lineitem, please feel free to call me Dudus. My friends and acquaintances do."

"Then with your permission, Dudus," Weasely continued, "the safe storage of money and the funding of investments surely must be ongoing challenges for your organization."

He paused and sipped his coffee as he waited for Dudus to either react or for him to ratify his opening statement. Dudus only stared at him in a deadpan manner, forcing Weasely to plow ahead with the reading he had hoped for.

"Greenbacks are physically impermanent. They are vulnerable to things like fire. They are also vulnerable to inflation, a phenomenon our government seems determined to create."

"I'm waiting for you to tell me something I don't already know," Dudus said and glanced at his watch.

"Let's say for the sake of argument you have $80 million. At the current 2% inflation rate, your $80 million will lose $1.6 million in purchasing power in just one year. Over twenty years it will lose a third of its value. And that's assuming inflation stays at a modest 2%."

"I am aware of that," Dudus said.

"But it doesn't have to be that way," Weasely said. "There is a solution – precious metals. Bullion is one financial instrument that requires no identification. It has no nationality and no records. It is tailor-made to solve your problem. Also, unlike paper money, bullion doesn't burn. And it's also great for storage. $80 million would be about 42,000 pounds. This could easily be buried at 15 or 20 different locations. Metals are one of the few assets you can own today that will give you complete privacy and anonymity."

"So what? Gold bullion has dropped in half from its peak a couple of years ago," Dudus said.

"But that was after soaring from about $250 an ounce over the previous eleven years. I have no doubt its prices will continue to be volatile. But the risk brought on by the volatility of gold pales when compared to the other alternatives. Harry tells me you have a real possibility of acquiring an extremely large amount of Spanish gold."

Dudus looked at Harry as if he shouldn't have been running his mouth out of school. Weasely saw the look and immediately jumped back in to reassure Dudus.

"Mr. President, I can assure you that my knowledge of this situation will never leave this office no matter what happens between us. You have my word."

"A man's life is worth no more to me than his word. I still don't see where this is leading," Dudus said.

"Let me go on. I will set up a refining company for melting scrap gold. I'll create a paper trail showing that my company is buying scrap gold for cash from multiple sources. In actuality the only source will be you. I will also set up a series of dummy corporations which will buy the cash gold from the refinery after it has been processed. In effect you will be buying back your own gold at market levels. I will take a 2% commission for processing the melt and handling the other details. Once the gold is melted down, it will be impossible to trace back to its origins. It will be up to you to find storage locations which do not require documentation. Then when you want money to spend or invest, you can cash out some of the gold. You will render it into legal cash, declare a capital gain on your tax return, and look to the world like a brilliant investor."

Dudus looked bored and reached into his pocket for a cigarette. Harry Dog immediately got out his lighter.

Dudus then said, "That's great assuming we find this cache of treasure that people have sought after for 400 years."

"True. But in the meantime, we can use this refinery for other purposes. Your agents can buy scrap jewelry from pawn shops or other sources with the cash you wish to conceal. My company will melt it down and resell it to you in a purely paper transaction, i.e. you still own untraceable gold which can be reconverted to legal cash at a later time."

"Sounds good, doesn't it Mr. President." Harry Dog interjected, seeking Dudus's approval.

Weasley again waited for Dudus' response. All he got was the same deadpan look. So, he continued.

"The gold doesn't have to be from the undiscovered treasure. The treasure just enhances the whole operation since the gold has resulted from a windfall find instead of having to have been purchased. Other than that, the process and results will be the same – clean cash. You will have converted hard-to-invest dollars into legal monies which can be spent anywhere by your having participated in something far less risky than the other alternatives you have available. I'd rather bury gold than bury cash any day, and gold is always liquid."

"I'll take your plan under advisement, Mr. Lineitem. Thank you for your time," Dudus said, abruptly concluding the meeting. "If I decide to proceed, Harry Dog will be in touch."

As they rode back to Tivoli Gardens in Harry Dog's king cab Nissan Frontier pickup, Dudus said, "I want you to pursue this Genovesa gold aggressively. What your friend, Mr. Lineitem, says seems to make sense. In the meantime, I will continue to mull over his strategy. My compliments, Harry. My first impression is that he seems like an intelligent man. I assume you do vouch for him, or you wouldn't have arranged this meeting, and I trust your judgment in people."

"Mr. President, I assure you I've done my homework. What he's saying makes sense."

"Whether I decide to employ Mr. Lineitem to execute his strategy or not, I want you to vigorously pursue finding the Genovesa gold. I am going to delegate this project to you. Use whatever resources and personnel we have available to accomplish your mission. You do not need to clear each and every action with me. If someone questions your authority, tell them I have given you discretion and that they are to follow your orders. You can report to me on a periodic basis. Harry, let me make this clear. I expect both accountability and results. If you produce, you have a very bright future with the Shower Posse. But if you let me down …."

"I appreciate your confidence. You'll see. I'll earn it. And let me say, I have been most satisfied with Lineitem. He's our kind of people," Harry Dog said. "And wouldn't you love to shaft Ferron Winter?"

"That's certainly an added incentive. That old bloodclaayt (fucker) cost me a lot of money on the Highway 2000 program. I'd like to return the favor."

"We'll get him this time, and you'll make lots of money doing it," Harry Dog said aloud, but silently he was having different thoughts.

*And while you're making money, sly old Harry Dog is gwan to mek coil (going to make a stack of money) as well, treasure or no treasure, on that one percent kickback Weasely promised me,* Harry Dog thought. *This is going to be sweet, but I need to get together with old Weasely again and see how he can use his 'paperwork magic' to set up accounts for my windfall money to be deposited that will not be able to be tracked back to me by either the authorities or Dudus. If this works, it could turn into my primary retirement fund.*

Harry had a very brief pang of guilt when he thought about Ferron Winter. It was fleeting however, coming and going from his brain almost before Harry realized he had had it. Ferron had been one of his mother's friends when she was a teenager. He certainly wasn't going to share this information with Dudus. There were many things best left unsaid, and potential conflicts of interest were one of them. When she was still alive, his mother had occasionally had nostalgia attacks about Ferron and what might have been. Apparently, they had had a Romeo-and-Juliet romance when she briefly dated Ferron before she met his father, Otis McLeon.

*Now there was a man. Otis taught mi how to survive on the streets.*

From what Harry could piece together, his mother's family thought Ferron and their daughter shouldn't carve out a future together since he was a backwards Maroon with little potential who would probably spend his life in Accompong. Her parents hoped she would eventually marry someone more in the mainstream of Jamaican life. The Winters were equally suspicious of her since she was a Maroon outsider.

*Just as well,* Harry thought. *Mi wouldn't have wanted to grow up as some back-a-bush butu (backwater hick) with few apachunitis (opportunities). After all,* women wanted a town man, not a sweaty mowly (stinky) bush butu.

He began to sing in his head the lyrics to Poser's popular Soca tune "Town Man".

*She like the town man; she love the town man*
*She want the town man; she say this man is mine*
*Mi de bloodclaayt (fucking) town man,* he said to himself.

16

```
┌─────────────────────────────┐
│                             │
│      WILKIE                 │
│                             │
│      GARAGE                 │
│                             │
│      BEET . OUT             │
│                             │
│      AND                    │
│                             │
│      WELDING                │
│                             │
└─────────────────────────────┘
```

## Chapter 4

By the time Mikey Mo stopped by Colonel Winter's house the following morning, The Colonel had decided on his next course of action. The Colonel gave him a synopsis of what he and Mrs. Halliburton-James had discussed. Mikey Mo sat and listened until The Colonel finished.

"Let's hope the treasure is hidden on our land," he observed. "Otherwise, we'll have to battle the Jamaican government as well as the Spanish government for it."

"I wouldn't rule that out anyway," The Colonel said. "Before Isabel Drain leaves town, would you introduce me to her? I would like to find out what more she knows about the diary Ruby instructed her to give to me."

"Of course. I do not have a cell phone number for her, but we can go to Ruby's house together. I'm sure Isabel'll be there since she said she has much to do to finalize her mother's affairs."

When they arrived at Ruby Drain's home, Isabel was bringing a box out onto the porch. The small, all-wood shotgun house was built on creosote posts about three feet above the ground. These posts became progressively shorter as they went towards the back of the house to compensate for the sloping yard. The front of the house had once been painted a bright electric blue that had now faded to a pastel blue and had peeled off in places; the side and back consisted of weathered unpainted planks. Red preformed concrete steps led up to the open front porch. The house had a partially rusted galvanized roof. There was an unpainted, free-standing outbuilding to one side. The front door and back windows were open to allow air flow. Isabel was dark, petite, and had short hair that had been left naturally curly. She was dressed in work clothes which were soaked through with perspiration. Mikey Mo made the introductions. She looked relieved that she had an excuse to take a break from her work.

"It's a pleasure to meet you," The Colonel said. "I thought a lot of your mother. I'm surprised we have never met."

"I was not raised in Jamaica," Isabel said. "Mi madda (my mother) emigrated to London where she met my father. I grew up there and still teach school there. After mi dada died, she returned to Jamaica, but England is the only home I've ever known."

"Sadly enough," The Colonel commented, "that is all too often the case with our bright young people. We educate them and someone else benefits. We lose too many of our youth because they find more opportunities abroad than we can offer them at home. But it is also common that Jamaicans wish to return to their homeland later in life. It is a dilemma Jamaica needs to solve if it wants to forge ahead."

"I'm certainly a case in point," she replied.

Let me begin by saying thank you for sending me the Spanish diary. Did you examine it before turning it over to me?"

"Not really. I gave it a cursory look."

"It's the diary of a seventeenth century Spanish sea captain," Colonel Winter said. "Do you know how it came to be in your mother's possession and what its significance is?"

"I only know it was a family heirloom – passed down for several generations." Isabel said. "She originally brought it to London with her from Jamaica."

"What about the calabash?"

"The same."

"There was a modern piece of paper in the journal that said "1 - 6 - 38." Do you know the significance of those numbers?" The Colonel asked.

"I really don't."

"It's also scratched onto the calabash," The Colonel added. "I think the inscription on the calabash was a modern addition while the design on the opposite side seems much older."

"Now that I think about it," Isabel said, "I found an index card in mi madda's papers which also had those numbers on it. Give me a second to flip through her file, and I think I can put my fingers on it. Oh yes, here it is."

She pulled out an index card that said "COMB. 1 - 6 - 38" and handed it to Colonel Winter. The Colonel showed it to Mikey Mo.

Mikey Mo commented, "Colonel, safe combinations have three numbers as a rule. Do you think the COMB might stand for combination?"

"Good thought, lad," The Colonel said. "Isabel, did your mother have a safe?"

"It's always possible. I know you don't have a crime problem here in Accompong, but she was robbed once in London, and after that she did become very security conscious. She bought a home safe there, but I haven't run across anything like that in this house so far."

"We would be very happy to help you search for one," Colonel Winter said. "Would you mind?"

"No, not at all. If something like that exists, I need to find it before I have to return to London," Isabel said.

Colonel Winter and Mikey Mo each began to search the house for signs of a home safe as Isabel continued to go through her mother's papers and pictures. They tapped on walls as well as the floor. They searched in and behind furniture as well as inside cabinets. Mikey

Mo checked to see if something were hidden in the refrigerator or freezer. Nothing turned up.

Isabel commented, "I really didn't expect you to find what you were looking for. I'm going to take a break. Would you join me in a cup of tea?"

"We would be delighted to," The Colonel said. "I'll just drink mine plain. Mikey Mo likes sugar in his."

"But what else would comb stand for?" Mikey Mo said as he accessed the internet via his smart phone to see if comb was an acronym for something else. It's got to be an abbreviation for a combination of some sort. The only other thing I see on Google is mathematical combinations."

Isabel brought each man a cup of tea and joined them at the kitchen table. They sipped their tea, each lost in a different thought.

Suddenly, Mikey Mo said, "Look around you. Do you see anything unusual?"

Both Isabel and Colonel Winter glanced around them, but neither detected what Mikey Mo was talking about.

"Look at that inside wall. See that return air conditioning vent," Mikey Mo said. "Why would Ruby have a vent in the wall if this house has neither central air conditioning nor heating?"

He snapped the plastic clips on the top corners and the vent fell open on its bottom hinge. A shallow wall safe that had been attached to two studs came into view.

"Dandimite (dynamite). Ku ya (look here)! Mikey Mo excitedly exclaimed. "Jus look ku pon dis. Mi mudda bwoy nuh bobo (just look at this. My mother's boy's no fool).

"Excellent – good work, lad, and I agree. Your mother raised a very intelligent son," The Colonel said. "Now let's see if 1 - 6 - 38 is the combination to it."

In less than a minute the hidden safe was open. Mikey Mo pulled out another book.

"May I see that?" Isabel asked. Mikey Mo handed it to her.

"This is my mother's handwriting," said Isabel. "I think it's a genealogy journal of some sort. It appears she's chronicling our family's history."

A Treasure Conspiracy

"Does she go back to 1740?" Colonel Winter asked.

Isabel began to flip through the book. She read a page out loud. The passage concerned Ned Phillips, a slave belonging to Thomas Partridge, the owner of the Potosi Estate.

"Does that name mean anything to you?" The Colonel asked.

"Yes. Ned Phillips was my great-great-great-great-great grandfather."

"And Potosi was one of the largest sugar estates in Trelawny," Mikey Mo said.

Isabel continued to read to herself. The Colonel and Mikey Mo waited to see what she would tell them next.

"It says here that Ned and two other slaves she calls John and Ben were kidnapped at gunpoint by a Spanish sea captain and made to unload most and possibly all of his valuable cargo he was taking back to Spain. They were then forced with three more slaves from the Wales Estate to carry this cargo inland and conceal it in the interior. One of the slaves knew some elementary Spanish and heard the seamen talking among themselves. They said the captain had ordered them to kill the slaves when their work was done."

"Bumbleclaat (holy shit), Mikey Mo uttered before he could catch himself.

The Colonel gave him a disapproving look for using profanity in Isabel's presence.

"Ned, John and Ben escaped into the forest, eluded their captors, and hid. They then tracked their captors and found the spot where the cargo was finally sequestered and then witnessed the murder of the other three slaves. After the Spanish left, they examined the cargo and found out it was gold and silver."

"That would have been the Genovesa," The Colonel said. "And the captain would have been Guiral. I can understand his paranoia since British Admiral Vernon was patrolling this area at that time, and since Spain and England were at war with each other."

"It goes on to say that Ned, John and Ben decided to record the location of the cargo so that if they were accused of being runaways when they returned to Potosi they could prove their story to their owner, Thomas Partridge, and escape punishment. To prevent any one of them from double-crossing the other two to save his own hide, they each recorded the cargo's location. Since each of them was illiterate and they had nothing to record the information on even if they could've written, they scratched a map on calabash gourds. Their check and balance was that each gourd only had part of the map. They also reasoned that a calabash was an item they could keep in their cabin and not have to explain to Partridge."

"So, the Genovesa treasure which salvagers have been looking for may not be in the Pedro Banks as thought, but instead it might be hidden on land in Jamaica," Mikey Mo said.

"Or at least a portion of it," Colonel Winter said. "But as we all know, Jamaica is a large, very remote island."

"With lots of places to hide something of value," Mikey Mo agreed.

"Would you trust me with your mother's journal?" The Colonel asked Isabel. "I promise to return it after I've had a chance to read it closer."

"Colonel Winter," Isabel said. "I'm a schoolteacher, not a treasure hunter or adventurer. My life is in London with my family and my students. Jamaica was my mother's home, not mine. I'll tell you what I'll do. I think the odds are very slim that you'll find this mythical treasure with this kind of sketchy information, and even if you did, you would have to fight the authorities for possibly a long, long time and spend who knows how much money to retain it. Mi mudda had a saying she used to tell me when I was a child. 'What sweet nanny goat a go run him belly' (the things that seem good to you now, can hurt you later)."

Both Mikey Mo and The Colonel smiled since each of them knew that proverb well.

"But if you *do* succeed," Isabel continued, "if you will promise me that the windfall will go for the benefit of the Maroon people and that my mother will get credit for the find, I'll let you have the diary."

"You have my word that we will build a community center in Accompong and name it for your mother," Colonel Winter said. "Will that do?"

"And we'll pay for you and your family to attend the dedication," he said as an afterthought.

'Shall we shake on it?" Isabel said.

Colonel Winter smiled, held out his hand, and said, "With no reservations."

TRESSPASSIES WILL BE
PROSECUTED BY THE ORDER
mRS LADY.THEWELL

# Chapter 5

When Colonel Winter returned home, his wife made him another cup of tea, and he took Ruby Drain's diary out under the Poinciana tree to read it for further information.

Ruby continued to mention the fate of slaves Ned, John, and Ben. Ned Phillips returned to Potosi to his wife, Delores, and his daughter, Hannah, and remained on the estate for the rest of his life. John later escaped and was given asylum by the Maroons. Recaptured and re-enslaved, he eventually died in Tacky's slave rebellion in 1760. Ben, the most literate of the three, was sold to a Marquis de Vaudreuil and taken to La Nouvelle-Orléans to be a house servant.

Thomas Partridge died, and Potosi was inherited by his son, Thomas Jr. In 1766, Hanover native John Tharp married Partridge's sister Elizabeth. He inherited the Potosi Estate. She bore Tharp four legitimate children before she died. After her death, Tharp had an illegitimate daughter, Mary Hyde Tharp, by the slave Hannah Phillips. Mary Hyde eventually evolved into being John Tharp's favorite child.

Colonel Winter carefully took notes as he read the diary. Some of the names were meaningful to him; others were not. He decided to mull over what he had learned before he attempted to form an action plan. He still didn't know any more than he had before about the location of the treasure, if it did indeed exist, but his gut told him this was far more than merely an old wives' tale. He called Mikey Mo to come by so he could tell him what he had learned.

That afternoon, Colonel Winter walked down to the local's hangout, Flashy's Place. It was a cross between a bar and a corner shop. Despite being no more than five meters square, it was one of Accompong's social hubs. The Colonel saw the usual domino game in progress on one rickety, leaning table. The table was loosely nailed to a tree and had rough planks for seats. Another group of men was watching an old muted television. Shaggy's hit song *In The Summertime* played on the juke box. Flashy as well as some of the regular customers greeted The Colonel.

"Whap'am, everything irie, Colonel? (what's up. Is everything okay, Colonel)" Flashy asked. "Red Stripe?"

"Everything's irie, Flashy. Thanks for asking. Yes, a cold Red Stripe would be nice."

Colonel Winter watched the men play dominoes and slowly sipped his beer. Mikey Mo entered.

"Your wife said I'd find you here," he said. "Mind if I join you for a brew?"

Flashy served one up.

"I've been researching what you told me this morning," Mikey Mo began. "First thing I learned was that the Drains and the Phillips are related. That's why Ruby was able to document the Ned Phillips story so well. I'm also sure that this is how she got the calabash she gave you. It has been passed down through the family."

"I had already guessed that," The Colonel said.

"It turns out that the slave John was more than a mere participant in Tacky's Rebellion. He wasn't on Tacky's side. He had been sold to the Esher Estate by that time and was the slave who sounded the alarm for his new master when Tacky and his men stole the munitions at Fort Haldane when he learned Tacky planned to use them to try to overrun Heywood and Esher Estates. This was the event that started the war. Tacky's men killed him in retribution."

"That clears that up," The Colonel said.

"Now the good news about John," Mikey Mo said. "He still has descendants in Jamaica today. I contacted the family posing as a historian. A calabash has been passed down through their family as well, and while they will not give it to us, they are willing to let us examine it and photograph it. They don't know its significance, and I didn't want to enlighten them."

"Great. Where do they live?"

"Montego Bay. I've made an appointment to drive up there tomorrow. Do you wish to join me?"

"No," said The Colonel. "If all you're going to do is take pictures of the calabash, and they have no knowledge of the gourd's significance, there's no reason for me to be there. My presence could only elevate its significance in their minds. I'll let you handle the matter."

"Consider it done," said Mikey Mo. "Now the third slave, Ben, the one who was sold to the Marquis de Vaudreuil in La Nouvelle-Orléans. It turns out that the Marquis is far from obscure. In fact, he was one of the pivotal figures in the history of the Louisiana Territory. His prominence simplified things greatly."

"Tell me more."

"The Marquis, Pierre de Rigaud, was governor of French Louisiana and was later named the last Governor-General of New France. His nephew, Louis-Phillipe de Vaudreuil, was second in command of the French naval units that supported the Americans during the American Revolution. He helped defeat the British fleet at the Battle of the Chesapeake during the siege of Yorktown."

"They were indeed prominent," The Colonel agreed.

"This should help trace slave Ben and discover if he has descendants who might have the third gourd."

"I sometimes envy the command you young people have of a computer and your ability to do in-depth research. I'm sure if Ben has a living relative, you will find him. Good Work."

"Thank you, sir. I'll show you the pictures of calabash number two when I return from Montego Bay."

```
┌─────────────────────────────────────────┐
│            WELCOME TO                      │
│             ELAINE'S                       │
│          THATCH ROOF PUB                   │
│         HOT & COLD DRINKS                  │
│     RUM PUNCH & OTHER FAVORITES            │
│     ALSO MUSIC TO WARM YOUR SOULS          │
│      POWER WATER ON WEEK-ENDS              │
└─────────────────────────────────────────┘
```

# Chapter 6

Betsy Black sat at the Hogfish Bar and Grill on Stock Island slowly sipping a Diet Coke. She was waiting for her husband, Will, and the Key West Police Chief, Walter Wanderley, to join her for lunch.

Betsy Black was the longstanding area president for WB Bank in Key West and now considered herself a bona fide freshwater Conch. She had originally been from Mobile, Alabama but she and Will were seasoned Floridians having lived in Vero Beach for a number of years. Betsy had met Wilson Black and married him in Mobile. Will, a native of the Mississippi Delta, had been a securities broker for Reynolds Smathers and Thompson, a New York Stock Exchange member firm, before being promoted to be resident manager of RS&T's Vero Beach branch. He currently managed RS&T's Key West office. Both the move to Vero Beach and the one to the Keys had turned out to be marvelous decisions.

Betsy sat at the picnic table on the pier at the Hogfish and watched the tarpon and angel fish swim almost an arm's length away. She was thinking about an incident that had happened that morning at the bank. As usual, it had involved one of Carson Crown's customers. Glad-handing, boisterous Carson, a multi-generational

Conch, was one of Betsy's most challenging and frustrating employees. Carson continually seemed to be involved in non-bank community activities which he justified and lauded as being his springboard to become what he termed to be a "super-banker." He was constantly dreaming and elephant hunting in lieu of working towards more down-to-earth, achievable goals. He was so preoccupied with his visions of grandeur he missed many of the more mundane opportunities around him. He constantly missed staff meetings and rarely listened when he did attend them. The accounts he did bring in were often marginal or high maintenance and all too often had to be serviced by other employees while Carson was out chasing rainbows.

That morning while Carson was attending a Rotary board meeting, Betsy had the occasion to talk for the first time to one of Carson's newer accounts.

The telephone conversation had begun with what seemed to be a reasonable premise – "I need to make a deposit, and I'm being told Carson's out of the bank."

"I can certainly help you with that," Betsy had responded. "What do you need to deposit, cash, check or money order?"

"I need to deposit money," the customer said.

"What type of money deposit? There are different ways to make a deposit depending on what you need to deposit."

"I need to deposit cash."

"I can find you our closest branch so you can make your deposit," Betsy had said.

"You mean I have to go somewhere to make a deposit?"

"Yes, if you are depositing cash."

"Well, can't I just deposit it over the phone?" the customer asked.

"No. I'm sorry. There is no way to deposit cash over the phone. I'm sure Carson will gladly explain this to you when he returns."

"You call yourself a full-service bank? What kind of service is this?" the customer asked before abruptly hanging up.

*Where does Carson find these people?* Betsy thought. *What planet do they live on?*

She looked up and saw Will coming through the tiki hut/bar center portion of the restaurant. Betsy waved at him to get his attention, and he smiled and waved back. As Will approached the table, he leaned over and bussed Betsy on the cheek.

"How is your day progressing so far, dear?" Will asked. After Will sat down and ordered a glass of tea, Betsy repeated the deposit phone conversation to him.

"Where does Carson find these people?" Will asked.

"You either must have ESP, or we've been together too long," Betsy said. "I just said those exact words myself."

She looked up again and saw Walter coming towards them. She waved to get Walter's attention. Walter had become the Blacks' close friend. Betsy had originally gotten to know him since WB was the primary bank for both the city of Key West and Monroe County. Will and Betsy had helped Walter on several occasions with criminal cases that were proving challenging to the police department. They had quickly learned to respect each other's judgment and intellect. Walter now had the habit of dropping over to Betsy's office at least once a week for coffee and often brought doughnuts for the staff. He and Betsy had both learned they could drop their guard and confide in or bounce ideas off each other with the assurance that their comments and observations would remain confidential.

"Sorry I'm running late," Walter said. "I had a last-minute matter I had to deal with along the way."

"So, you're having one of those days too," Betsy said and gave Walter a synopsis of the conversation she had had with the unsophisticated bank customer.

"Not that I'm trying to top that," Walter said, "but my stop on the way over here was equally abnormal. I was called by a motel in New Town. After a guest checked out of the motel today, housekeeping went to clean the room and turned on the ceiling fan. The departed guest had poured ketchup and mustard on the fan blades and left the fan speed on high. When she turned the fan on, it redecorated the room with mustard and ketchup from one end to the other. The maid fainted thinking the red was blood."

"So, what will you do?" Will asked.

"Try to find the guest and make him responsible," Walter said. "And this might not be easy. The guest was from way up north. We'll see what happens."

"Always something," Betsy commented.

"Yeah, that's my second oddball situation this week," Walter said, "and I've still got four more days to go. An incident which hasn't made the paper yet was a woman who caused a car wreck while crossing North Roosevelt Boulevard. She was wearing a black one-piece bathing suit and had pulled the top down to her waist. She stood in the middle of the crosswalk and tried to flag people down to bum a cigarette. When they wouldn't stop or if they told her they didn't have one, she cursed and gave them the finger. One guy stomped on his brakes to cuss her back and got rear-ended."

"Surely she was drunk," Betsy said.

"Oh, yeah," Walter said. "She reeked of alcohol. The paramedics got there first. She told them she was running from someone who had been beating her, but they couldn't find any bruises on her."

"Another tourist?" Will asked.

Walter nodded and said, "I sometimes think my divine maker put me on this earth primarily to babysit delusional or drunken grownups."

The waitress came by and took their orders. Will got hogfish sliders, Betsy a Cobb salad, and Walter ordered fish tacos. As they were waiting for their food, Betsy's cell phone rang.

"God, please don't let this be Carson," she said. "Hello. ... Mikey Mo? ... My God ... You're the last person on earth I expected to hear from today."

She covered the phone and looked at Will. "Mikey Mo Mullins from Jamaica," she said.

"Mikey Mo," Betsy continued. "Gud mawning (good morning). Great to hear from you. Is everything all right? ... Colonel Winter would like to meet with us at our earliest convenience? Is he OK? ... The Colonel is paying for our airline tickets? Mikey, you're beginning to worry me. Are you sure everything's all right? What's it all about? ... You can't discuss it over the phone? ... But he says it's important? And we won't have to stay long? Hold on, Will's right here."

Betsy covered the phone and glanced over at her husband.

Will said, "Tell him that we'll try to rearrange our schedules. I can break loose for a few days if it's that important. See if we can stay at Sundance. Will Henry pick us up at the airport?"

Betsy got back on the phone with Mikey Mo. "Will says he thinks we can work something out. Can we stay at Sundance? Will Henry be picking us up? He won't? … Colonel Winter wants to keep this meeting confidential for the time being? And you'll be picking us up instead? Please tell me everything's all right. Do you promise? We'll be back to you. Yuh walk gud (take care). Wi luv yuh (we love you) too."

Betsy hung up and said, "What in the world could that be all about? Colonel Winter's never asked us to make a special trip to Jamaica before."

Walter gave her a puzzled look.

"Colonel Winter is the leader of the Accompong Maroons," Betsy explained. "He's not a foolish old man who takes things lightly. This must be important. Will and I owe him a lot. My Jamaican assignment for WB Bank would not have been successful without The Colonel's assistance. In fact, Will and I might well have been killed down there without his and the Maroon's intervention. Mikey Mo is his top lieutenant and will probably be the next Colonel."

"I remember you were close to being in over your head while you were there," Walter said. "If you'll remember, I warned you at the time about the viciousness of the Jamaican underworld."

"Colonel Winter made us honorary Maroons before we left," Will said. "He pledged to help and protect us going forward, and we promised him the same thing. I really didn't expect him to ever need our help. He can pretty well handle most situations, but if he needs us, I'll do whatever I can for him."

"So will I," Betsy agreed. "He went the distance for us when we needed him – even before we knew we needed him, and he was both a father and a protector to us."

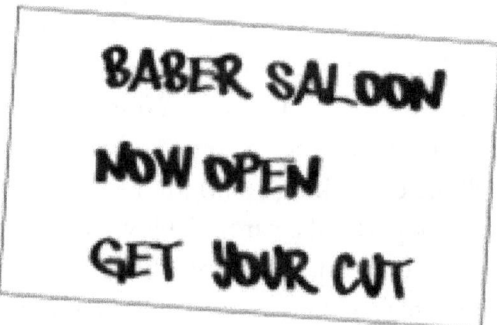

# Chapter 7

"Ladies and gentlemen, welcome to Sangster International Airport. Local time is 10:56 and the temperature is 29 degrees Centigrade or 84 degrees Fahrenheit.

"For your safety and comfort, please remain seated with your seat belt fastened until the Captain turns off the Fasten Seat Belt sign. This will indicate that the plane is no longer in service and that it is safe for you to move about the cabin."

Will was listening to the singer Half Pint's *Welcome* on the airline-provided headphones when the announcement came on. He handed the headphones back to the passing flight attendant in preparation for landing.

The flight attendant on the jet PA system continued.

"On behalf of Air Jamaica and the entire crew, I'd like to thank you for joining us on this trip, and we are looking forward to seeing you on board again in the near future. For you first time visitors, 'Welcome to paradise.' For you returning visitors, 'welcome home.' Have an irie stay."

"Well, we're back," Will told Betsy.

"I *do* feel like I'm coming home."

"Look across the runway at the mounds of dirt. Probably the same ones that were there the last time we were here."

"I'm sure they have plans to get a bobcat and move them mañana."

"Yep. We're back on island time."

Will and Betsy crossed the tarmac and entered the terminal. Despite the long queue, it didn't take long to clear the "nothing to declare" line. When they emerged, Mikey Mo was waiting. He was wearing a green and yellow Usain Bolt t-shirt.

"Welcome to Jamdown (Jamaica), mi bredda and sistah," he said with a huge grin on his face. "Everyting criss on flight (did you have a good flight)?"

"Everything is everything (all is well)," Will responded.

Mikey Mo's grin grew.

"Boy, are you a sight for sore eyes," Will said as Mikey Mo hugged each of them in turn.

"Luggage?"

"Everything we have is right here," Will said, patting their carry-ons.

They walked across the parking lot to Mikey Mo's dirty, white, right-hand-drive 2003 Toyota Ipsum. Will jumped in the front to ride shotgun while Betsy sat in the back seat.

"Your hair's grown back out," Betsy commented.

"Yah, you'll remember mi had a slight problem the last time you were here," Mike Mo replied, referring to the incident when rogue policemen had cut off his dreadlocks.

"Are you at liberty to tell us what's so urgent and secretive that The Colonel would bring us here?" Betsy asked.

"The Colonel prefers to discuss things with you himself," Mikey Mo said and glanced in his rear-view mirror as he pulled away from the curb.

"You've had us worried," Betsy said.

"Feel no way (don't worry). It nuh bad. It may be bad like yaz instead (it may be awesome instead)."

"That's a relief," Betsy said. "Where will we be staying? The Colonel was just as mysterious about that."

"Half Moon in Montego Bay. He wants you to be comfortable."

"Wow. He is going all out," Will said. "We haven't been there for years … decades actually."

"Mehbe you can have a second honeymoon," Mikey Mo said and grinned as he looked in his mirror again. "He rented one of the oceanside villas for you. Dont worry about de bill. He has made arrangements. Jus relax an enjoy."

"The Half Moon was the first place we stayed in Jamaica back in the '80's," Betsy said.

"And then it took a major hit in a storm," Will added.

"Yah, Hurricane Gilbert in 1988. Mi just a child then."

"I've noticed you keep looking in your rear-view mirror," Will said. "Is something wrong?"

"Probably not," Mikey Mo said. "Mi pretty sure that car was behind mi as mi traveled to the airport to pick you up, and mi see it again now. Probably a coincidence. Dont fret."

"Will we see The Colonel today?" Will asked.

"No, mon. He said for you to just get settled in an relax this afternoon. Mi take you to Accompong in the mawning. Mi will pick you up at 8:30."

"If you come early, we can all have breakfast together," Betsy said.

"Thenk yu. Dat be cool."

The following morning after an outdoor breakfast under the trees at the Half Moon Hotel, Mikey Mo and the Blacks left for Accompong. Mikey Mo drove west on A1 through Reading until they picked up B8, which would take them into the interior. He put a CD in the car and began to play Peter Tosh's cover of *Johnny. B. Goode*. Mikey Mo practiced his DJ toasting technique as the song played. They passed through Anchovy and at Marchmont, picked up B6, and headed back east. He headed south again until they reached Jointwood and turned east one final time to take them into Accompong.

When they reached Marchmont, Will commented that Mikey Mo seemed to be peering again into his rear-view mirror more and more often.

"Something amiss?" Will asked.

"Yah, dat same car that followed us from the airport is behind us again. Now mi know it was more than a coincidence. We'll see if he turns on B6."

A couple of miles later Will asked again, "Still there? Did he turn onto B6?"

Mikey Mo grimaced and nodded. He reached under the seat, pulled out a pistol, and laid it beside him. Betsy looked alarmed.

"Dunna worry. Mi just not taking any chances."

Betsy and Will exchanged concerned looks anyway.

The last thirty minutes of their drive on the pitted, unpaved back road into Accompong challenged even Mikey Mo's driving skills. An American driver would probably have rattled his car to death on the road's irregular surface, but Mikey Mo was used to it. He slowed down to a crawl and seemed to be able to anticipate the worst of the potholes. There was no oncoming traffic.

"I see some things never change," Betsy commented. "This road is every bit as lousy as I remembered it. Reminds me of the road to the Rio Grande River near Port Antonio. Henry used to hate that road."

"Yah, because we don't pay Jamaican taxes, they have no reason to upgrade it."

Despite having been here before, Will and Betsy were still awed by the sudden slopes and jagged limestone face of the rugged Cockpit country.

"As rough as this countryside is now, can you imagine what it must have been like for the British troops in the 1700's when they were trying to locate and fight the Maroons?" Will said. "There was no road at all then."

Mikey Mo peered out his rear-view mirror. "Mi dunna see our follower. He knows it would be impossible for him to follow us and mi not notice."

Suddenly they saw the open gate and the blue and white "Welcome to Accompong" sign.

"We're here."

Mikey Mo tooted his horn as they passed Flashy's. Some regulars waved back.

"The Colonel said to bring you directly to his house," Mikey Mo said.

When they pulled up to Colonel Winter's modest home, they could see The Colonel under the Poinciana tree. He rose and walked with his arms extended towards the Toyota to greet them.

"Some people wish blessings; others pray for them. I have sent you my blessings, and now my blessings and prayers have become one. Welcome home, my children," The Colonel said as he hugged Betsy with one arm and Will with the other. "I hope you had a nice flight."

"Yes, we did," Will said, "despite being concerned for you. This whole trip has been shrouded with so much mystery, we couldn't help but worry. And we think someone followed us from both the airport and the hotel."

The Colonel gave Mikey Mo a sideways glance, Mikey Mo said "Mi explain later."

The Colonel nodded.

About that time Harry Dog's henchman who had been following Mikey Mo for the past two days passed Colonel Winter's house. He did not slow down, and the driver did not overtly look their way. Mikey Mo recognized the car, said nothing, but noted his car's license plate.

"You've had us worried," Betsy said.

"Unlike what many people think, mysteries are not necessarily bad," The Colonel said, "but sometimes unless maximum discretion is exercised, a good thing can turn sour, and a rare opportunity may escape forever. Why don't you join me for some tea, and we'll sit out here in the fresh air while I explain?"

Colonel Winter's wife brought out some tea, greeted them warmly and then excused herself, saying she had something on the stove.

"Have you ever dreamed of finding Spanish treasure?" Colonel Winter asked after each had had a few sips from their tea.

"Of course. Who hasn't had that dream?" Will said. "After all, we have lived in both Vero Beach and Key West, cities made famous for treasure discoveries by the greatest treasure hunter of them all — Mel Fisher."

"We have a possible opportunity to discover treasure of the magnitude of what Mel Fisher uncovered," Colonel Winter said. "I do not hope to profit from it personally but instead see it as a windfall for the Maroon people."

"This is exciting. You've got my attention," Betsy said. "I'm already optimistic. After all, Mel always began each day saying, 'Today is the day.'"

"One of Accompong's long-term residents … a widow … died a couple of weeks ago. After her funeral, her daughter, who lives in London, gave Mikey Mo some items that her mother wished me to have. One was a Spanish diary from 1740. The other was an extremely old calabash gourd which had been passed down through their family for generations."

The Colonel paused to sip his tea. Despite their eagerness to hear more, Will and Betsy knew from experience not to rush him. He would tell the story in his own manner, at his own speed.

"When I examined the journal, its author turned out to be the captain of the Genovesa, a Spanish galleon that sank that same year. The Genovesa's treasure has never been recovered. It is thought to have gone down in the Pedro Banks about a 100 miles from Kingston. It carried several tons of gold and silver. Experts have put a value guesstimate of roughly $600 million in today's dollars," The Colonel said.

"That's about as large as the Atocha," Will commented.

"Maybe even larger," Mikey Mo said.

"So did the diary tell where the ship went down?" Betsy asked.

"No, but it told something equally interesting," Colonel Winter said. "According to the journal, all of the treasure may not been on the ship. Captain Guiral was more nervous about losing his cargo to the British than he was to a storm. In 1840 Spain was at war with Great Britain – the War of Jenkins' Ear – and the British commander of Jamaica Station had been having a considerable amount of success against Spanish ships. So, the Spanish captain put all or part of the treasure ashore in Jamaica with the intention of recovering it after the cessation of hostilities. However, he never got to do that since the Genovesa sank in a storm a few days later in the Pedro Banks."

"Wow!" Will exclaimed. "Was all of the treasure offloaded in Jamaica?"

"The journal does not make that clear."

"Do you know where it is?" Betsy asked.

"No. Not at this time," Colonel Winter said, "but there's more to the story."

He paused to take another sip of his tea.

"Mikey Mo and I called on the daughter ... Isabel Drain ... to see if we could learn more. Someone had scratched the numbers 1 - 6 - 38 in the design carved on the calabash. At first, we thought it was a commemorative date ... that was the date Captain Cudjoe agreed to cease hostilities against the British ... but the numbers turned out to have a different significance. Thanks to my associate here," he paused and patted Mikey Mo on the arm, "we have learned differently."

"This keeps getting better and better," Will said.

"Isabel Drain told us that her mother had been paranoid about home invasions since she had experienced a very frightening house robbery in London. After that incident, she bought a home safe and kept items she owned of value in it. Mikey Mo suggested that the calabash numbers might be the combination to a safe and asked her if her mother had had a safe put into her house in Accompong. Isabel didn't know, but she gave us permission to conduct a search. Mikey found a safe disguised as an air conditioning vent. There was no reason for Ruby ... Isabel's mother ... to have an air conditioning vent since the house had no air conditioning."

Mikey Mo beamed since The Colonel was graciously giving him the accolades he deserved.

The Colonel cleared his throat.

"In the safe, we found Ruby's own personal diary. When I examined it, I learned of a fable that had been passed down through their family - that kidnapped slaves had been used to take the treasure inland. When three of the slaves learned that the Spanish captain had given his men orders to kill them after they had served their useful purpose, they escaped and disappeared into the bush. They then tracked the Spanish and learned where the treasure was finally stored."

"Much like the Maroons had done to the British for years," Betsy mused. "Did the slaves kill the Spanish?"

"No, but they recorded clues as to the treasure's location on the only thing they had available to them – calabash gourds. One of the slaves was one of Ruby Drain's forbears. The calabash Isabel brought to me was one of those original gourds."

"Then why did Isabel give it to you?" Will asked.

"Because her mother told her to," Colonel Winter said, "and because until we discovered her mother's journal, she didn't know the significance of what she had."

Will and Betsy just shook their heads.

"To cut the remaining portion of this story short, Mikey Mo and I have used a local history and genealogy expert to help us to identify the descendants of the other two calabash owners and have been able to photograph one of the two. We discovered it is still here in Jamaica."

"So, where do we come into this?" Will asked.

"I'm coming to that. The third slave was later sold to a prominent citizen in what is now the New Orleans area. Primarily because of the new owner's prominence, we have identified one of that slave's descendants and have been in touch with her. She does not know the calabash's significance. I have talked with her and have made her a very generous offer to sell me the gourd. I told her it is a historic relic which will be used as part of a permanent Jamaican museum exhibit – which is not entirely untrue – assuming we are able to find the Genovesa's precious cargo.

"The favor I now ask of you, since I trust you implicitly, is to take this woman the money I promised her and to pick up the gourd. I will pay all the expenses of your trip. The transaction will take place during the New Orleans Jazz Fest. You will gift-wrap the gourd safely and deliver it to a staff member of a Jamaican band who will be performing at the Fest. He will then bring it back to me. He does not know the nature or value of what he is bringing me … and you are not to tell him. If word gets out about what is potentially at stake, who knows what might happen. This friend of the Maroons will be told only that it is just a souvenir that a relative of mine is sending me as a gift."

"Is that why you didn't have Henry Davis pick us up at the airport, and why you didn't want us to stay at Sundance?" Betsy asked.

"Yes, as much as I love and trust Henry and the staff at Sundance, the fewer people who know about this affair for now the better. As we say in Jamaica 'Bushes have ears, walls have eyes.' Don't you agree?"

"Yes, from what you've told us about how much is at stake, I'm sure you're right," Will said. "Which Jamaican band will be at the Fest?"

"Jimmy Cliff. One of his mixing engineers, Yonni Taylor, is of Maroon heritage. Mi will arrange passes for you to go back stage and will let you know where the band and its entourage will be staying. He and mi have worked together on shows in the past," Mikey Mo said.

"We'll be glad to bring it back," Betsy volunteered.

"No, my dear friends. I wouldn't want to use up all my good will with you all at once. This old man needs for you to have reason to visit him."

"You couldn't live long enough for that … ," Will began.

Colonel Winter put his hands on both Will's and Betsy's and gently squeezed.

"No. My way is best. They will be returning in a private plane and avoid customs."

Will nodded his understanding, knowing that when The Colonel's mind was made up, it was made up.

"We've never been behind the scenes at Jazz Fest," Will said to change the subject.

"Wi will see that you are extended every courtesy.".

"So, good. If we are in agreement, go in peace," Colonel Winter said, "and please be vigilant and careful, my children. Mikey Mo will be your primary contact going forward. I do not wish for you to come to any harm, my precious ones. Remember 'wherever there are bones, there are dogs.'"

```
NOTICE
CHECK UNCLE VIN
FOR THESE ITEMS
BISCUIT'S        PEANUT'S
PENCIL'S    COMB'S   PEN'S
RUBBER'S        EXCERSICE -
BOOK'S    SWEET'S    ECT.
BUSINESS NOW BACK IN OPERATION
```

# Chapter 8

Will was listening to Doug Kershaw's *Louisiana Man* on Delta's oldies music service when the flight attendant came on the air.

"Ladies and gentlemen, welcome to the Louis Armstrong New Orleans International Airport. Local time is 1:26 PM. The temperature is 82 degrees. For those of you coming to New Orleans for the Jazz and Heritage Festival, the weather looks like it is going to be clear and mild, a perfect weekend to enjoy music and New Orleans hospitality."

"Well, we're here," Will commented to Betsy. "I've really missed coming to Jazz Fest since we moved to South Florida. Do you realize the wide lineup of performers we've heard here that we would never have heard otherwise?"

"Sure do," Betsy said. "Just landing here is already bringing back memories – Roy Orbison, Keely Smith, Al Hirt, and Bob Dylan. The list seems almost endless."

"The Allman Brothers and War or Fats Domino."

"What about Rod Stewart and Van Morrison?"

41

"Van Morrison was a major surprise. Just like Dylan was a disappointment."

"Don't forget … James Brown, the hardest working man in show business or the Killer, Jerry Lee Lewis."

"My God in heaven. The list just goes on and on. We've sure been blessed. Have I told you lately that I love you?"

"No."

"Then remind me, and I'll tell you sometime."

"Asshole."

And elderly lady across the aisle only heard the last word in Will and Betsy's conversation and peered disapprovingly over her glasses at them.

"And of course, the regulars like Dr. John and Marcia Ball," Will said, "and a few I'd just as soon forget."

"You mean like Joan Baez," Betsy said. "I'll never forget her show where she used her time on stage as a weapon against President Reagan."

"Another asshole."

The flight attendant continued.

"If you require deplaning assistance, please remain in your seat until all other passengers have deplaned, and one of our crew members will be pleased to assist you."

"I can't believe The Colonel just told us to pick wherever we wanted to stay," Will said. "He didn't blink an eye when I suggested our old favorite in the French Quarter, the Royal Sonesta. It's certainly no budget motel, but we'll be walking distance from virtually everywhere we want to go."

"Hey, he didn't skimp in Montego Bay either. The Half Moon certainly ain't no flop house."

"You can say that again. Well, it's really to his benefit. Jimmy Cliff is staying in the Quarter as well."

"Yeah, he and his band are renting an apartment. I always wanted to do that."

"Then I could stand outside in my undershirt and yell 'Stella, Stella' or maybe 'Betsy, Betsy' like a N'awlins native."

"You better not," Betsy said and laughed. "I'll drop a blooming flowerpot on your head. And I won't give you any warning either."

"You'd drop a flowerpot on my head? As much as you love plants?"

"I love my self-respect and dignity even more."

"On behalf of Delta Airlines and our entire crew, we would like to thank you for flying with us today …"

Will and Betsy caught a cab to the French Quarter. They took I-10 into the city, getting off on Basin Street at the Vieux Carre exit before turning onto Conti Street. All this area of the city was so familiar to them. They squeezed each other's hand in their excitement to be back in the city. The cab pulled up to the door at the Royal Sonesta, and a doorman smiled as he helped them get their things out of the car.

"Oh look, Betsy," Will said, "Desiré Oyster Bar. I'd almost forgotten about it until this instant."

They entered the regal lobby and looked around. "Now this is elegance," Will said. "They don't make 'em like this anymore."

Soon they were settled in their third floor room.

"I could eat some oysters," Will said. "Wanna begin our N'awlins experience at Desiré?"

"How 'bout Acme Oyster House on Iberville instead? We'll save Desiré for after we're tired of walking. I'd like to get out on the Quarter and walk around after being trapped in the plane. Besides, maybe we can find Voodoo Blues for The Colonel."

"You're on."

Will and Betsy walked over to Acme. They didn't notice, but a dreadlocked man followed them from a distance.

"Let's sit at the counter," Betsy said.

"You up for raw, or would you rather have an oyster Po-boy?" Will asked.

"Raw for me. I figure we'll get a Po-boy at the fairgrounds during Fest tomorrow. Do they still sell oysters by the each?"

"Damned if I know. I'm going to get at least a dozen anyway. Bring on the saltines, the horse radish, *and* the hot sauce!"

After they placed their order, Will asked the woman manning the counter is she had ever heard of Voodoo Blues.

"Oh, yes," the woman answered. "Back over on Bourbon Street – 700 block I think."

"Perfect," Will said, "since the Sonesta is only a few blocks away."

Voodoo Blues had an oval neon sign with a skeleton dressed in a suit, pork pie hat and sunglasses backing up the lettering. It hung beneath a rusted corrugated tin overhang. The stucco building had once been a pastel green, but now it was peeling and dilapidated. The faded pink doorway was completely open to the street, and the transom above it had another neon skeleton peeking out over the doorway. The eerie strains of Dr. John's *Gris-Gris Gumbo Ya Ya* played on the shop sound system. A six-foot skeleton leered at them as they entered the store. Under a giant neon guitar ceiling fixture, a skeletal Elvis strumming a guitar dominated the middle of the store. Tables throughout the shop were piled high with a wide array of voodoo concoctions, knickknacks, and souvenirs. The dreadlocked man following them didn't enter but instead loitered on the sidewalk across the street and smoked a cigarette.

Will asked the black teenage-looking clerk if Erzube Blanton was in the store.

The clerk responded, "Not at the moment, but I can call her. I think she's only a few doors down. May I ask who would like to see her?"

"Will and Betsy Black – a mutual friend in Jamaica asked us to look her up. I think she may be expecting us."

"Let me see if I can find her. You're welcome to look around the shop in the meantime."

Within minutes a tall, dark woman walked in. She looked even taller since her hair was piled high under a head wrap wound up like a turban. She had full eyebrows and lips. Her long-sleeved, white, cotton peasant blouse was accented by a large cameo. A blue wrap was around her shoulders. Orb-like earrings dangled from a gold chain. All in all, the woman had a commanding, subtly frightening countenance.

"My name is Madame Erzube Blanton," she said in a flat even voice. "You wish to see me?"

"Madame Blanton, my name is Betsy Black; this is my husband, Will. I believe you spoke on the phone with Colonel Ferron Winter in Jamaica recently about a calabash gourd heirloom which has been passed down through your family."

She handed Madame Blanton a business card.

Erzube simply stared at it and then nodded slightly.

"We're his emissaries. We're here to finalize the transaction you discussed," Betsy continued.

"Certainly not what I expected," Erzube said quietly as she gave them a deadpan stare. "Two young, white Americans representing an elderly Jamaican gentleman."

"I can understand that we are not what you might have expected, but Colonel Winter has sent a letter of introduction with us and has authorized us to pay you the amount of money the two of you agreed on," Will said.

"Have you brought cash?" Erzube asked.

Will nodded and said, "Of course."

"I understand this will be part of a historical exhibit in Jamaica. Will my family get recognition?"

"Colonel Winter didn't discuss that with us, but I can't imagine that it would become an issue. We will convey your wishes and ask him to call you to confirm the matter," Betsy said. "If you wish to email him a written message, we'll be here for the rest of the weekend attending Jazz Fest."

"Please come into my office," Erzube said after another pause.

Erzube led them into a cramped back room office, and Will opened his soft-sided leather briefcase to retrieve the letter from Colonel Winter. An old, scarred desk took up most of the room, leaving just enough space for two guest chairs and a filing cabinet. A mahogany wood carving hung behind the desk. In the lower center was a conch shell. Facing the shell were three African-looking heads. Above this scene was a cluster of bananas being eyed by a cat and a parrot. The top of the carving consisted of an elephant carrying a large round container, possibly a water jar. The elephant's trunk seemed to keep the jar balanced so it wouldn't fall off the elephant's back.

"That's an interesting wood carving," Betsy observed as she tried to make small-talk conversation. "Do those figures have any symbolic meaning in voodoo or magic?"

"No," Madame Erzube said, "not to my knowledge. It's a family heirloom."

"From Jamaica?"

Madame Erzube nodded in agreement.

"Well it's certainly eye-catching," Betsy said. "Jamaicans are such creative people. Will and I have a house full of Jamaican carvings that we would never part with."

Will found The Colonel's letter and handed it to Madame Erzube. She put on her reading half-glasses and read it. Then she unlocked the cabinet drawer and took out the calabash. Will handed her a sealed envelope containing the cash. Erzube opened the envelope and patiently counted the money. Satisfied that the funds were the correct amount, she handed them the gourd. Will and Betsy took a moment to examine it.

"Do you mind if we photograph it here?" Betsy asked. "And may we take your picture as well so we can show it to Colonel Winter?"

"I have no objection," Erzube said and posed with the calabash. Betsy then put it on top of the filing cabinet and photographed each side. She checked afterwards to make sure the legends on the gourd were legible in the pictures and then emailed them to herself.

"Do you have something we might put the calabash in?" Will asked, "And perhaps some packing that we might put around it? Do you have gift wrapping in the store?"

"May we also have a sales receipt for customs purposes?" Betsy asked. "Would you simply call it a souvenir? $50.00 would be a good stated value."

"I'll ask Marie to take care of these things," Erzube said and took the gourd out to the clerk. Within minutes, she brought back the gourd gift-wrapped and in a shopping bag and gave it Will. She handed Betsy a handwritten receipt.

Dr. John's *Zu Zu Man* now played in the background as Will and Betsy stood on the sidewalk outside deciding where to go next. The dreadlocked man crossed over the street and followed as they walked down the block.

When Will and Betsy paused in front of The Embers Steak House to read the sidewalk menu posted by the entrance, Harry Dog's protégée thought he saw his chance. He elbowed a tourist on the sidewalk into bumping into Betsy, and when she momentarily lost her balance, he grabbed the shopping bag and turned to run with it. An oblivious teenager eating an ice cream cone stepped in front of the would-be robber. As he dodged to avoid the teen, the thief slipped on the spilled ice cream and stumbled into a mime dressed as a Mardi Gras court jester. When he stepped on the mime's foot, the mime suddenly found his voice and began to scream profanities.

The confusion gave Will time to react. He habitually carried a kubatan fighting stick disguised as an ink pen in his shirt pocket. Will grabbed the kubatan and stabbed out with it catching the surprised thief in the ear rupturing his ear drum. The miscreant yelled and dropped the bag. The teen who had unintentionally collided with him accidentally kicked Betsy's parcel back in Will's direction as he grabbed a handful of the thief's dreadlocks for balance. This momentarily threw the mugger off kilter again. Will snatched up the bag and struck a second time with his kubatan. This time he caught the would-be thief on his Adam's apple. He screamed in pain before throwing up in the open guitar case of a street performer, covering the singer's hard-earned tips with puke.

Will struck out a third time. The hapless thief dodged Will's blow but in doing so collided with a fire plug. He careened off into a Lucky Dog street cart. The Lucky Dog vendor was serving a hot dog when the thief jostled him and made him squeeze down on the bun. The ketchup, mustard and sauerkraut laden Lucky Dog squirted out and down the already miserable thief's shirt, burning his chest as it went down. The thief began to shake his shirt trying to dislodge the scalding hot dog. When he clenched his stomach muscles, it slid on down into his pants.

"Mi manhood on fire!"

The robber began high-stepping to try to dislodge the scalding wiener. It slid on down his pants leg and out onto the sidewalk. He inadvertently stomped on it, leaving a red-tinged meaty blob. He stared at the gory-looking mess, not realizing what it was, but thinking the worst.

By this time, the mime had produced a knife and stepped forward aggressively growling. He slashed the scoundrel's outstretched left forearm, opening a gash in it. The surprised thief automatically pulled his own knife out of his waistband with his right hand to defend himself. The agile mime chopped his wrist, sending Betsy's would-be assailant's knife clattering to the sidewalk. Now unarmed, the man thought better of his situation and decided to cut his losses by fleeing into the astonished crowd, leaving a trail of blood and ketchup on the sidewalk.

Will turned to see if Betsy was injured.

"You OK?"

"I think so. I may have sprained my wrist slightly when I bounced off the brick building."

Then she noticed Will had their package.

"Oh great, I see you got our package back."

"Thanks to a little luck and my trusty oak kubatan. Let's get this gourd back to the Sonesta before something else happens. I don't want to complicate matters by having to explain this situation to the NOPD."

When they got back up to their room, Will said, "Do you think that was just a random street mugging, or does someone want our calabash?"

"Hopefully, it was just a street mugging. The crime rate in the Quarter is bad," Betsy said. "No one is supposed to know why we're here except Colonel Winter and Mikey Mo."

"I find it strange, though, that the thief was dreadlocked. Do you think he might possibly have been Jamaican?"

"I thought I might have heard a Jamaican accent when he screamed. I hope that's a coincidence as well. People everywhere wear dreads nowadays."

"A little too coincidental for me," Will replied. "Let's get back to the hotel to lock this thing up before something else happens."

"Excellent idea. This favor for The Colonel is turning out to be anything but routine."

"Well, we'll be getting rid of the calabash soon, and then we can kick back and enjoy Jazz Fest. In the meantime, why don't The Colonel and I treat you to some crab-meat Sardou at Galatoire's?"

"And some shrimp Remoulade as well?"

"Works for me. I didn't come to the Big Easy just to eat Lucky Dogs."

```
┌─────────────────────────────────┐
│                                 │
│    TOMBSTONES                   │
│                                 │
│    ROWE                         │
│                                 │
│    BARBERING SALO               │
│                                 │
│    -N AFRO AND                  │
│                                 │
│    STYLE SCOND                  │
│                                 │
│    DOOR UPSTAIRS                │
│                                 │
└─────────────────────────────────┘
```

# Chapter 9

On Thursday morning Will and Betsy caught the Jazz Fest Express shuttle bus from the Steamboat Natchez Dock on Decatur Street and went directly to the Fest held each year on the 145-acre New Orleans Fair Grounds and Racetrack on Gentilly Boulevard. They got off the shuttle and walked towards the gate.

A head-shaven black man in a sleeveless, tie-dye t-shirt got off the bus and followed discreetly from a distance. Will carried a canvas tote bag containing a beach blanket, sunscreen and other items they might need during the afternoon. Betsy had their admission tickets and the pass to get backstage to see Yonni Taylor, Jimmy Cliff's mixing engineer. Jimmy was scheduled to play at 3:50 pm at the Congo Square Stage.

Will and Betsy came in the gate by the Gentilly Stage and walked down past the Fais Do Do Stage towards Congo Square. They could hear Big Al Carson singing his signature song, *Take Your Drunken Ass Home*.

"Whoa! Stop!" Will said. "I've got to hear Big Al for at least one or two songs."

They each bought a beer and listened to Big Al and his band before resuming their stroll. They marveled at the seemingly endless array of vendors selling everything from food to crafts and Jazz Fest souvenirs. They passed the Louisiana Folk Life Village. The man from the bus stayed well behind them, but they were never out of his sight.

Since they wanted to see a couple of acts before Jimmy Cliff and another one afterwards, Will and Betsy had mapped out an agenda over drinks in the Royal Sonesta's Mystic Den lounge the night before. They were tempted to see the Isley Brothers and Irma Thomas on the Gentilly Stage but decided it'd be prudent to pick shows nearer to Congo Square. They chose instead to go see Buckwheat Zydeco and Galactic at the Acura stage before Cliff went on and to see Paul Simon afterwards.

"It's always frustrating to try to pick which shows you want to see," Will said. "I want to see them all, but twelve venues going on simultaneously forces you to be selective. Keep in mind, we can't even see the blues tent, the gospel tent or the jazz tent from this side of the racetrack."

"I think we picked out some pretty good shows. Let's not forget we're here primarily to represent Colonel Winter."

"I'm going to duck into this porta-potty for a second since it doesn't have a line out in front of it. This beer's going straight through me."

"Go ahead. Give me the bag."

When Will closed the door to the porta-potty, the man trailing them saw his chance. He dropped his cigar on the ground and quickly slipped up behind Betsy. He stiff-armed her shoulder blades from behind, snatched the bag, and fled into a crowd of people. Betsy wasn't sure what to do — try to chase him or wait for Will to come back out. She decided she needed to get Will's attention immediately and ran up to the porta-potty door and banged on it.

"Will!" Betsy yelled. "Our bag! Somebody stole it!"

Will was still zipping his pants when he threw the porta-potty door open.

"Who? Where?"

"A black guy … and he took off that way. He came up behind me and snatched it out of my hand."

They took off in the direction Betsy was pointing. The man was nowhere to be seen.

"What'd he look like?" Will asked.

"Didn't get a good look," Betsy said. "He came up behind me. I saw mostly a tie-dye t-shirt."

"Did he have dreads?" Will asked.

"No, but he was kind of young and his head was shaved."

"Not the same guy as yesterday, but that description describes a helluva lot of people around here. Thank goodness we didn't have anything of real value in the bag."

"No shit. I'm sure glad our credit cards or driver's license weren't in it."

"Or Colonel Winter's calabash. We almost brought it out here today to give to Yonni Taylor. Thank God we decided it might not make it through the security bag-check at the gate."

"Yesterday could have been a random street crime … but two days in a row … uh-uh … that's more than coincidence."

"I agree. For two people who were supposed to be flying below the radar screen …"

"Somebody knows why we're here and wants what we have," Betsy said, finishing Will's thought. "Let's think this situation out."

They decided to go to Congo Square as they had already planned to talk to Yonni Taylor and arrange to give him the "present" somewhere other than the fairgrounds. They decided not to trust Yonni by telling him about anything that had happened to them in New Orleans since they weren't sure now just who they could rely on. He might not be as trustworthy as The Colonel thought. After all, there was more money at stake than any of them had ever seen … or were likely to ever see again. In the meantime, it was imperative to contact Mikey Mo and tell him about their unexpected shit-storms.

```
Orgo   Vitamal
    hERBAL  DOCTOR

HERBS TAKEN FROM VARIOUS COUNTRIES
BLENDED BY EXPERT HANDS TO GIVE YOU
THE BEST IN CURE FOR GASPHITES.COLD
NERVE ETC. ASWK HERE FOR THE FAMOUS
ORGO VITAMAL ROOTS TONIC WINE
    WORKING DAYS EVERY FRIDAY
       FROM 12-3 WESLEY ROAD
```

# Chapter 10

"Should we call Mikey Mo from the fairgrounds on our cell phone?" Will asked, "Or should we wait until we get back to the hotel? On second thought, let's take a cab to RST's New Orleans branch. Our hotel room may be bugged. Jim Lenaghan, the branch manager, is a former broker I worked with in Mobile."

"You're dead right on that since someone seems to know more about The Colonel's business than he should. I think it's prudent to be more careful than we previously thought. And I agree. Let's not use the landline from the hotel."

Will sighed.

"I guess this means Paul Simon is out. Well, hell. You can't see everyone, but you were right when you said that Colonel Winter's business is more important. We can come back and see Elvis Costello and Red Hot Chili Peppers tomorrow to make up for it. Let's go over to Congo Square before we leave, act like nothing's wrong, and see if we can get a feel for this Yonni Taylor before we talk to Mikey Mo."

"Then we'll catch the shuttle back into town. I also want to revisit Madame Erzube."

"Why her?"

"Just call it woman's intuition. Let's not dawdle at Congo Square. We've got a lot to do."

Later when they walked into Voodoo Blues, Madame Erzube didn't seem happy to see them. Her arm was bandaged.

"Get out of here," she said shrilly. "You bring bad juju with you. Go, or I'll release Lenglensou on you."

"What in the world happened to you?" Betsy asked.

"Two men came to my home yesterday demanding to know what I had sold you and how much I got for it.

"I told them it was none of their damned business. Then the bastards tied me to a chair and began to burn me with a lighted cigar. The other a-hole threatened to burn my shop.

"I finally told them that I'd sold you my calabash family heirloom, but that I didn't know your name or where you were staying in New Orleans. The one with the cigar then threatened to burn my eyelid so I told him I thought you were going to Jazz Fest."

"Black guys? Did one have dreads?" Will asked. "Did the other have a shaved head?"

Madame Erzube nodded.

"They apparently already knew who we were and also where we were staying," Betsy said. "One followed us when we left here and tried to steal your shop bag. He wasn't successful, but the other man did manage to steal another bag from us today at the Fest."

"I hope you didn't come back here because you thought these people were working for me. Did you?"

Betsy took a step forward and reached out to try to comfort the almost hysterical woman. Madame Erzube stepped back.

"No. We thought you were very straight with us."

"You damned right I was."

"We're sorry. We didn't know what to think," Betsy said. "That's why we decided to pay you another visit, but if they tried to torture you for information, it seems unlikely either was connected to you. Please accept our apologies for the pain you've suffered."

"I don't think you'll be endangered again. We're the ones they're after," Will added.

"Why are these people willing to go to this extent for an old gourd?" Erzube asked. "It's been in my family for years and was nothing more than a family curiosity. Now, all of a sudden, it's become dear enough for your Colonel to pay me money and for these thugs to want to destroy my shop and kill me for it. What've you not told me?"

"You're asking the wrong people," Betsy said. "We were only doing an old friend a favor and saving him a trip to the U.S. when we agreed to represent him in this matter. We were as surprised by the attack as you were. My apologies again. We'll report these incidents to Colonel Winter. I'm sure he'd prefer that the police not be brought into the matter."

"They don't do me no good anyway. If these men are local, I *will* find them. We have ways of dealing with people like that. We also have ways of dealing with people like your Colonel if he's been lying to me. I may not live in the Caribbean, but that don't mean I still don't have contacts there."

Will and Betsy left Voodoo Blues and got a cab to RST's New Orleans office so they could use the phone to call Mikey Mo. Will walked in and asked the receptionist if they could see Jim Lenaghan. After introducing Betsy to Jim, Will asked if he could have a private office to make a phone call.

"It's international," Will told Jim. "I'll have it charged to my office."

"Don't worry about it. We all work for the same firm. I don't guess one international call's going to destroy this month's P and L."

Will dialed Jamaica.

"Chicken," Will said, calling Mikey by his street name, just in case someone could possibly be listening. "We've run into some unexpected issues."

"You weren't able to get the 'present'?"

"Oh, we got it alright, but someone else wants it as well. I think we can talk freely on this phone. I'm not at our hotel but on a friend's landline that I think is safe."

Will told Mikey Mo about finalizing the calabash transaction and how they had had the shop gift-wrap it for them. He then explained how they had then almost lost the gourd in what at first appeared to be a random street mugging, but how he and Betsy had become convinced after a second incident at the Jazz Fest that someone was willing to go to great lengths to steal the calabash from them. He then told Mikey Mo that their revisit to Voodoo Blues had confirmed their suspicions.

"You'll remember that mi thought we were being followed in Jamaica. Someone other than us three definitely knows about this. How is it that when lots of money is at stake, it's impossible to maintain a secret? Mi haven't spoken to a soul."

"Nor have we. As you Jamaicans say, 'someone have two faces under one hat'."

"But who?"

"That's for you and The Colonel to find out.

"Have you delivered the package to our mutually agreed contact?"

"Nope. We'd hoped to do so tomorrow."

"Don't do anything until you hear back from me," Mikey Mo said, his English suddenly becoming flawless. "I'll talk to The Colonel immediately and will call you back at this number at 10 a.m. tomorrow."

He repeated the number back to Will.

"Shouldn't be a problem then, but you can't call me here during the weekend. This business isn't open on Saturdays," Will said. "But if a problem does arise about Friday, I'll give you a heads up before ten. Inna di morrowz (see you tomorrow)."

"Til den, walk good, mi frens (until then, stay safe, my friends)."

"Same."

Jim gave Will permission to use the phone again the following day for the incoming call. He seemed curious about why Will felt he needed to use this phone, but when Will avoided volunteering the information, he let the matter drop. As a brokerage veteran, he, like Will, respected the fact that some matters must be kept confidential even from friends.

# A Treasure Conspiracy

Mikey Mo called promptly at ten the next day and got right down to business.

"Since we've got a leak on this end and won't be able to identify it possibly for some time, Colonel Winter wants to change the plan. You'll deliver a package to your contact, but instead of the real package, you'll take him a gift-wrapped Jazz Fest or New Orleans souvenir about the same size as the original package. If you could find another calabash or gourd and wrap it, it'd be even better. You'll then deliver that fake package but keep the real gourd for yourself. I assume it's in a secure place."

"It's locked in the hotel safe."

"Good. Now, The Colonel has the biggest favor of all to ask of you. Will you deliver the real gourd to him personally?"

"We didn't expect that. Any particular time frame?" Will asked with a sigh.

"We'll work out those details. He's aware that this is asking a very big favor and needs to make it as convenient for you as possible. He'll be forever in your debt. After all, he knows that 'too much hurry yu get dere tomorrow; take time, get dere today' (if a person takes his time, he will get to his destination sooner than if he rushes about)."

BARGIN'S

# Chapter 11

The next morning, Will went out on Bourbon Street and collected tourist newspapers and brochures to see if he could find an acceptable calabash substitute to deliver to Jimmy Cliff's Yonni Taylor. He came back to the room, and they flipped through the circulars looking for ideas. Betsy's first couple of brochures were unproductive. She called a couple of Caribbean grocery stores and a basket shop entitled Lucky Clover Trading Company. Then she hit pay-dirt, a shop called Ah Ha on Magazine Street in the Irish Channel area. They said they handled decorative gourds and that they also did gift wrapping. Within the hour, Will and Betsy had their substitute package. They called the house on Conti Street being rented by Cliff and his entourage at the cell phone number Mikey Mo had given them and made arrangements to deliver the package to Yonni before everyone left to go to the fairgrounds for the day.

"Let's walk since it's just over on Conti," Betsy suggested.

Will and Betsy turned the corner off Bourbon onto Conti Street. Soon they saw the sign for the Bombay Club.

"Look," she said pointing.

"That brings back some memories. I'll never forget the night Marc Turk, your old Murphy High School classmate, treated us there. He really rolled out the red carpet for us. First time I'd ever even heard of black-eyed pea hummus. I remember you had scallops and I had seared fish with dirty rice."

"Don't forget the smoked cheddar jalapeño cornbread muffins. I guess he should be able to treat his friends royally though – after all he did own the place."

"Small world when a former Mobilian owns a New Orleans landmark. I'm glad he liked you in high school."

"Do you realize that was the last time we ever saw Johnny Bachemin alive?" Betsy asked. "The piano player for the trio who normally played the Bombay Club had the flu, and it was Johnny's night off, so he filled in as a favor to Marc."

"Yep. You're right. The French Quarter may be a tourist's party heaven, but it can also be a pretty rough place. By the time we visited New Orleans again, Johnny had been tortured and killed in his apartment by some homophobic scrum-bums looking for money ... probably to feed a drug habit. Best I remember, the law caught up with them out in Colorado with Johnny's credit cards. And remember, Johnny played *Basin Street* that night just for you."

"And *Take Five* for you."

Will stopped and took Betsy by the hand. "My love, I don't know if I've told you lately, but thank you for marrying me. Being married to you has been one adventure after another."

"I can't imagine what my life would have been like without you either, my darling,"

She squeezed his hand back.

Will and Betsy didn't notice, but they were again being followed by another black man. When Will and Betsy paused near the Bombay Club, he ducked into a doorway to keep from being seen.

After a few more blocks, they identified the address of Jimmy Cliff's rental. Jimmy Peart, the band's bass player, answered the door. After they identified themselves and gave him Betsy's business card, they were admitted. The band was lolling about as they took their time getting ready for the day. Yonni introduced Will and Betsy to the band members before inviting them to join him for a cup of tea. Betsy commented that this rental house compared very favorably to their room at the Royal Sonesta. Will, the consummate music fan, had brought his Jimmy Cliff greatest hits compilation with him and asked the members present to sign it for him. They gladly passed it around as Will and Betsy sipped their tea.

"Your rendition of *Light My Fire* really seemed to light a fire with the crowd yesterday," he told Ansel Collins, the keyboard player. "The Doors broke that song on the charts when I was in college. It seemed that you couldn't go to a dance anywhere that year without some band playing it."

Yonni questioned the Blacks on how they had gotten to know Colonel Winter and Mikey Mo. Betsy told him about her assignment in Jamaica to represent her bank's interest in financing the Jamaican Highway 2000 project.

Yonni smiled.

"I remember the Highway 2000 program well. Some heads really rolled because of it—all the way to the top—some of the most ruthless and powerful men in Jamaica went down."

"And deservedly so," Will said. "But Betsy couldn't have exposed the corruption by herself. Without The Colonel's assistance, it never would have come to light. There were too many powerful people making money by plundering the project. Without his involvement, the best-case scenario would have been finding a scapegoat, but the graft would have continued anyway. And Betsy and I would probably not even be alive. Like The Colonel says, 'All kind of fish eat man, only shark get blame.'"

Yonni smiled and put, "Well said. I see you have been acclimated as a Jamaican. But unfortunately, that was merely a battle in a never-ending war. Crooked politicos and their backers will continue to find ways to enrich themselves on the backs of the Jamaican people ..."

"Backers ... You mean parasites and vultures, don't you?"

I was being tactful, but to use another Jamaican proverb, 'You can stop a bird flying over you, but you cannot stop it building a nest.'"

It was Will and Betsy's turn to smile.

"So, what have you brought me today?" Yonni asked.

# A Treasure Conspiracy

"A package Colonel Winter wishes you to take back to Jamaica. He didn't tell us the nature of the package, only that it's nothing illegal and nothing that should get confiscated by the airlines. He said it is something he can't get in Jamaica, and if the matter comes up, for you to tell Jamaican customs that it's a gift, which it is. You will note the box *is* gift wrapped, and I have a sales slip for you to show customs. It should be pretty straightforward."

"I don't mind at all. Chicken and I go way back together. He's done me plenty of favors, and I have nothing but respect for Colonel Winter. I'm glad I can be of service to either or both of them."

After chatting for a short period longer, Yonni said, purposely lapsing into patois to test Will and Betsy's command of the dialect, "If wi don, mi have odda ting mi need to hangle dis mawning (if we're finished, I have some other business I need to deal with this morning). Go wi' Jah. (go with God) Hope wi link in Xaymaca (hope we meet again in Jamaica). Respeck."

"Respeck," Will replied, bumping fists with Yonni. "Lata den (later then). Tank yu for everting (thank you for everything)."

Yonni nodded slightly; Will had passed the test.

Returning to the Royal Sonesta to change into attire more appropriate for the fairgrounds, Will and Betsy walked back over to Decatur Street to catch the Jazz Fest Express again. As they rode the bus, Will asked Betsy if she would mind if their first show would be to see "Frogman" Henry at the Gentilly Stage. The performance was being billed as the Frogman's possible final one before he retired from show business.

Frogman did not disappoint them, but they wondered about what to expect momentarily when Frogman came out on the stage on a rolling four-wheel walker with a helpmate beside him to assist with his balance. Frogman was wearing an ivory cab-driver cap and had on a muted, untucked and mostly unbuttoned tropical shirt over plain white t-shirt and dark slacks. Once Frogman was in the middle of the stage and his assistant handed him a microphone, all doubt was erased about his ability to perform. With a nine-piece group backing him up, Frogman launched into his signature song, "Ain't Got No Home", hitting the falsetto notes as well as he had done when he was younger.

He then rolled nonstop through his repertoire of familiar songs. The mostly baby-boomer audience sang along with such familiar Frogman Henry songs as "(I Don't Know Why I Love You) But I Do" and "You Always Hurt The One You Love."

"Damn, it's a shame Frogman's about to retire," Will said. "The old boy's still got his pipes."

When Frogman completed his set, the same man returned to the stage and walked along beside him as he left. The crowd roared its approval.

Later that day, Will and Betsy saw Miami's Arturo Sandoval, Red Hot Chili Peppers, and Elvis Costello before deciding to return to the hotel to relax before going out to dinner.

Will had just dozed off for a quick nap, when he heard a rap on the door.

"Who is it?" Betsy asked through the closed door.

"New Orleans Police Department," came the curt response. "Open the door."

Will and Betsy looked at each other questioningly.

"May I ask what this is all about?" Will asked.

"Open the door, and we'll explain."

Two burly detectives entered the room, showed their IDs, and introduced themselves.

"Do you know a Yonni Taylor?" the lead detective asked.

"Why, yes," Will said. "He works with the Jamaican singer Jimmy Cliff. They played Jazz Fest yesterday. Why do you ask?"

"Have you seen him here in New Orleans?"

"Yes, we saw him earlier today. What's the problem, officer? Has he been hurt? He was fine when we saw him this morning," Will said.

"I'm afraid he's been the victim of a homicide."

"Whaaa …! When? How? We saw him late this morning before going out to the fairgrounds for today's Fest. In fact, we had a nice visit."

"So, you've been at the fairgrounds since then?" one detective asked.

"Yes, here's our Jazz Fest bus stubs."

Will reached over and picked them up off the room desk.

"What was your business with Mr. Taylor?" the detective asked.

"A friend of ours in Jamaica asked us to buy a present and send it back with Yonni when he leaves Jazz Fest," Betsy said.

"What is that present?"

"A New Orleans souvenir."

"No contraband?"

"Of course not."

"Do you have a sales receipt?"

"No. It was gift wrapped. We gave the receipt to Yonni in case he needed it for Montego Bay customs."

"How was he killed?" Will asked. "Were any other members of the band harmed? The house was full of band personnel when we were there."

"He was tortured before being killed with a knife, and the house was ransacked," the detective said. "He apparently was there alone after everyone else had gone to the Fest when the incident occurred."

The detective failed to mention that Yonni's skin was covered with round burn marks about the size of a quarter or that he was bound when his throat was slit.

"He was stabbed like there'd been a fight?" Will asked.

"Can't comment" the detective said. "You say you left a gift-wrapped package there. We didn't find one in the house."

"What led you to us?" Betsy asked.

"Your business card. He'd jotted Royal Sonesta on the back of it."

"Yes, I did give him my card this morning," Betsy admitted. "This morning was the first time we'd ever met him. He's a friend of a friend."

"Thank you for your time. If we have any further questions, we will get back to you. Will you be here for a few days?

"No sir, we're here only for Jazz Fest. We live near Key West."

"But you have mutual friends in Jamaica?" the confused detective mused.

"It's a long story," Will said.

"Hmmm."

The detectives took down Will and Betsy's contact information before they left.

"We need to call Mikey Mo again," Betsy said.

"I agree, and the sooner the better."

They dialed Mikey Mo. He came on the line.

"Chicken, we've got a *real* problem up here," Will explained. He brought Mikey Mo up to date on the events which had occurred since they had last talked.

"This is extremely disturbing. So, let's make sure I understand this right. You delivered the dummy package to Yonni, and someone killed him for it. Where's the real gourd?"

"Still in the hotel safe."

"Stay where you are. I'm going to call Colonel Winter, and I'll be back to you."

After hanging up, Betsy asked Will, "How in the world did the word get out about the calabash? This means our enemies are convinced that the calabash is a vital link in finding a treasure that we thought was our secret."

"And will go to any lengths to get it. Duh! I must've had my head up my ass not to realize that. I really hate it that an innocent person like Yonni gets dragged into this mess."

"Not just dragged in – killed."

"But you never know. He might have been on the other side. I just don't know who to trust anymore – other than you."

"I know this is heresy to bring up, but do you think the lure of unbelievable wealth could have turned Mikey Mo from a good guy to a baddie?"

"Surely not. But who else knows?"

"Mikey did say something about consulting some research people. Money does funny things to people. Remember what The Colonel said that when it comes to serious money 'Bushes have ears, walls have eyes.'"

"And 'wherever there are bones, there are dogs.'"

Mikey Mo called back within minutes.

"American has a flight leaving New Orleans at 12:45 for Mo Bay. If I can get you on it, can you make it? I'll pick you up in Mo Bay."

TO DO LOND SCAPING

EDGEING

LAWN AND

GARDENING

Tel 76220

# Chapter 12

"Ladies and gentlemen, welcome to Sangster International Airport. Local time is 7:21 PM and the temperature is 27 degrees Celsius or 81 degrees Fahrenheit. For your safety and comfort please remain seated ..."

Will looked at Betsy and smiled. "Did you think we'd be back in Montego Bay so soon?"

"No, but I guess I shouldn't be totally shocked. The way things have gone since we left here last."

They walked into the airport from the tarmac and down the hall to the customs area. They had no trouble getting the gift-wrapped calabash through customs by showing him the photocopy of Madame Erzuma's sales receipt.

"Boy, I'm glad I kept a copy since we gave the original away," Betsy said.

"Amen. Remember the time we were bringing in Christmas presents for Henry and Rose and the customs official gave us total hell?" Will asked.

"Uh huh – he wanted to unwrap all our gifts to verify that we weren't bringing in products for resale."

"Just shows you how subjective all that is. The lady we got this time didn't even hesitate."

"That's what smugglers and terrorists count on. Inconsistencies in the system."

As they left customs, they looked for Mikey Mo. Instead they saw their old friend and driver Henry Davis beaming at them. After immediately concluding his conversation with another driver with his usual "tak care of the road (goodbye). Mi brudda and sistah here."

He held out his arms to greet them.

"Welcome home, mi Jam-Merican brudda and sistah. Too long time mi nuh si yuh (it's been too long since I've seen you)."

As usual, Henry was informally but neatly dressed. He was still as thin and fit looking as he had been the last time they'd seen him. His mustache was neatly trimmed. He seemed to have a bit more salt in his salt-and-pepper hair than they remembered. He was wearing the Los Angeles Dodgers baseball cap the Blacks had given him several years before.

"My God, are you a sight for sore eyes," Will said. How yuh bin dween (how have you been doing)?"

Henry smiled again, "Very good. I see you have not let your patois lapse."

"I was taught by the master," Will said.

Betsy said nothing. She just continued to hug Henry's neck.

"As much as we've wanted to see you, we were expecting Mikey Mo."

"Chicken had car trouble."

The Blacks looked at each other.

"I'll tell you in the bus," Henry said and looked around. "When yu go a Jackass yard, yu noh fi chat 'bout big iyaz (it's not smart to talk about important business here)."

They got in Henry's red Nissan van and pulled away from the airport.

"I'm aware that you're here on a mission for The Colonel," Henry said.

Will and Betsy looked at each other and were glad Henry had cleared the air somewhat. They hadn't been sure what they could or could not say around him.

"No one is supposed to know we're here," Betsy said. "What's wrong with Chicken's car?"

"Seems to have been vandalized," Henry said. "And I'm supposed to be the only other person who knows you are in Mo Bay. I know part of the story, but I'm sure I don't know it all."

"So, you don't know the nature of our mission?" Will asked.

"Only that it's important to Colonel Winter. He said too much knowledge on my part might put me in needless danger. He also said he'll tell me more on a need-to-know basis to minimize the chances of a leak. 'Plantain ripe, can't green again' (leaked information will never be a secret again)."

"We've already had a few close calls," Betsy said. She and Will then related the series of events which had transpired in New Orleans. "No one was supposed to know we were there either."

Henry just whistled "whew" followed by "Jezzam" as he looked in his rear-view mirror.

"Someone behind us?" Will asked.

"Looks like one of The Colonel's men. He must have sent one for security. I think it's Fireman."

Will and Betsy gave each other an alarmed look before Betsy responded. "I'm not surprised after what we've been through the last few days. Where are we going to spend the night tonight?"

"My house," Henry said. "We'll take off for Accompong in the morning."

"Great. That'll give us a chance to see Rose," Betsy said. "We have a package for The Colonel. Do you have a secure place to keep it for the night?"

Henry nodded and said, "Yes, I do as long as it's not too big."

"Shouldn't be an issue," Will said.

Close to an hour later, as they neared Henry's house on Primrose Hill, he drove up the steep incline by the Columbus Plaza shopping center in Discovery Bay. Will and Betsy began to playfully sing a spontaneous rendition of the old Jerry Wallace hit song *Primrose Lane*.

*Primrose Lane, life's a holiday on Primrose Lane*
*Just a holiday on Primrose Lane with you*

Henry laughed and said, "You're not supposed to be old enough to remember that song."

Henry pulled into his driveway and tooted his horn. The name of the villa, Club View, had been worked into the design of the wrought iron gate and fence. Will and Betsy could see the house through the gate. Rose had turned on the spotlights. Will got out and opened the gate so Henry could drive through and then closed it again.

"Like I said at the airport, this villa, just like you, is a sight for sore eyes," Will said when Henry had parked the bus. Henry's wife, Rose, had heard the horn and was coming out of the back door with her arms spread to greet them. Rose had on slippers and a housedress. Even in this informal dress, she was her usual neat self. Rose had the same coloration as Henry and was about the same height and age as her husband. Her accent was always definitely educated Jamaican. Both Will and Betsy rushed over to hug her.

"I'm assuming you ate on the plane," Rose said when they got in the house, "so all I prepared is some Solomon Gundy and of course some welcome-back-to-Jamaica rum fruit punch."

"Perfect, as always," Will said. "You have a knack of knowing just what we want and need, but the main thing we mostly want is to just spend a lovely evening with you and Henry. But you won't hurt my feelings if you cook fritters for breakfast in the morning."

"You mean flitters don't you?" Betsy teased her husband.

"Then flitters it is," Rose said as she laughed.

The foursome spent a delightful night catching up on news with each other. Rose did not bring up anything pertaining to the Black's mission for The Colonel. She knew that if they wished or were permitted to discuss it, they would open the topic. She did ask however if she could accompany them to Accompong.

The following morning, after a special Jamaican breakfast of cornmeal porridge and saltfish fritters, the foursome left to drive into the Cockpit Country to go to Accompong. Henry took Highway A1 to Runaway Bay and then turned to go into the interior on B3. There they picked up B11 and stayed on it until they picked up B5. The trip was pleasant and uneventful. Will and Betsy didn't notice a car following them, but Henry did. After driving for about ten miles on B5, as they were about to top a hill on an isolated stretch, Henry slowed. There appeared to be road construction ahead. A trench had been dug across the highway, and a man waved for them to stop.

"Wha the …" Will exclaimed.

"Dutty renk rent-a-dread (dirty stinking shyster)," Henry mumbled to himself, referring to the Jamaican habit of digging potholes in a road and then pretending to repair them as an excuse to extract contributions from gullible but sympathetic passing motorists. "Just digging up the road so he can dig some money out of us. It's de usual fuckery (it's the usual bullshit)."

The man approached Henry's bus and said, "Can yu gimme lickle frackles to help repair de hiway (can you give me a little donation to help repair the highway)?"

Before Henry could respond, the man pulled a gun out of his waistband. "Mehbe dis matic convince yu (maybe this automatic pistol will convince you)."

Two other men suddenly appeared out of the brush. Each of them was holding a pistol. One man opened the side door to the bus and reached across it, grabbing the bag with the calabash in it. He also grabbed Betsy's cell phone off the seat, dropped in on the shoulder of the road, and stomped on it. As the first man began to demand Henry's phone, a shot rang out. The first man dropped in his tracks. Blood and brain matter splattered on Henry and the side of his van from the pin-point accurate head shot. The other two men didn't hesitate or try to find the shooter and return fire but instead took off running over the hill. Moments later, the Blacks heard an engine crank as the unseen car threw gravel off the shoulder in its attempt to speed away.

The shooter ran up and said, "A (is) everyone ok?"

"Yes. Thanks to you, we're still on the right side of the grass. Mr. …?" Will asked.

"Mi fren dem call me Fireman."

"Yah. Mi deh yah (I'm okay). Sure betta dan we did a minute aguh," Henry replied. "Mi shirt been betta though."

"And I just washed it," Rose commented.

"If you hadn't shown up when you did, I might've done something unladylike in my panties," Betsy commented.

"Glad that didn't happen. Yah, Fireman. We seem to be fine … except for what they broke and stole," Will said. "Thank goodness you came along when you did."

"He didn't just come along," Henry said. "I've noticed Fireman following us since we left Discovery Bay."

"And you didn't say anything?" Betsy asked.

"I couldn't be positive who he was and didn't want to alarm you. I was hoping he worked for Colonel Winter."

Fireman was already on his cell phone making a call. "Chicken, this is Fireman." He went on to explain to Mikey Mo what had happened.

When Will heard who Fireman was talking to, he asked to use the phone.

"Mikey Mo, this is Will. They got away with the package."

"That's not good, but it won't do them any good if they don't have the other two gourds," Mikey Mo said, "but it certainly puts a crimp into The Colonel's plans."

"Not as big a crimp as you might think," Will said. "Betsy took pictures of the calabash and emailed them to herself. Thank God she did that because the a-holes who attacked us this morning smashed her cell phone. And by the way, before I forget, thank you for having your man follow us. I'm not sure what would have happened otherwise. We might all be dead."

"Nah a problem. We'll talk about this more when you arrive. May I speak to Fireman again?"

Will handed Fireman the phone.

"Were there any witnesses to the incident? No? Good."

Mikey Mo then told Fireman to bring the body so they could try to identify it and learn more about who their adversary was. Fireman said he had planned to bring it anyway.

"We don't want to leave a body on the side of the road for the constabulary to find," Fireman said. "Help me lug him into my trunk."

Fireman followed Henry's bus into Accompong, but instead of going to Colonel Winter's house, he first detoured off and took the body elsewhere before rejoining them. Mikey Mo and The Colonel were waiting for them when they arrived. After cleaning up in The Colonel's bathroom, they rejoined him to sip some tea at the table under the poinciana tree. Colonel Winter apologized profusely for the danger he had subjected the Blacks to. He asked them to repeat their experiences so he could be sure he had all his facts correct.

"I had planned on studying the three calabashes together today, but that won't be possible now until I get the pictures from you," he said. "Thank you, my dears, for having the foresight to photograph the missing one. Otherwise, we'd be back to square one. Henry will take you back to Discovery Bay. Do you have to leave Jamaica immediately?"

"No, we've both arranged to stay here for a while in case you needed us," Will said. "Besides, I don't get a chance to look for a half a billion dollar treasure every day."

"Then I'll be in touch," Colonel Winter said. "Do you mind having some guests for a few days, Henry?"

"Mind?" Henry said. "Rose and I are thrilled. We'll take care of our Jam-Merican friends."

"We won't be in your way?" Will asked. "Don't feel like you have to entertain us. We don't want to wear out our welcome and smell like old fish."

"Never," Henry said. "In Jamaica, when visitors come a wi fireside, wi mek wi pot smell nice (in Jamaica, when we have guests, we treat them the best we can)."

```
┌─────────────────────────────────┐
│                                 │
│        'TAILORING'              │
│        BOB DAVIS                │
│       COSTOM TAILOR             │
│      Renivating done            │
│           Here                  │
│      pants, shirt, ect.         │
│                                 │
└─────────────────────────────────┘
```

# Chapter 13

Will thought he heard a bump and imagined for a moment that either he or Betsy had accidentally knocked something over in the dark of Henry and Rose's guest bedroom, but then he decided it had maybe come from farther away. He had been sleeping soundly, dreaming of having a Sundance reunion with the staff. He and Betsy had really wanted to see Leva and E.J. while they were in Discovery Bay but understood why The Colonel had been insistent that as few people as necessary should know of their presence in Jamaica. The problems he and Betsy had had in both New Orleans and Jamaica had reinforced with the two of them just how much was potentially at stake and what lengths people would do to get their hands on the Spanish treasure. He had also lamented to Betsy earlier how he would hate to think that he had put Leva and E.J. in danger by selfishly wanting to socialize with them. It was bad enough that they had potentially exposed Henry and Rose to unknown hazards by drawing them into the increasingly perilous picture. He consoled himself by thinking it was not the Blacks but Mikey Mo who had involved the Davises.

After drinking too much rum before, during, and after dinner, Will had slept more soundly than usual. He partially awoke when he heard the thump coming from somewhere in the house. He glanced at the digital clock on the bedside table and saw it was 12:16.

"Did you hear something?" he muttered to Betsy.

She gave him a mumbled response which he interpreted as go-back-to-bed.

"As long as I'm awake, I'm going to the bathroom," Will said.

Another mumbled response sounded like just-don't-wake-the-whole-house-up-doing-it.

Betsy almost dozed back off until she was jolted fully awake by what sounded like footsteps.

*My dufus husband's bumped into something coming back.*

Instead of Will, a tall brawny, black man stared down at her.

Betsy gasped.

His face was partially obscured by a hoodie, but the message he sent was instantaneous since he was holding a machete. Another man grabbed her in the dark, pulling her upright in bed, and securing her with duct tape while the first man wound more duct tape around her mouth.

*Oh, my God! I'm about to get raped or killed.*

Instead of ripping her nightgown off as she expected, the man merely held her while the first man finished securing her arms. They then turned on the light and looked in the closet for her shoes and clothing.

Betsy could now see both men more clearly.

The second man was shorter and more slightly built than the first assailant. He had dreads. She could see a pistol in his waistband. The man with the hoodie had scraggly, unkept facial hair. The long sleeves on the hoodie had been irregularly chopped off, and she could see tattoos on both brawny arms. When he noticed that Betsy's clothing was still in her suitcase on the fold-up wooden luggage caddy, he gruffly told the second man to close the suitcase and bring the entire thing. He was obviously the person in charge.

She gasped recognition. Now she was more scared than ever.

*Shit! The men who ambushed Henry's van and stole the gourd!*

The men marched Betsy out into the hall where she saw that Will had been bound up in a similar manner.

*So that's what Will heard.*

Will was wearing the t-shirt and gym shorts he had gone to bed in. Other than being trussed up, he appeared to be OK. When they got downstairs, Will and Betsy saw Henry and Rose duct-taped to their dining room chairs.

*So that was the first noise.*

The Davises were still in their bedclothes and had pillowcases tied over their heads. They did not appear to have been harmed. Things looked in order. The house had not been ransacked, making Betsy think that robbery was not the motive.

The man who appeared to be the henchman said to the leader, "Gabriel, yu know wha villa wi gwan take dem to (do you know which villa we're supposed to take them to)?"

The leader said nothing but gave the speaker a dirty look like he had talked too much when he called him by name. The men then turned the lights back out in the house, leaving Rose and Henry in the dark with pillowcases still tied over their heads.

They marched Will and Betsy barefooted out of the house, prodding them as they stumbled along. Will stubbed his toe and lost his balance almost making Betsy lose hers. One of the men caught him before he could fall and jerked him back up, almost causing him to lose his balance a second time.

Betsy came close to slipping on something liquid. Both Will and Betsy almost retched when they looked down.

*Blood and an intestine.*

Henry and Rose's dog lay dead in the yard. Its throat had been deeply sliced, almost severing its head, and it had been hacked and gutted. They were roughly shoved into the back seat of a Honda minivan, and a pillowcase was put over both of their heads. They could hear their suitcase being carelessly thrown into the back.

The men went back into Club View and planted listening devices. When they had finished in the house, they planted a GPS and another listening device in Henry's bus.

Will and Betsy heard the van doors open and then slam shut as the two men got into the vehicle. The man in the hoodie finally spoke to them for the first time.

"If yu bruk out (misbehave), mi trow you in back of car (I'll throw you into the back of the car). Undastan (understand)."

They both nervously nodded their assent. The backseat was certainly better than the rear of the vehicle.

The speaker drove, leaving the more slightly built man to watch the Blacks. The driver laid his pistol beside him, and they backed out of Club View's driveway. They heard the driver tell the other man to close the gate.

Instead of going back down the hill past the Discovery Bay Police Department and past Columbus Plaza to A1, the men took the road in the opposite direction. It was a truck route used primarily for hauling bauxite but would merge back into A1 several miles away. When they reached A1, the driver turned and headed towards Runaway Bay. In the closed confines of the vehicle, both Will and Betsy could smell the nauseating scent of the unwashed man nearest to them. Will's tailbone hurt as they bounced down the pothole-pitted mining road. Betsy felt lightheaded as she struggled to breathe the foul air.

After what seemed like an eternity, they heard a gate open, and the car drove into a driveway. They were led still blindfolded across some pavers and into a house. The men roughly pushed them into a second room before taking the pillowcases off their heads. When the leader released Will and Betsy, they saw he was holding his pistol. They looked around them. They seemed to be in a large bedroom in what appeared to be a villa. Iron bars were on the windows, partially obscuring an ocean view.

"Why are we here?" Will asked. "What do you want?"

The leader turned to the Blacks and said as he left the room, "Don ask and don be chupid (don't ask and don't be stupid). Yu will do tings wi way if yu waan live (you will do things our way if you want to live)."

With that simple statement, he closed and locked the door behind him.

"PLEASE DON'T PEA HERE"

# Chapter 14

"We've identified the body of the person who was killed in Henry Davis' ambush," Mikey Mo reported to The Colonel. "'Knuckles' Biddle – a Shower Posse member. A bad dude the world is better off without."

"So, our adversary is our old nemesis Dudus Coke," Colonel Winter responded. "Dam ... nation. I hate to hear that we're in an altercation with 'The President' again. He's one vicious bastard."

"Well, if yu play wid puppy, it lick yu mout."

"Dudus in no puppy. He's a meaner-than-hell pit bull who does more than lick."

Colonel Winter had cost the Shower Posse millions of dollars and eliminated some of their stalwart members in past confrontations, so he was not pleased that he was now confronting them again. Their last conflict had exposed Shower Posse induced graft in the Jamaican Highway 2000 building program.

"As we all still vividly recall," Mikey Mo said, "the Blacks were drawn into our last battle with the posse."

"How well I remember, and I hate that it's happening again," Colonel Winter said, thinking back to the bid-rigging and bogus reporting which had almost compromised Betsy's bank and resulted ultimately in bringing down politicos high in the Jamaican government. It had also almost caused Will and Betsy's deaths.

Mikey Mo's cell phone rang. It was Henry Davis calling.

Henry skipped the preliminaries and went straight to the reason for his call.

"Chicken, the Blacks were abducted from my villa last night."

Mikey Mo held the phone away from his face and repeated Henry's statement to The Colonel. Colonel Winter winced.

"Do you know if they have been killed or hurt?" Mikey Mo asked. "Are you and Rose OK?"

"Jah be wid wi. We're both shaken but otherwise OK. I don't think the Blacks were harmed either – at least not here. If our intruders had wanted us dead, they'd have done it right here. The men marched them out of my house. It was after midnight after we had all gone to bed. Two men broke into my house, tied up Rose and me, and then kidnapped the Blacks."

"Your dog didn't warn you someone was on your property?" Mikey Mo asked.

"They killed him – cut his throat."

"Mon, I'm so sorry. But thank Jah they only cut the dog's throat instead of yours. So, how'd you get loose?"

"Big Boy came by this morning to borrow some tools," Henry said, referring to his youngest child. "He found us. He just released us a few minutes ago"

"Did you call the constabulary?"

"No – because I'm pretty sure I recognized the lowlifes as Shower Posse and thought we'd have better luck handling this matter discreetly. Besides, we need to fight fire with fire no holds barred. That's all Dudus understands. Sorry for maga dog, maga dog turn roun and bite yu. We both know Dudus Coke has tentacles which extend into the constabulary. Rose is more rattled than I am. I put her to bed. After I made sure she was fine, I called you. The kidnappers were two of the same thugs who attacked us on the highway."

"We've identified the third one – the dead one. Knuckles Biddle."

"The Shower Posse's Knuckles Biddle?"

"The one and the same," Mikey Mo said. "He answers to Harry Dog."

"So, I'm right. This is a Shower Posse matter. Thought so. That may give us a clue as to where the Blacks are being held. Let me find out from my street contacts what locations the Shower Posse uses around here. Do you think the Blacks are being held for ransom? Surely the Shower Posse has bigger fish to fry than two visiting Americans. Any ransom would be chump change to Dudus Coke."

"There are relevant facts which The Colonel has withheld from you until now. I can't discuss them without his permission. Let me just say that I don't think the Shower Posse will harm the Blacks for the time being, as long as we do not involve John Law – which, as you pointed out, would probably be fruitless anyway since many of members of the constabulary are on Dudus' payroll. We have something Dudus Coke wants, and he's using the Blacks as a bargaining tool. I think it's time Colonel Winter and I told you more about the errands the Blacks have been running for him, but I don't want to do it on the phone. In the meantime, I'll put out my own feelers as well to try to identify posse-owned locations. When can you get up here to Accompong?"

"Let's try to find Will and Betsy first and make sure they're safe," Henry said. "Then I'll listen to what you and Ferron have to tell me."

"Give me a few hours to see if I can narrow down where they might be holding them. You do the same. Let's set a time for us to report back to each other," Mikey Mo said.

"No later than three this afternoon. I'll initiate the call."

"I'll be listening for your call, but we still want to meet with you as soon as possible."

```
R. BENE

GURAGE

MECHINEC

WELDING ON BODY

                    WORK
```

# Chapter 15

After several hours, Will and Betsy heard a key turn in the bedroom door of the villa where they were being held. Two men walked in flanked by their abductors. Both were beefy men who appeared to be approaching middle age. Then men were clean-cut, wearing both their hair and beard short and neatly trimmed. Their dress was conservative. The apparent leader looked at the Blacks with penetrating eyes, and they recognized him immediately.

"Please sit," the man said, pointing to the love seat in sitting area of the bedroom. "My name is Christopher Coke; many people call me Dudus. My associate here is known as Harry Dog."

Harry Dog nodded but still said nothing. His dark, silent, homicidal demeanor made the Blacks shiver slightly.

Dudus continued, "We will be your host for the next several days until we can resolve a situation involving you and us."

He rose and walked towards Will and Betsy with his hand extended. His lips smiled, but his eyes did not. "It is a pleasure to finally meet you, Mrs. Black. Your reputation as an astute banker has preceded you. Our paths have crossed in the past, but there have always been intermediaries between you and me. I am glad to finally meet you in person."

Betsy shuddered to think of the possible outcome of this meeting. When she was representing WB Bank and trying to protect the bank's loan interest in the Jamaican road financing project, she and Will, with Colonel Winter's assistance, had cost Dudus and his partners millions of dollars. Also many of the governmental contacts Dudus had kept on "retainer" who had enriched him in the past and would have enabled him to make even more millions in the future on upcoming Jamaican government contracts were now either dead or serving long prison terms. This had forced Dudus to retrench and reorganize much of his operation. Betsy had played a part in costing Dudus more money than she and Will would ever see in a lifetime. Questions raced through her mind. Was it now time for Dudus' retribution? Were she and Will now condemned in a revenge move? Did Dudus plan to kill or mutilate both of them slowly? He had a reputation for doing such things. If his intention was simply to settle the old score, why didn't he just have them murdered at Club View? Or did he have a sadistic desire to prolong their suffering? She shuddered to think what could be in store. Will was having similar thoughts.

As if he was reading her mind, Dudus said, "Your invitation to join me here is purely business not personal. Your friend, Colonel Winter, has some things I want and that I mean to obtain. Your fate depends on my ability to negotiate with him for those items. I think you know what I'm referring to."

Will and Betsy relaxed slightly. Dudus did not plan to kill or torture them immediately. They were being held hostage for the remaining two gourds. But would Dudus kill them once he got what he wanted? At least for the time being they had a chance. He was not simply getting revenge for the money he had lost on the Highway 2000 program. Their relief was short-lived, however.

"But if you value your lives, you will help me convince Colonel Winter to turn the calabashes over to me. Also, if you attempt to escape, my men have orders to shoot to kill … and I can and will arrange less comfortable accommodations for you."

With that statement made, the meeting was concluded. Dudus and his henchmen left the room, locking the door behind them.

Will and Betsy did not speak to each other since they did not know if listening devices had been planted in the room. They went to the window and looked out. They did not recognize the coastline. They listened at the doorway and heard one of their abductors talking to the villa's cook.

"Pansy, give dey bully beef and bread fi lunch (give them canned corned beef sandwiches for lunch)."

Within the next hour, a middle-aged Jamaican woman in a uniform brought the sandwiches in the room. One of their abductors accompanied her. She said nothing to the Blacks, nor did she make eye contact; she simply put the tray down on the table in the sitting area and left.

~ ~ ~

"Henry, I'm still shaking," Rose Davis told her husband. "I don't remember just when I've been so scared. It's a miracle those people didn't kill us."

"That's because we weren't the targets," Henry said. "We were just a minor inconvenience who happened to be in their way."

"What did Chicken say when you called him?" Rose asked.

"That the men definitely worked for Dudus Coke and that he'd get back to me after they formulate a plan of attack. Neither of us want to endanger the Blacks further by bringing the law into the picture since no one knows who among the deputies might be on Dudus' payroll. Mikey Mo wants me to come to Accompong asap so he can explain more about why all this is happening, but I told him I would first do what I can from this end to find the Blacks before driving down there."

"Do you know what to do to find them?" Rose asked.

"No, honestly I don't. All I know is 'blood follow vein'."

Shortly thereafter, Rose said, "Henry, you have just given me an idea."

"Gwan (go on)."

"We heard the rude bwoys (thugs) refer to a villa?"

Henry nodded.

"We both know that villa staff members are a small, close-knit community and are often bench an batty (very close friends) who will go to great lengths for one of their own. I also know from what people say at the market that the Shower Posse uses rental villas not only as an investment but for other purposes as well."

"Like to launder money into legitimate areas," Henry added.

"We both know that Leva Carter and E.J. at Sundance Villa adore the Blacks and would do anything for them."

Henry nodded and said, "And also for Mikey Mo. He's Kingtoo's (E.J.'s street name) parri (best friend). The Blacks have been wanting to see Leva and E.J since they arrived but haven't done so because of the sensitive nature of their commitment to The Colonel."

"But at this point, secrecy about Will and Betsy being in Jamaica is less important than getting them released unharmed."

Henry nodded again.

"So why don't we get Leva and E.J. to see if they can use their contacts who work in other villas to try to identify if the Blacks are being held as a guest at one of the Shower Posse's villas."

Henry smiled broadly and said, "Mi Rose not ongle smart but cyaan gi rude boys macca jook (my Rose is not only smart but knows how to give the bad guys a thorny poke)."

Rose beamed at her husband's compliment and said, "A little axe can cut down a big tree. I'll go down to Sundance right now and get the ball rolling."

"Discreetly, my dear. C'mon, I'll drive you down the hill."

```
┌─────────────────────────────────┐
│      RED HAT                     │
│         VULCHINIZING             │
│      COFFEES SHOP                │
│      BOTTLE DEPT                 │
└─────────────────────────────────┘
```

# Chapter 16

Henry and Rose approached the gate at Sundance, the rental villa that had been Will and Betsy's residence when they had lived in Jamaica. The bank had rented the villa for the Blacks for the duration of their previous extended stay. Betsy had been on special assignment for WB Bank to handle loan disbursements, progress inspections and accounting for WB's loan participation with Royal Bank of Commerce and the Inter-American Development Bank on the Jamaican Highway 2000 highway building program after it was determined that her predecessor had local conflicts of interest that had prevented him from properly representing the bank's interests. Will had gotten New York Stock Exchange permission to work out of Jamaica as a remote Key West satellite office for the duration of Betsy's assignment.

Highway 2000 had been part of Prime Minister Patterson's Millennium Projects Programme and had been designed to upgrade Jamaica's infrastructure. WB's loan had helped finance a toll road that had passed through six parishes including the Maroon country to connect Kingston on the south coast with Ocho Rios and Montego Bay on the north coast. Will and Betsy with the assistance of Colonel Winter and the Maroons had uncovered a gigantic multi-million dollar swindle to defraud not only WB but the other lenders involved in the program as well. The ripple effects had resulted in a vote of no-confidence in Jamaica's government and had forced the election of new government officials. Many people had either gone to prison or had died before the affair was concluded. Among the central figures who had never been indicted but had lost millions because of Betsy's efforts were Dudus Coke and his Kingston and St. Andrew Corporation arm, a fraudulent contractor on the Highway 2000 project.

The domestics at Sundance, along with Henry and Rose Davis, had become more than staff to Will and Betsy. They had become friends and comrades who had helped assimilate the Blacks into the Jamaican community. Each looked at the other as extended family. Will and Betsy had set the tone for their relationship almost immediately by insisting that the staff join them for each meal instead of merely being servers. They had also insisted on helping the staff clear the table after each meal.

Leva Carter was the cook and housekeeper for Sundance, meaning she was also in charge of the household. Leva was a neat and tidy, middle-aged, full-figured Jamaican who people were immediately drawn to because of her beaming smile and twinkling eyes. Leva was a good-hearted person whose broad grin almost always made strangers feel immediately at ease. Appropriately enough, her street name was "Honey-pye". Leva had a husband and family, but she lived most of the time in the bedroom provided for her at Sundance. She would go home on her days off. Her family often came to visit her at the villa. Leva loved to cook and loved just as much to hear compliments on her meals. She was also a rabid gospel music fan. When Will and Betsy formed a mental image of Leva in their minds, almost inevitably they could picture her almost waltzing with the broom around the villa merrily singing a religious song like *Jesus Is My Rock*.

E.J. "Kingtoo" Aarons, Sundance's houseboy and gardener, was a dark-complected, clean-shorn, single Jamaican in his early twenties. He also took care of the villa's dogs. He lived in an apartment adjacent to the carport. He was a six-foot tall, baby-faced beanpole. His impish grin made him look even younger than he really was. E.J. had first introduced the Blacks to Mikey Mo "Chicken" Mullins, his best friend since childhood.

Will and Betsy had learned E.J.'s full name one day when Will was teasing him about his Elvis fascination.

"I would have thought you'd be a Bob Marley or a Michael Jackson fan," Will had said. "You weren't even born when Elvis was alive."

That was when E.J. had explained the significance of his name to them. He had been born in St. Ann on the tenth anniversary of Elvis Presley's death. The Obeah man had told E.J.'s mother that this was a sign that he would grow up to be a king. So she had named him Elvis Jessie. People either called him E.J. or his street name Kingtoo. E.J. had taken the Obeah man's pronouncements to heart. He had become an ardent Elvis fan and impersonator and especially loved Elvis's gospel music since he was a devout Christian. His room was stocked with Elvis paraphernalia and posters and his closet contained costumes that he would wear on special occasions or on his day off in lieu of his white-shirt-and-dark-slacked houseboy uniform. Will and Betsy were always amused when E.J. reverted to his Elvis persona.

Henry honked his horn for admittance. Leva was in the kitchen when she heard the familiar horn beep. She looked out the kitchen window and saw that it was indeed Henry's bus.

"Kingtoo. It's Mr. Davis at the front gate. Go open it, and let him in."

E.J. opened the gate, and Henry and Rose drove up the driveway to the turnaround in the front yard. They got out and walked into the house while E.J. closed the gate again.

"Wud yu lak some tea (may I offer you some tea), Mr. and Mrs. Davis?" Leva asked.

"Dat be goodas (nice)," Rose said as she sat on a stool at the kitchen pass-through. "Lemon and sugar, please, Mrs. Carter."

While they were waiting for the water to heat, Rose brought up the reason for their visit after E.J. came back in the front door. She told Leva and E.J. that the Blacks were in Jamaica for a brief visit and had been staying at her house. Both Leva and E.J. momentarily seemed to have their feelings hurt that Will and Betsy had not come by

Sundance for a visit. Henry quickly explained that the Blacks were taking care of some confidential business for Colonel Winter who had asked everyone involved to keep the Blacks' presence and the nature of his business a secret.

"I'll be very honest with you and tell you that The Colonel has not even shared with us what this affair is all about," Rose said. "It is very hush-hush, but sumady deh talk (somebody is talking) because the Blacks were taken from our house at gunpoint last night."

"Boxcova (oh, no)! Yu don mean," Leva exclaimed. "Du yu know who?"

"I'm afraid we do," Henry said. "They were almost certainly kidnapped by the Shower Posse."

"Mi reah (my God)! Dat bad, bad, bad!" E.J. said. "Deh ah very bad men (they are very bad men)."

"Big massa mek dem rude boys fyah fi yuh (God will make those scoundrels burn in hell) for sure," Leva agreed.

"From what we overheard them say," Henry said, "we think they are probably holding the Blacks at a Shower Posse owned villa."

"We know that you and other villa staff members are bench an batty (a close-knit community) and that you talk to each other," Rose said. "Do you think you can discreetly find which villa is being used to hold the Blacks?"

"As you know, we will do anything for Will and Betsy ... and for The Colonel," Leva said. "Dem gud people in the hands of some very rude boys (very vicious thugs)."

"Mi true brethren (true friends) all right. Mi hab always big up dem (I have always respected them), and they hab always big up wi in return (they have always respected us in return)," E.J. said.

"Amen. I'll get right on it and let you know what I find out," Leva said. "I pray they will be all right."

"Remember – be discreet," Henry said. "Their lives might depend on it."

```
┌─────────────────────────────────────┐
│                                       │
│             VERNE'S                   │
│          BEAUTY SALON                 │
│       SPECIALIZED IN ALL:             │
│       BEAUTY CARE; WIGS               │
│     CLEANING. PRESS & KIRLS           │
│        COLD STRAIGHTEN . SHA-         │
│      MPOO AND CONDITIONED             │
│         MEN HAIR ALSO                 │
│                                       │
└─────────────────────────────────────┘
```

# Chapter 17

After the Henry and Rose left Sundance, Leva immediately dropped everything she was doing, got on the phone, and began calling. One of her calls was to her husband's aunt Florence. Florence not only knew the staff members in most of the area villas but visited them on a regular basis. She and her husband Wilbert lived near Fisherman's Beach in Runaway Bay. She helped her husband, a commercial fisherman, sell his catch door to door to cooks so they would have fresh seafood for their guests. Cooks knew they could buy seafood from Florence and Wilbert with confidence. Florence's daughter was the newly hired cook at Whistling Villa, a villa in the Runaway Bay area. Florence's nephew, Nakomis Kyle, also known as Ruddy-Puss, was the houseboy at Almond Hill, the villa next door to Sundance.

She asked Florence if Dudus Coke or the Shower Posse had any investment villas in the area.

"Yeh, mi dawta Pansy now du di wuk fi deh at Whistling Villa (yes, my daughter Pansy is working for them at Whistling Villa)," Florence replied. "Dey also own Almond Hill nex' door to yu."

"Where's Whistling Villa located?" Leva asked.

"Near Jerky's – Runaway Bay."

"Hab yu godeh to see har (have you visited her there)?" Leva asked.

"Yeh, jus this mawning (morning). Shi see mi at de gate. Shi say mi cyaan visit todeh. Shi say dem bring two white people inna de villa laas night (she came to the gate and said I couldn't come in the house since they had brought two white people in the night before)."

Leva was excited as she hung up the phone. Pay-dirt! She was positive she had located the Blacks.

"Jeeezam," she screamed excitedly. "E.J., E.J., cum ya (come here)."

E.J. came running in from the yard, and Leva told him what she had found.

"Mi back foot (great)!" E.J. shouted excitedly.

"Yu go to Whistling Villa an pree it (check it out)... But don get ketch (don't get caught)."

"Wooiii! No problem! Dis anancy rope wi tie anancy (this spider's web is going to tie itself). Leh mi use de fone (let me use the phone) please."

E.J. called his good friend Mikey Mo, asked him to come by Sundance, telling him he would explain an idea that was jelling in his mind. E.J. then went to his room and found a small snapshot of Will and Betsy.

Mikey Mo drove E.J. to Whistling Villa. Before they arrived, they went to Fisherman Beach and picked up Aunt Florence's husband Wilbert. They told Wilbert to go to the front gate at Almond Hill and try to sell some fresh fish. Pansy came out to the gate. She looked like she was afraid. Before she could greet Wilbert, he held his finger to his lips; Pansy nodded that she understood. Wilbert talked to her in a voice loud enough to be heard from the villa.

"Yu need fish, pretty gal, fi yu guests?"

Then in a lower voice only Pansy could hear he said, "Promise yu fadda yu a hol mi dung (promise your father you'll keep my secret). If dem be yu guests, nod."

He quickly flashed E.J.'s picture of Will and Betsy.

She nodded.

"Numba qwengas (number of gangsters)?"

Pansy held up two fingers.

"Eba dehayah (are they always here)?"

She nodded.

"Anyone else?"

She shook her head.

Wilbert then said out loud enough for the men in the villa to hear, "Mi bring sum back annuda day. Tanks, pretty gal. Jah bless (I'll bring some back another day. Thanks, pretty girl. May God bless you)."

Now that what he needed to know had been confirmed and he had actually seen the villa, it was time for E.J. to get Mikey Mo to help him turn his idea into a plan. A silk cotton tree in the yard with ripe fruit on it had given him the nucleus of an additional idea as well.

CATERATERS FOR
. BANQUETS . PARTIES
. WEDDINGS . DINNER

# Chapter 18

E.J. and Mikey Mo spent the remainder of the day collecting the items they would need to rescue the Blacks. They planned to return to Whistling Villa after dark and put the plan into motion.

It took an hour when they returned to do the preparation work, but when they were finished, E.J. was confident that it would be "mission-accomplished" before the evening concluded. Fortunately there was a new moon that night, and the yard was almost pitch black. When Mikey Mo and E.J. were satisfied that they were about as ready as they would ever be, they climbed onto a low-lying branch of the silk cotton tree in the villa's front yard. The canopy of the twenty-five foot tree made that section of the yard shadowy dark. Mikey Mo began to whack rhythmically on the trunk of the tree with a three-foot long 2x2 pine picket. It wasn't long before one of Will and Betsy's captors came to the front door.

"Gabriel, deh sup'm nah gwan but mi cyaana see shit (Gabriel, there's something going on out here, but I can't see shit)," LeVar called out to his partner.

"LeVar, don just stan der, fassy. Gwan guh check out du rupshun outa door (LeVar, don't just stand there, dickhead. Go check and see what the disruption is)."

Mikey Mo beat the picket on the tree again and began to make a whooping sound. E.J. threw a piece of the fruit from the silk cotton tree and hit LeVar in the chest. Mikey Mo pounded on the tree again.

"Mi nah guh ova deh (I'm not going over there)," LeVar said. "Mi hear Whooping Boy duppie man over deh (I hear a Whooping Boy ghost)."

Yu claffy (you idiot). Dats no duppie (that's not a ghost), Gabriel said. "Get yuh mawga rass deh, or mi smack yuh head back (get your skinny ass out there, or I'm going to smack you in the back of the head)."

LeVar stepped out of the door. When he did, he tripped a wire and a bucket of fish guts, over-ripe mango and glue came down on top of his head.

"But a wah di rass (what the fuck)?" he screamed as he kicked the bucket as he slid down.

Gabriel came running out with a pistol, and when he did, he hit the marbles E.J. had spread all over the front steps just as Mikey Mo whacked the tree again, simultaneously whooping for joy. Gabriel's pistol flew out into the dark, and he toppled forward face-first, straight into a puddle of goat manure that Mikey Mo and E.J. had poured there.

Gabriel screamed, "Fuckery (bullshit)" just as a bucket of birdseed in quick-drying concrete came raining down on him.

The laughing E.J. could resist uttering to Mikey Mo, "Nah, de goat hab running belly (the goat has diarrhea)."

Mikey Mo sniggered and whooped and beat even louder on a tree branch. E.J. threw silk cotton fruit at both of the downed hoodlums. Gabriel attempted to stand by grabbing the stair railing that E.J. and Mikey Mo had sawed almost in half. When Gabriel grabbed it, he went face first into the flower bed into the puddle of wet concrete Mikey Mo had just poured.

"Who evah yu be out dere, ya rass fi mi (whoever you are out there, your ass is mine), he screamed.

E.J. responded by turning on his Bluetooth boom box which began to play Elvis's *Suspicion.*

*We're caught in a trap, we can't get out ...* , blared out from the tree. E.J. giggled loud enough for everyone to hear.

By this time, LeVar had managed to struggle to a standing position. He immediately went to try to get Gabriel out of the flowerbed. Mikey Mo and E.J. rained bang-snap fireworks down on him as he did so.

The furious thugs charged the silk cotton tree. Just as they got under the main trunk and began to attempt to climb it, Mikey Mo poured a bucket of used sludgy motor oil on them. He followed this by beaning Gabriel with the bucket that had a large limestone rock left in it. E.J. followed this with a torrent of feathers he had gotten from tearing up an old bed pillow at Sundance and then clobbered LeVar with the bucket he had had the feathers in. It had also been weighted with a rock. Both kidnappers lay stunned in a tangled heap at the foot of the tree.

E.J. jumped down from the silk cotton tree and ran around the house to rescue the Blacks. He cut around the back to the bedroom where they were being held. When Gabriel and LeVar saw him running, they took up the chase. E.J. stayed on the grass, but Will and Betsy's abductors took the as-the-crow-flies short cut across the pool patio to try to cut him off. When they did, Gabriel and LeVar hit the bb pellet's that E.J. and Mikey Mo had spread on the pool deck. They skidded for the water. LeVar grabbed the pool ladder just as Gabriel collided with him. E.J. had unscrewed the ladder from the deck, and when LeVar grabbed it, both he and Gabriel plunged headlong into the pool. Within seconds, both men were screaming and trying to get out of their clothes as the caustic soda Mikey Mo had poured into the pool began to make them burn and itch.

Mikey Mo followed E.J. with a machete in his hand. When they got into the bedroom, they saw that Will and Betsy had both been tethered to chairs. As E.J. held the backs of the chairs away from the Blacks, Mikey Mo hacked up their wooden backs with the machete. When Will and Betsy were free, E.J. told them to run, that they did even though they were still attached to small remnants of the formerly nice villa furniture. E.J. paused only long enough to grab his Bluetooth boom box. Both of the kidnappers had managed to get out of the pool, but their only thought at that moment was trying to wash the burning caustic soda off of themselves with the villa water hose and to scream a torrent of curse words. The water failed to come on since Mikey Mo had beaten the handle off the hose bib.

The last words the Blacks heard as they headed for the car were a string of virtually indecipherable epithets from the suffering Shower Posse members.

"Bongopushdigrasskvaat!"

"Bamborasspussyholeclaat!"

E.J. jumped in the front passenger seat and told the Blacks to get in the back. Within moments they were all in Mikey Mo's car as he sped down the bumpy road.

```
CAUTION:
NO   ONE   SHOULD   FOUND
COMING IN THIS PREMISES AT NIGHTS
ONLY IN THE DAYS ON BUSINESS
```

# Chapter 19

Mikey Mo was elated as he drove the Blacks safely back to Club View. Ever the D.J., he tried to raise everyone's spirits by playing Barbara Jones' reggae version of The Dells hit song *Oh, What A Night* and accompanying it gleefully with E.J. joining in an off-key duet. After the adrenaline wore off, they all felt drained. Even though Henry and Rose were still somewhat shaken, they were fine otherwise. They were relieved to see that Will and Betsy had been successfully rescued and that no harm had befallen them. Mikey Mo reported in to The Colonel and told him for the first time of the evening's activities. He apologized profusely for not keeping Colonel Winter in the loop on E.J.'s plan but justified his actions by telling Colonel Winter that time had been of the essence. The Colonel said he understood and was secretly relieved since his own contacts had produced no meaningful leads on the Blacks' whereabouts.

"I'll stay with Will and Betsy at the Davis residence tonight," Mikey Mo told The Colonel. "We will not be caught unawares again.... And I don't think LeVar and Gabriel want to have another showdown with us tonight anyway."

"Doesn't sound like they're in much shape for a rematch with you right now," Colonel Winter said, "but don't forget that they work for The President, and he has very deep resources available to him. LeVar and Gabriel's next altercation will most likely be with The President's unofficial vice president, Harry Dog, and from what I've heard about Harry, I would not want to be in their shoes when they report they lost custody of the hostages he had entrusted them with."

"Harry Dog may be pissed, but I doubt if he would be able to mobilize the posse's resources tonight," Mikey Mo said. "Keep in mind, he doesn't know who Kingtoo and I are, and he doesn't know where we took the Blacks."

"Valid points, but be vigilant nevertheless. The hungry fowl wakes early. Please bring the Blacks to Accompong in the morning. Now, be safe."

The following morning Mikey Mo drove to Accompong while E.J. returned to Sundance to fill Leva in on the prior night's activities. Thankfully, the trip was uneventful. The Colonel had his wife serve tea under the Poinciana tree when they arrived.

"It has been bothering me how Dudus Coke found out that we had Francisco Guiral's diary and that we were trying to locate the Genovesa treasure. I also have been wondering just how he seems to know about our plans and always seems to be one step ahead of us. I went to great lengths to keep this matter a secret with a very small inner circle of people. Well, I still don't know who gave him heads-up on the whole matter, but I did find out how he has been monitoring our plans."

Everyone looked at each other and thought, *I'm not the weak link*.

"He's been bugging my house," Colonel Winter continued. "I hired an expert, Link Ledingham, to help solve the mystery. He found listening devices both in and out of my house. I'm not sure how Dudus did it, but somehow, he has managed to bug my home as well attach one to the underside of this table. Link removed the devices and assured me he thinks he found them all."

"That certainly explains our near fiasco in New Orleans. We knew it wasn't a random street mugging," Will said, "and it explains how they knew about our contact, Yonni Taylor in Jimmy Cliff's band.

We've been thinking that Erzube Blanton, the owner of Voodoo Blues, was somehow responsible and had double-crossed you."

"My conscience has been bothering me since then after Yonni was brutally murdered trying to do me an innocent favor," Colonel Winter said. "I've paid my respects to his family and told them I would try my best to locate Yonni's killers."

"And it also partially explains our ambush on the road, and how they knew we still had the real gourd," Betsy said. "But why were we kidnapped?"

Dudus planned to hold you hostage to force me to give him the other two gourds," Colonel Winter said. "He made his demands while you were being held."

"I didn't know that," said Mikey Mo.

"You didn't need to know it at that moment," Colonel Winter said. "Besides, you were busy trying to rescue our friends here. I didn't want to add more stress to an already stressful situation and have that possibly affect your judgment. Sometimes less knowledge gives you the extra sense of urgency that then forces creativity. Too much knowledge sometimes leads to despondency since obstacles seem insurmountable. As a wise man said, 'If you saw what the river carried, you would never drink the water'."

Mikey Mo still looked somewhat like he had his feelings hurt.

"The main thing is, thanks to you and E.J., everything worked out and no one on our team was hurt. I would still like to know who made Dudus aware of the treasure to begin with. But now we should not have the eavesdropping problem going forward - assuming Link found all of Dudus' listening devices, but I do not expect Dudus to give up. He is a very formidable opponent who is very motivated when he wants something. After all, we did cost him a lot of money as well as damage his network when we exposed the graft in the Highway 2000 project. But enough analysis, and on to new business.

"I have been fortunate enough to find and obtain the services of a Dr. Hardy Pushcart," The Colonel continued.

"Who's that?" Mikey Mo asked, feeling once again that he had been kept out of the loop.

"Dr. Pushcart is an expert in ancient European and African history and an African dialect expert. One of his primary fields of expertise is the Ashanti dialect. He also wrote a book entitled "Atlantic Africa and the Spanish Caribbean." I have asked him to study the two diaries as well as the two calabashes we have in our possession along with the photos of the third calabash the Blacks delivered from New Orleans."

"Aren't you worried that he might talk to someone about the affair?" Betsy asked.

"Well, it's apparent that our secret is no longer a secret, since President Dudus has become involved," Colonel Winter said, "but I did make Hardy sign a confidentiality agreement making him legally responsible for damages if he divulges any information on the matter without my consent and made him liable for reimbursing me for his consulting fees. I can only hope dishonesty and loyalty will not become issues with him. We do need assistance, so I've got to trust someone. Hardy is supposed come here this morning and give me his initial feedback. I was hoping we could all meet with him together."

"We would really like to be part of this affair going forward," Will said. "This is a once in a lifetime opportunity for Betsy and me to be involved with an adventure of this magnitude. We have both told our employers we wish to use the vacation time we have coming to us to help a family friend."

"I'm glad you feel that way," Colonel Winter said.

"But we've got one request," Betsy said. "We don't feel right about imposing on Henry and Rose for an extended period of time. So, if at all possible, we would like to live at Sundance while we're here."

"There are no guests in it currently," Mikey Mo said.

"I will pay the rent," Colonel Winter said. "And you will accept Dr. Pushcart as a part of our team going forward. Agreed."

"Agreed. We will finalize our arrangements in Key West," Betsy said.

Will and Betsy heard a noise behind them. When they turned, they saw a yellow and black Honda CBR motorcycle turn onto Colonel Winter's yard. The driver was neatly dressed in chinos and a pale blue golf shirt and was wearing a helmet. He tooted his horn and parked his bike. When he took off his helmet, the Blacks saw a neatly-groomed, short-haired Jamaican who appeared to be in his late thirties. He had mostly nondescript features and straight white teeth. He was clean-shaven except for a pencil mustache. His one eye-catching feature was that his ears stuck straight out from the side of his head.

"The professor has arrived," Colonel Winter said and rose to greet their visitor. After introductions were made and the initial get-to-know-you was concluded, they all sat at The Colonel's front-yard concrete table.

"In my opinion, the gourds are authentic," Pushcart began. "The verbiage on them is 1700's vintage Ashanti, and the words are words that reflect the slaves' station in life. I think the words were added to supplement and clarify the pictures to denote landmarks."

"Excellent, Dr. Pushcart," Will said. "This is getting more and more exciting."

"If we are going to be working together on the same team," Pushcart said, "please call me Hardy, Mr. Black."

"Then we are Will and Betsy."

"I believe the lines on the three gourds are a rough map of sorts," Hardy continued. "There is a flower carved on one gourd. I believe that the flower may be meant to mark our final destination. Each

calabash contains an image that I find very puzzling. It looks like a crude image of a human face. He produced an internet picture he had printed on his computer.

"Now examine this picture and compare it to the ones on each calabash," he said. "It is called the Makapansgat pebble or the pebble of many faces. It is about the same size as a baseball and has been dated approximately 3,000,000 years Before Present. It could very well be the world's oldest known manuport. The name is derived from a cave in Makapansgat, South Africa. I have no idea why this image seems to be on each of the gourds, but it is there. I've got to believe it was put on there for a reason."

"Like being a clue to the treasure?" Will asked.

"Possibly, but at this point I really don't know. The pictures and the verbiage lead me to believe they were possibly describing Long Mile Cave in Trelawny Parrish."

"Is that good or bad?" Betsy asked.

"It's actually good but strange. It is not near the southern coast. It would have been a long walk," Hardy said.

"Especially lugging a heavy load," Will interjected.

"Let me fill you in a little more on Long Mile Cave," Hardy said. "The reason I said it is good is that it is an easy-to-access, mostly collapsed limestone chamber on private property, very close to Coxheath-Windsor Road, and getting to the cave from the road requires that you merely park your car and scramble over some boulders. I know the property owner, and he has let me explore it in the past. What is left of the cave is an overhang about three by six meters. Most of the original roof is in the form of boulders over a circular floor. There is no dark zone or biota to contend with. Some locals call it Hell's Gate Cave. Others call it Pick'ny Mama Cave because of a legend about some woman giving birth to a stillborn baby in it or some such nonsense."

"I haven't heard you mention any insurmountable obstacles so far," Will said.

"The last time I was in the cave it seemed to have been used as a shelter for some homeless people," Hardy said. "I saw some bags of clothes, along with some assorted bottles and other garbage, but no one had attempted to wall-off part of the cave behind the overhang and there were no signs of any recent digging."

"Doesn't sound like there's a whole lot to it," Betsy said. "Why's it so well known?"

"Because of the artifacts that have been found there. Archaeologists have found the bones of an extinct monkey there as well as human bones and pottery shards. One explorer even found the remains of a Taino kitchen there."

"So it sounds like we're heading for Long Mile cave," Mikey Mo said.

"And the sooner the better," Betsy agreed.

"I don't need to remind you to keep yu secret in yu own gourdy (that you are not to discuss this matter with any outsiders)," Colonel Winter said. "We've had enough unexpected company so far, and we don't need another incident."

"Did you tell Hardy who the source of our problems has been?" Will asked. "I think Hardy has a right to know what he is getting himself into."

"No, but I will now. The President – Dudus Coke," Colonel Winter said to Hardy.

"Whew and ouch," was all that Hardy could think to say.

"And Dudus' associate Harry Dog."

"Double ouch."

"If their involvement changes things and you don't want to proceed, I will understand," The Colonel said. "I don't want any more of my friends getting killed because of this lost treasure-trove. Remember please, be careful. And if yu yearry debil a come, clear de way (if you hear the devil coming, clear the way)."

```
┌─────────────────────────────┐
│  L.J. HYATT                 │
│  GOLDSMITH                  │
│  REPAIR WATCH CLOCK         │
│  SEWING MATCHINE            │
│  TYPE WRITER ECT.           │
└─────────────────────────────┘
```

# Chapter 20

Bunny Witter and Garfield Williams of the Spangler posse met at their Matthews Lane headquarters in Kingston.

"Dudus Coke has something big pending – something real big," Bunny said.

"And what dat be?" Garfield responded.

"I'm not completely sure, but one of mi "friends" says it's huge. Mi mole over there says the same thing. And he's got Harry Dog on special assignment."

"Maybe mi should assign someone to kind of keep a tab on things," Garfield said.

The Spangler Posse and the Shower Posse had been traditional adversaries. The Spangler Posse was a powerful Kingston gang founded in the Matthews Lane neighborhood in the 1970's. It and Dudus Coke's Shower Posse were considered by many to be the two most powerful gangs in Kingston. Whereas the Shower Posse was closely affiliated with the right-leaning Jamaica Labour Party and had been a large factor in making Edward Seaga Prime Minister of Jamaica, the Spangler Posse had been created and propagated by JLP's opposition, the left-wing People's National Party (PNP). Like the

Shower Posse, the Spangler Posse was notorious for being violent while at the same time being very generous in supporting west Kingston residents – another "Robin Hood" of sorts.

The Spangler Posse was very involved in the Jamaican political scene, and had been recruited recently to use strong-arm methods to help PNP Prime Minister Portia Simpson's campaign efforts. Bunny Witter had a more direct involvement in politics as well. On more than one occasion he had been the PNP's unsuccessful candidate for the West Kingston seat in Parliament long occupied by Edward Seaga.

The Spangler Posse had been founded by "Early Bird" Phipps and for many years the higher echelon of the gang consisted of other members of the Phipps family. For much of its existence, the gang had specialized in trafficking marijuana and crack cocaine. It had soldiers in both Great Britain and North America and was a major factor in the illegal drug business in New York City and New Jersey. Many members of the Phipps family had been killed in gang wars, many of which had occurred with the Shower Posse, or had been imprisoned through joint efforts of the U.S. government and the Jamaican government. With "Zekes" Phipps serving a long-term prison sentence, the day-to-day operations of the Spangler Posse were now being run under his prison-led direction by Bunny Witter and Garfield Williams.

A period of peace between the Shower Posse and the Spangler Posse had ended when "Rooster" Robinson, the under-boss of the Spangler Posse, had changed sides and joined the Shower Posse. Gang warfare then raged and soldiers from both sides lost their lives. Now Bunny and Garfield sensed they had an opportunity to even the score with Dudus Coke and profit handsomely at the same time.

"How'd you find out something might be up?" Garfield asked. "Fill me in on the details."

"As these things so often are, the story is a little complicated," Bunny said. "I haven't mentioned it to you before now because I was trying to make sure I understood it first myself, but here's the skinny. It all started with Colonel Ferron Winter."

"The Maroon Colonel in Accompong?"

"The same. It seems that a long-time resident in Accompong, a lady named Ruby Drain, died and her daughter, Isabel, approached Mikey Mo Mullins about a bequest her mother had made. Ruby's heritage was early Maroon, and she left behind a historical diary and a family heirloom. She also left instructions for Isabel to turn them over to The Colonel upon her death."

"So how did Dudus Coke get into this picture?" Garfield asked. "I never thought of him as a history buff."

"I'm coming to that. Well, it turns out that this diary was more than just another family curiosity. It was written in 1739 during the War of Jenkins' Ear between the Spanish and the British just before the First Maroon War concluded. It was written by the captain of the Spanish galleon, the Genovesa. The Genovesa has always been thought to have been sunk in a hurricane along with all its cargo in the waters off Kingston, but in the diary, Captain Guiral claims to have offloaded either some or all of his cargo before the Genovesa sank and to have hidden it in the Jamaican interior."

"So what kind of cargo are we talking about?"

"Maybe as much as $400 to $600 million in gold and silver."

"Rhatid! You don't mean! No wonder Dudus is suddenly a history buff," Garfield said, "but Jamaica is a big country to hide a treasure in."

"Yes, it is. And the story gets better. Colonel Winter has supposedly unearthed other clues giving him an idea as to where the treasure might be buried."

"This is getting *very* interesting," Garfield said. "So how did Dudus Coke get wind of all this. I'm sure Ferron Winter tried to keep a lid on this whole matter. He's a codgy old bastard, you know."

"Oh, Winter tried all right, but the diary was written in Spanish so he had to bring an outside translator into the picture. He hired Juanita Halliburton-James, an assistant professor from the University of West Indies Mona campus to translate it for him and educate him on the historical facts. What he didn't know was that the Shower Posse had anonymously endowed professor Halliburton-James' chair at the university so she owed Dudus big-time. She decided to use her knowledge as payback."

"Dudus and Harry Dog have a way of calling in their good deeds. They do very little out of the goodness of their black hearts."

"Sheeit, mon," Bunny said and laughed. "That's an understatement. Dudus Coke will never suffer from a heart attack. To have heart attack, you got to have a heart. But let me continue. Harry Dog told Dr. Halliburton-James to plant listening devices in Winter's house and yard."

"So how'd you get in the loop," Garfield said. "You're not on speaking terms with any of these people."

"I first started getting involved by wondering why Knuckles Biddle died. He was Shower Posse."

"I didn't hear Knuckles was dead," Garfield said.

"That's because he was killed trying to rob the tour guide Henry Davis – one of Colonel Winter's childhood friends. I heard through sources that Winter probably put the hit on Knuckles, and now Knuckles is assumed to be buried in a hole somewhere in the cockpit country."

"Why would Winter risk staring a war between the Maroons and the Shower Posse?"

"I asked myself the same thing and decided to monitor the situation. There had to be a good reason. After all, a war would be in our best interest since a war between those two could only benefit the Spangler Posse."

"You're right about that."

"Then I got an unexpected break. We both know that bushes have ears and walls have eyes. I am on speaking terms with Dr. Halliburton-James' secretary, Delores Packard. She owes me. A while back her son "Picker" Packard …"

"How's old "Picker" – haven't heard his name in a while – has he been around?" Garfield asked. "He was one of the best security-system and lock-pickers I ever knew. Didn't he emigrate to London?"

"Oh, he's still here. You know why he's gone underground, don't you? He was disabling security systems and robbing north shore villas until he got caught. I used my political influence to get him off, and he promised to go straight. He went straight all right – straight to becoming a security expert and changed his name to Link Ledingham.

Clothes may cover up character, but Link will always be Picker. As I said, that family owes me. I got Delores to make copies of a lot of Dr. Halliburton-James' notes on the whole matter and also got Delores to listen in on her boss's phone calls. And I got one of our mutual friends to introduce Link to Colonel Winter and to make sure The Colonel knew Link was a security expert. Well, to make a long story short, I had our mutual friend plant some suggestions with Mikey Mo Mullins that one of Link's areas of expertise was locating listening devices and disabling them. Mikey got Winter to bite, and we replaced Dudus' bugs with our own. I had him plant a GPS and a listening device on both Mikey Mo and Henry Davis's vehicles as well."

"Very good. Damn that's a lot of money! I'd *sure* love to find that mother."

"You mean that mother-fucking-load," Bunny interjected.

"… But it would be almost as sweet putting the screws to Dudus and Ferron. Neither one of those batty holes (assholes) ever did me any favors and never will."

"Colonel Winter has now gotten a white couple from America involved as well as his old buddy Henry Davis."

"Let's see what we can learn about the Americans. And if any of them get in our way, we can always take them out."

"Well, woo-iii, let's do it. The best thing we've got going for us right now is that none of this group knows that we know anything about this whole affair so we've got the element of surprise on our side."

"I agree. Let's take advantage of that fact. Jeezam (Jesus), $600 million! If it's only half that …"

"Or even a fourth of that," Bunny said. "That's a shit-pot load of money, and *I* mean to take it."

"We would never make that kind of money off selling ganja to Rastas."

"Beggar beg from beggar, him nebber (never) get rich."

"Amen, my brother."

# Chapter 21

The morning after their strategy session with Colonel Winter, Mikey Mo's expeditionary force departed for Long Mile Cave. They traveled west until they picked up Highway B6 and then went through Retirement, Vauxhall, and Siloah before coming to Windsor. Hardy called ahead and got clearance to visit the cave from its owner. They took Henry's bus so he could be there to watch their transportation and protect it from vandals while the rest of the group explored the cave. He would also serve as their lookout in case of trouble. Will gave Henry a loud whistle attached to a lanyard to wear around his neck so he could warn them if he sensed trouble developing.

The shoulder of the highway was narrow where they had to park the bus. Henry couldn't pull completely off the highway, but he assured them them it was "no problem" since he would be staying with the vehicle. Just as Hardy had explained to them the previous day, it was an easy climb over some boulders to reach the cave itself. They were thankful that their hike wasn't many kilometers into the craggy, snaggy bush. Hardy nimbly scrambled down into various breakdown boulder voids located along the inner edge as he led the party. It was soon apparent what he had told them about the cave had been accurate. They were not able to penetrate the cave more than several meters vertically when they got to it. Within a few minutes they stood on the circular floor of the mostly now collapsed cave. A fire pit was in the middle of the floor with some broken Red Stripe bottles in it.

"Now what do we do?" Will asked. "What are we looking for?"

"Just start looking, and don't get frustrated," Hardy replied. "Remember, time longer than rope (your patience will be rewarded)."

Will and Betsy began to run their hands across the dirt and rock wall while Hardy and Mikey Mo examined the floor. There seemed to be nothing of interest. Will sat on a boulder and opened a bottle of water.

"I'm starting to think this may be a wild goose chase," Mikey Mo commented as he wiped his sweaty brow on his sleeve.

"Don't be too quick to judge," Hardy said. "If the clues had been easy to find, they would have been found a long time ago. Open yu eyes and look. Ongle dos who cyaah dance blame it on de music (only losers make excuses)."

Will felt something crawling up his leg. When he looked down, he saw it was a wasp. He jumped up as he tried to swat it. When he did, his foot slipped on some loose pebbles throwing him backward, banging his head against the wall. The boulder he had been sitting on rolled forward, and he found himself in an awkward position sprawled between it and the cave wall. He tried to get up but couldn't seem to get his feet back under him.

"Are you hurt?" Betsy cried out.

"Mostly hurt my pride," Will said. "I don't guess a bump on the head and a skinned elbow is going to be fatal."

"Now I know what they mean when they say pride goeth before a fall," Betsy said and laughed as Hardy reached down to help Will back up.

As Will dusted himself off, he tried to move the boulder back to its original position. When he did, he saw something under it and started scratching at it to see what it was.

"Look!" Will called out excitedly to his companions. "I've found something."

He pushed the small pry-bar he had brought for digging under the object.

"This looks like a smaller version of one of those Makapansgat pebbles Hardy showed us on the calabashes," Will cried out.

"You're right," Mikey Mo said. "See if anything else is down there. Try not to break it."

Within minutes, Will had unearthed a small, green, glazed stoneware olive jar. Cowhide had been stuffed into the top of it. Other than one handle on it being broken, it was in remarkably good condition. The tattered cowhide crumbled when they tried to remove it. A calabash was in the jar. When they held it up, they saw it had inscriptions carved into it.

"I guess this is the clue that's hidden in the cave. Do you think the treasure might be here as well?" Betsy asked.

"My guess is that it would've been too lucky for us to find it on this first attempt," Hardy said. "Let's get this back to Accompong so I can study the gourd when I can concentrate, and if we need to come back to Long Mile Cave after that, we will."

Suddenly they heard Henry's whistle.

"Something's up," Will said. "We better hide this thing."

"I'll put the jar back in the hole and roll the rock over it," Hardy said, "while you find some place to hide the gourd. Hurry! Henry might be in trouble."

Betsy dropped the Makapansgat-like rock down into the pocket of her vented Columbia fishing shirt. Will clamored out of the cave searching for a hidey-hole. He saw a cluster of banana trees growing wild in the undergrowth not far away. He ran over to it and jammed the gourd into the thicket. It blended right in with the brown aging banana corms. He jumped back when a hairy, poisonous banana spider scurried out of one of the corms, grabbed a rock and smashed it.

"I hate those things."

Mikey Mo, Betsy and Hardy scurried over the boulders to get back to the road while Will finished covering the calabash with banana leaves. They saw two motorcycles parked behind Henry's van. Henry was on the ground. One of the uniformed men was holding s leather sap while the other was snatching the whistle off Henry's neck. Mikey Mo immediately recognized the white-seamed blue serge trousers and the blue-striped, short-sleeved shirts as belonging to the Island Special

Constabulary Force. Each man also wore a black hat with blue stripes around the top.

*Odd,* he thought. *Why would the ISCF be out here? This area is normally patrolled by the Jamaica Rural Police Force. And don't they usually use patrol cars?*

The ISCF was the primary backup reserve force for the Jamaica Constabulary Force. It was normally given tasks requiring minimal skills like preserving peace and keeping order in urban neighborhoods. Almost two-thirds of the ISCF officers were used in Kingston and St. Andrew. The JRPF or District Constables whose powers extended to all parts of the island were much more likely to be patrolling this rural area.

As Mikey Mo approached the car, his suspicions increased. One of the men clearly had a gang-related tattoo on his forearm. One man standing over Henry turned and through clenched teeth said, "Tan right deh and don't back chat unless yu waan de sed, batty hole (stand right there and don't talk back unless you want the same, asshole)."

*This is definitely not how an ISCF officer is taught to treat or speak to a citizen,* Mikey Mo mused, his thoughts reverting to a past incident in which rogue officers had once beaten him and cut off his dreadlocks just because he was a Rasta.

"Is dat a Spangler Posse tat on yu arm?" Mikey Mo asked, hoping to send a message to his companions that these men were not legitimate law enforcement officers. The others glanced down at the man's arm and knew what Mikey was trying to tell them. At that second, Will came running up the hill, momentarily distracting the man. Mikey Mo grabbed at the thug's arm.

The man reacted by swinging his leather sap at Mikey Mo. Just as he did, Hardy produced a pocket pepper spray container and squirted it in the man's eyes. The man howled in pain and dropped the sap. Betsy took this opportunity to kick the man in the knee. She heard a snap as the tendons gave way, and the man tumbled to the ground screaming in agony. When he hit the ground, she kicked one more time, this time catching him in the groin. He screamed like a wounded cat, but this time two octaves higher.

Hardy turned and sprayed the other man with the pepper spray. At the same time, Will pulled his kubatan from his pocket and stabbed the man in the Adam's apple with it. The man didn't know whether to clutch his eyes or his throat. He grabbed at Betsy's shirt hoping to get something to wipe his eyes, ripping it off. Betsy, now with only her bra on, grabbed the shirt back and swung it as hard as she could, the rock still in the pocket. The rock hit the man in the teeth sending him to the ground, unsure what was hurting him worse – his eyes, his throat or his mouth. Hardy grabbed the leather sap off the ground and hit the man in the head, giving him one more place to hurt and then kicked the man again. The man moaned through his bloody mouth as he lost consciousness.

Hardy then grabbed one of the motorcycles and pushed it off the side of the road. It bounced off the shoulder and down the steep, strip-mined incline. Mikey Mo grabbed the other one and did the same thing. The bikes tumbled at least 20 feet before coming to rest as a twisted mass of metal on top of each other at the foot of the hill. Will and Betsy grabbed Henry and helped him to his feet.

"Are you hurt?" Betsy asked.

"I don't think so, at least not permanently" Henry said. The first man seemed to be recovering so Henry kicked him in the groin a second time. He too passed out.

"Are you dizzy? Can you drive?" Will asked.

"I'm fine. I just have a headache," Henry said. "A little rum will cure that when we get back."

"Everyone – in Henry's bus - now," Mikey Mo shouted. "Let's get out of here before these guys cause us any more trouble."

Henry cranked the engine.

As they pulled away, Will said, "What about the calabash?"

"We'll get it later," Mikey Mo said. "They don't know where or what it is, and I don't think they're in much of a mood to begin a search.

Mikey Mo called The Colonel on his cell phone and told him what had just happened. After Mikey Mo assured him that everyone was OK, Colonel Winter said he would send someone to retrieve the lost gourd.

"How did they find out you were going to Long Mile Cave?" Colonel Winter asked Mikey Mo. … "And when you'd be there," he added as an afterthought.

"I don't know, but they were sure here waiting on us."

"But they don't know what you found?" Colonel Winter asked.

"I don't see how they could," Mikey Mo said. "We didn't even know ourselves what we were looking for."

"And still don't know the significance of what you found," Colonel Winter added.

"You're right. Hardy was planning on studying it when we got back."

"I guess you know the Constabulary uses the ISCG to patrol Tivoli Gardens, Dudus Coke's stronghold," Colonel Winter said.

"But these guys were Spangler Posse," Mikey Mo said. "I recognized the tattoo."

"You must be wrong. You mean Shower Posse, don't you?" Colonel Winter said.

"Uh-uh," Mikey Mo said. "I know Spangler Posse symbols when I see them."

"How'd they get into this picture? Our activities are turning into the worst kept secret on earth. I guess Queen Elizabeth will know next."

"Damned if I know how the Spangler Posse got into the act," Mikey Mo said, "but I know what I saw."

"I trust you to know your stuff. Neither posse has an exclusive on corrupting the regular ISCG patrolmen. I've been told that some of ISCG people are also sometimes secretly members of various posses."

"No wonder people think posses controls armies," Mikey Mo said. "They do."

```
┌─────────────────────────────────────────────┐
│              NOTICE                           │
│      1 ACRE & 2 PURCHASE                       │
│      OF LAND FOR SALE                          │
│      APPLY TO .... MR & MRS GRANT              │
└─────────────────────────────────────────────┘
```

# Chapter 22

Henry's cell phone then rang. It was Colonel Winter.

"Are you OK, my friend? Do you need to see a doctor?" he asked Henry.

"I'm fine. Just a little bump on the head, not as bad as some of the bumps we used to get as children," Henry said.

"Maybe so, but we're not children anymore."

"Don't tell Rose. I don't want her worrying any more than she already is."

"I'll let you tell her the story your way. There's no use bringing the Blacks back to Accompong until I can retrieve the calabash and give Hardy time to study it. I'd rather they not stay at Club View and put you and Rose at risk again. Drop them off in Discovery Bay and stay with them until my men arrive. They'll bring Mikey Mo and Hardy back up here. I've made arrangements with Leva Carter for the Blacks to move into Sundance. She is thrilled to have them as her guests again. I'm sure she's preparing a grand reunion, but make sure there's not too much celebrating. Keep your guard up. Our enemy is determined and able."

A Treasure Conspiracy

"I know, chicken deh merry, hawk deh near (even in the happiest of times danger is lurking and one must be watchful)," Henry said.

"Precisely, mi parri (my old friend). Once you have the Blacks moved, then you can bring Chicken and Hardy back to Accompong."

"Will do. We be talk soon forward. Mi gaan for now (we'll be in touch soon. Goodbye for now)."

"Soon come, mi fren. And tanks again (see you soon, my friend. And Thanks again)."

Henry drove back to Club View, and they said goodbye to Mikey Mo and Hardy when their ride arrived shortly thereafter. As Mikey Mo and Hardy were leaving, Mikey Mo's phone rang. He answered it and listened silently before hanging up. Will and Betsy went into the house to pack their things for the move to Sundance.

When they arrived at Sundance, Kingtoo opened the gate. Leva was still scurrying around trying to make sure the villa was just perfect for their arrival. She was in a grand mood as she mopped the front stoop and was singing *Put Your Hand In The Hand* merrily to the radio as she almost danced with the mop. As soon as Henry stopped his bus, she put the mop in the pail and rushed out to greet Will and Betsy. After everyone hugged and commented on how good the other person looked, E.J. took the bags into the house and put them in the master bedroom. He then returned to the yard to close the gate, briefly patrol it for any irregularities, and then feed Gina and Samantha, the house Rottweilers.

"I've planned a special dinner for you tonight," Leva announced proudly. "All your favorite dishes.

"And I hope you made enough for Henry and Rose," Betsy said.

"Of course. The Davises are family."

"I hope you saved me something to do in the kitchen," Betsy said.

"You and Rose just stay out of my kitchen. Get on out of here and enjoy yourself," Leva said and wagged her finger. "I have a pitcher of fruit rum punch waiting for you on the back porch."

"Which you and E.J. *will* help us drink when he gets back up to the villa," Will said. "God, it's great to be back home at Sundance again. And I'm torn as to which view is better – the one from the porch or seeing you two."

"The porch view can't light a candle to the sight of my favorite Jam-Mericans," Leva said. "Now, go put some music on the stereo. Make it light and happy. I feel like I won the lottery having you folks back."

"Then I've got just the song for you. How about some Keys music? I've got a Leo Dean album with me which is sure to bring a smile to your face," Will said.

Soon Leo Dean's *Six Lucky Numbers* was playing on the house stereo system.

About that time E.J. returned to the house. He was now wearing his "Jailhouse Rock" t-shirt showing Elvis gyrating in his prison stripes. He looked mildly disturbed.

"When Jamaica's Elvis is in the building, it's time to party," Will said with a laugh.

"Anything wrong outside, E.J.?" Leva asked.

"No, Mrs. Carter. Mi just dash weh (throw away) a snakeskin ova (over) de fence. Samantha was playing with it. Mi didn't want her to eat it and get sick. It might be Ol' Hige's skin," E.J. said.

"If it Ol' Hige's skin, yu shouldn't have thrown it away but should have put salt and pepper on it instead. Then Ol' Hige won't put its skin back on because it burn it so bad, and then it would go away," Leva said.

To change the subject, E.J. said, "You do know, don't you, that Honey-Pye here is the person who found out where you were being held."

Leva beamed and put the snake skin out of her mind.

"But Kingtoo here is the person who conceived of the plan on how to rescue you," Leva said.

Now it was E.J.'s turn to beam.

"Thank you; thank you; thank you. And we want to hear the details about both," Betsy said. "And don't leave out one little thing – we want to hear every word."

They all hugged again, and Leva poured each person a drink.

Will raised his glass and said, "I'd like to offer a toast to lying, stealing, cheating, and drinking. When you lie; lie for a friend. When you steal; steal a heart. When you cheat; cheat death. When you drink; drink with me."

"Cheers," Henry said in agreement.

In short order, the group killed the pitcher of fruit rum punches, and Leva made another one. E.J. and Leva took turns telling about each of their involvements in the Blacks' rescue. Then she announced that dinner was served. Leva began the meal with pumpkin soup. Then she served jerked chicken, peas and rice, callaloo, and plantains, some of Will and Betsy's favorite dishes. She capped the meal off with a cornmeal pudding. After dinner, Rose and Betsy helped Leva clean up in the kitchen before the exhausted group decided to call it an evening.

With their attention on the reunion, the Sundance revelers were oblivious to the fact that their party was being monitored from Almond Tree, the empty six-bedroom villa next door. Almond Tree's co-owner and property manager, George Kirby, was an "exporter" who had dealt with Dudus Coke on many occasions. They also sometimes bought rental properties like Almond Tree together to launder their profits. It had only taken one phone call from Coke to Kirby to get the key to Almond Tree. Harry Dog had gone to pick it up. Now one of Harry Dog's men sat in the dark next door waiting for an opportunity to plant listening devices in Sundance.

After midnight, a still somewhat tipsy E.J. awoke to a sound in the yard. He turned on a flashlight and nervously walked out into the dark. His light shined on Gina who lay still in the yard.

"Who godeh (goes there)?"

Samantha, their other dog, began to bark and chase something or someone in the dark. E.J. couldn't tell what she was chasing.

"Mi raahi (oh, my God)," the superstitious E.J. screamed "Ol' Hige! Yu come back. Mi should have put salt and pepper on yu skin dis afternoon like Leva say. Please do nuh get mi. Yu mek mistake. A nuh mi yu waan (please don't get me. You're making a mistake. It's not me you want)."

The surprised, now-exposed apparition ran in the dark towards the villa until it suddenly tripped on a giant cotton tree root. It jumped back up before Samantha could reach it and took off for the nearest structure, E.J.'s garage apartment, not knowing that after seeing the snake skin that afternoon E.J. had been taking protective measures before bedtime to protect himself from a possible return of this duppy. Leva's warning confirmed in E.J.'s mind that the snake skin had indeed been a sign that an Ol' Hige might be on the property, and he had taken steps to protect himself from that possibility. His fan had been running on high in case the Ol' Hige was there to suck E.J.'s air out of him as he slept. The interloper slipped on some salt E.J. had sprinkled on the floor. E.J. had sprinkled it out liberally so that if he was right about the snake skin, the Ol' Hige's burning sensation resulting from contact with salt would keep it from putting his skin back on, thereby leaving him temporarily vulnerable. The hapless intruder then stumbled into a shelf containing granular ant poison. It spilled, and E.J's fan blew it into his sweaty face. As the insecticide blew in his eyes and temporarily blinded him, he inhaled more poison, and it went down his throat. As he began asthmatically wheezing and simultaneously rubbing its burning eyes, Samantha burst into the room. The would-be thief screamed loudly in a high voice, further convincing E.J. that there was an Ol' Hige in his apartment. E.J. dived under his car belly-first and skidded on a driveway oil spill being soaked up by cat litter. The intruder swung at Samantha with a yard rake, but after missing the dog, he began to run for the gate. Samantha, however, grabbed one shoe and pulled it off. The man then ran gimpy-legged on his remaining shoe towards the closed gate. As he tried to climb the unlocked gate, it swung open leaving him dangling from it until it stopped swinging long enough for him to jump down, spraining his ankle.

By this time, all the lights in the house were on. Will, Betsy and Leva came running out the front door to see what the excitement was. They heard a metal-on-metal crunch in the dark outside the gate when a Toyota Corolla driven by one of Colonel Winter's trusted men, Cooley Man, turned into the driveway. He had been dispatched to Sundance in case security was needed.

Cooley Man jumped out of his vehicle and ran up the driveway. Leva shouted, "Mi raahi, whaap'm (my God, what's happening)?

"Mi just run ova bike in da dark (I just ran over a motorcycle in the dark) outside the gate," Cooley Man said. "Don't shoot. I work for Colonel Winter."

"Whaaap'm bike driver (what happened to the motorcycle driver)?" Leva asked.

"'Blacka mon run weh (a black man ran away). Wen mi call 'im but 'im seem fraidy fraidy (when I called out to him, he seemed afraid)," Cooley Man said. "'Im be hut (hurt)."

"Tank raad yu dehyah (thank God you're here)," Leva said in a panicked voice.

Leva began to search for E.J.

"Kingtoo, Kingtoo! Where yu at (where are you)?"

E.J. climbed out from under the car. His entire front was covered with oil, grease, and cat litter.

"Ku paan yuh tu (look at you). Are yu hut (are you hurt)?" Leva asked worriedly.

"I and I mek Ol' Hige gwey (I made Ol' Hige go away)," E.J. said proudly.

"Looks to me like you and Samantha did - with a little help from The Colonel," Will said. "Where's Gina?"

"Mi raashi (oh, my God)!" E.J. exclaimed and ran to where Gina was lying. "Mi forget. Did Ol' Hige queng (kill) Gina by sucking the air out of her?"

"Gina's not suffering from Ol' Hige," Will said. "I thinks she's been poisoned with that rancid meat next to her. Our nighttime intruder was definitely a burglar – and not a duppy."

"Hurry! Bring Gina to the side of the house by the water hose," Betsy said. When E.J. just stood there paralyzed, she shouted, "Now!"

Moments later, Betsy began to squirt water down Gina's open mouth. Gina didn't react at first, but finally she vomited, expelling the poisoned meat she had eaten. Gina tried to stand up but slumped back to the ground. Samantha whimpered as if she knew something was wrong with her companion and licked Gina in sympathy.

"I think we got to her in time," Will said. "That was good thinking, Betsy. I think you just saved Gina's life."

"What do you want to bet that E.J.'s Ol' Hige was one of Dudus' men," Betsy asked, "looking for whatever we found at Long Mile Cave?"

"Kingtoo, you may believe in duppies," Will said, "but I don't think Ol' Hige has taken up motorcycle riding nowadays."

```
special new rates
Paradise Park Sawmill
for custom cutting timber
SAWING LOGS = $ 60 PER  100BOARD FEET
*** PLAINING AND THICKNESSING ***
= $50 PER 100 BOARD FEET
*** 24 Hour Express Service ***
```

# Chapter 23

Will sipped some tea, as he explained the previous night's encounter at Sundance to Colonel Winter. Betsy filled in parts of the story.

"Dudus or Harry Dog somehow knew we had moved from Club View to Sundance," Betsy said. "But how did they find out so quickly? They seem to know our every move as quickly as we do. I'm getting to the point I don't know who I can trust anymore."

Will looked at Mikey Mo and said, "I'm sure glad Cooley Man showed up when he did."

"The Colonel told me on the phone as we were leaving Long Mile Cave to keep an eye on you," Mikey Mo said. "We *will* get to the bottom of how Dudus is able to track our every move. I promise you."

"Maybe Dudus sold his soul to the devil to get his own duppy," Will said and laughed.

"You mean the Shower Posse has a house duppy," Betsy said. "Maybe it's a rolling Faust."

"I was thinking more like 'now playing wide receiver for the Shower Posse we have Whistling Cowboy and his giant three-legged horse,'" Will said. "Itty-itty-hop; itty-itty-hop."

"In that case maybe we need an obeah man as our quarterback," Betsy said with a smile.

"Nah, 'if there's something strange in the neighborhood, who you gonna call?' "

" 'Ghostbusters,' " Betsy answered.

" 'If there's something weird and it don't look good, who you gonna call?' " Will said.

" 'Ghostbusters,' " Mikey Mo now chimed in.

"All kidding aside," Betsy said. "With everything that keeps befalling us; I'm getting paranoid about anything and everything. If Dudus' men show up one more time, I might even begin to believe in duppies myself."

Colonel Winter just sat silently and smiled as his younger colleagues bantered back and forth and tried to relieve their stress and frustration as they all waited for Hardy to arrive.

Finally The Colonel said. "Just remember, no ebery chain you hear a fe rollin' calf (every chain you hear is not a rolling calf)."

"I know you're right, and I'm overreacting. But thank the good lord we didn't have the calabash at Sundance," Betsy said.

"At least that was one thing President Coke didn't know," Will said.

Hardy drove up, parked his car and walked across The Colonel's front yard. He was carrying the Long Mile Cave calabash with him. After greetings were exchanged and he was served some tea, they got down to work.

"First, let's look at the drawings. You will notice this primitive face. Look familiar?"

"Sure. It looks somewhat like a Makapansgat pebble," Will said, "but something doesn't seem right."

"The mouth – the mouth is different," Mikey Mo said.

"Precisely," Hardy replied.

"This one's got a great big mouth," Betsy said.

"Yeah, it looks like a big old happy face with an upturned banana mouth," Will said. "What does that mean?"

"At this point, I really don't know," Hardy said, "but I'm sure there's a reason it was carved that way."

"Maybe the artist was just happy he wasn't a slave anymore," Will said, "or because the sight of all that gold made him think about what he could do with it and this made him a very happy camper."

"I don't think so, Will," Betsy said.

"Or maybe he's drawing a picture of his – you-know-what – because he got a little lovin' the night before," Will said and winked.

The group laughed. Betsy blushed and said, "My husband is all class. Too bad so much of it is low."

"Let me continue. This gourd has some interesting inscriptions," Hardy said. "For instance, notice these words – nson and gu."

"Which mean?" Betsy asked.

"The words are Ghanese Akan. Many of the early slaves in Jamaica were originally imported from Ghana. Much of Ashanti is derived from Ghanese Akan. Nson means seven; gu means falls. This made me concentrate on Jamaican waterfalls. As you know, we have many. I think the clue is about YS Falls in St. Elizabeth Parrish. It's comprised of seven waterfalls."

He paused to see if there were any questions or if anyone wanted to play devil's advocate with his conclusion. Instead, the group sat silently and thought about what Hardy had just told them.

Hardy continued. "Here is another inscription - Ohu du nsia susuw anee kwadu. That translates as '117 measurement west banana.'"

"And you clowns laughed at me for saying it looked like a banana," Will said. "I may not know Akan, but I recognize a banana shape when I see one."

"I would say you don't know a banana from your you-know-what," Betsy said, "but I won't stoop to below-the-waist humor."

"What is your interpretation of that?" Colonel Winter said, as he tried to get the conversation back on track.

"Once again, I wish I knew," Hardy said. "Something is obviously 117 paces west of something else. The only thing I know to do is to make another expedition and see if we can get to the bottom of the puzzle. One thing's for sure, we're not going to do it from here. By the way, once again YS is private property. I looked up the owner's name, but it's not anyone I know personally."

"Give me the owner's name, and I'll take care of things," Colonel Winter said.

"Since YS is open to the public, why don't we just pay to go in, and Will, Betsy and I can pretend to be American tourists while Mikey Mo will pretend to be our tour driver. That way we won't set off and any bells and whistles which might bring us to the unwanted attention of our opposition," Hardy suggested.

"It's an easy trip from here," Mikey Mo said. "We just get on B6 and head west to the Black River. YS is between Maggoty and Savanna la Mar."

"Sounds like a good plan," The Colonel said. "You guys up for another field trip?"

"Do one-legged ducks swim in circles?" Will asked.

"Can a middle-aged stockbroker become a threat to Henny Youngman?" Betsy retorted.

The verdict was a unanimous "no-way" followed by "Will, don't give up your day-job for stand-up comedy."

"At least this group isn't a bunch of hypocrites who talk about me behind my back," Will said.

Colonel Winter got in a final playful jab with, "Will, just remember, my friend. Behind the dog, it may be 'Dog'. In front of it, it's 'Mister Dog'."

# Chapter 24

Leva Carter cut up tropical ingredients to make a fresh fruit cocktail for Will and Betsy's breakfast. They had told her not to prepare her usual morning feast since Mikey Mo had told them to save their appetite for a surprise he had in store for lunch. Henry drove them to Accompong. Hardy and Mikey Mo were waiting. After a brief meeting in Colonel Winter's front yard, a change of plans was agreed upon. Since they were going to be masquerading as tourists and since a tour driver normally waited in the parking lot for his guests to enjoy their outing, Henry would drive the group to YS instead of Mikey Mo. This way Mikey Mo could diplomatically enter the park with the others, and they'd have an extra set of eyes and hands when needed.

Henry got back on Highway B6 and headed west towards Negril.

He traveled through a mile-long avenue of bamboo and turned off at Santa Cruz onto the main road to the Black River at Howie's roadside cook-shop. Howie's was the surprise Mikey Mo had been saving for them. They could hear Inner Circle's *Sweet Jamaica* playing in the background.

"Howie's is one of St. Elizabeth's great well-kept secrets," he told the Blacks. "Their pepper shrimp is to die for, and they also make great

123

curried goat stew. But I'm telling you right now, you can't go wrong with anything in there. I hope you brought your appetite like I told you to."

Hardy agreed with everything Mikey Mo said about Howie's, and they quickly arrived at a consensus to order enough pepper shrimp for the entire group.

Howie's was a low shed with a dozen steaming, smoke-blackened, steal cauldrons set in a row. Each was balanced over a few burning logs on its own tripod of rocks. Several cooks tended savory pots of conch, fish and oxtail. Mikey Mo walked up to a gaunt man he knew who called himself Peckes and gave him a finger-interlocking thumb-rub handshake.

"Hail up, mi fren. Yuh gud (hello, my friend. How are things)? Mikey Mo asked.

"Everting is everting (all is going according to plan)," the man responded. "And yuh?"

"Mi nice, mi nice," Mikey Mo responded. "Mi group need pepper shrimp fo five."

Peckes consulted a woman named Vila, who then picked up a cell phone and placed an unintelligible phone call.

"Soon come," Peckes said. "Red Stripe?"

Mikey Mo held up five fingers and said, "Yah, mon. Dat be gud."

He then ordered bowls of a sweet, almond-and-bay-leaf-scented peanut porridge for his friends to eat while they waited. Fifteen minutes later there was no sign of the pepper shrimp. Vila placed another phone call.

"Soon come. Soon come," she said after she hung up.

Ten more minutes passed, and just as Betsy began to wonder if they would ever be served, a tall woman emerged from a house on the hill. She introduced herself as Margaret Stone and set down a large stainless-steel bowl heaping with flaming red 'shrimp'. They were actually large river crayfish topped with chilies that looked more like tiny lobsters. She shoveled several pounds into a black plastic sack and then spooned in some more.

"Dese extra spoonfuls for waiting," she explained.

They took their bounty back to Henry's bus. When Will and Betsy looked into the bag they could see and smell that the 'shrimp' had been stir-fried in minced Scotch bonnet peppers, coarse sea salt, pepper and vinegar.

"Boy, do these look good!" Betsy commented.

"And smell even better," Will agreed and tasted one. "Chicken, yu did gud, my friend. Dis eat gud (this tastes wonderful)."

The pepper shrimp were spicy, sweet and addictive and turned out to be the most delicious – as well as the messiest car snack Will and Betsy had ever encountered.

When they finished, Will announced, "Now I'm ready for whatever YS Falls has in store for us."

"Then let's get gone," Henry said. "Now that our bellies are full, time's a-wasting."

They left Howie's and drove along a bumpy back-road lined with some of the tallest logwood trees in Jamaica. Despite the potholes, the view was fresh, green and soothing.

"YS Falls soon come," Mike Mo said, and he was right.

After they arrived at the YS ticket office which doubled as a bookshop, bar and grill area, they bought four of the $17 admission tickets. Henry stayed with the bus. Everyone else put on a bathing suit. Will carried some garden tools in a backpack. A scenic but bouncy jitney ride took them to YS Falls themselves. After the group had spent a few moments taking in the wonder of the falls, they realized that there was something there for virtually every kind of tourist. Visitors could swim or just hang out in the pools at the bottom of each cascade or swing, jungle-style, from a looping rope into the falls and then splash down feet-first. Kids and adults both cavorted in the pools.

YS's grounds were lushly landscaped and picnic tables dotted the grounds here and there. Some people were snapping pictures while others were just relaxing and reading a book.

"I'm impressed," Will said. "This is very nice."

"Nice enough to almost make you forget why you're here," Betsy said, "but we better get to it. Let's split up and start exploring."

Hardy noted a rough, local-looking man eyeing them through binoculars. When Hardy looked his way, the man immediately turned and began observing another group.

"I wonder if he's an employee," Hardy said.

"Probably a lifeguard," Mikey Mo answered. "Or maybe security."

"Funny. The people in the ticket office were all wearing YS t-shirts. This guy's not. Hmmm, makes me wonder, but OK, gang; let's get busy."

Hardy pulled a pocket compass from his shirt pocket and oriented himself.

"That way is west," he said and pointed. "Whatever it is we're looking for is supposed to be 117 paces west of something. Let's each take a waterfall and try to identify what might appear to be a meaningful landmark. When and if you see something, walk 117 paces west of it and see what you find there. If you don't find anything, pick something else that might have been here 300 years ago and walk west of it. Don't know what else to do. We'll meet at that picnic table, in say … 30 minutes and compare notes."

He pointed at the empty picnic table he was referring to and then pulled out the guide map of the property to give each of them their assignment.

"If someone is using the picnic table 30 minutes from now, just hang out near it under that tree until the rest of us can get there. If you find something, don't create a stir and attract attention. Wait and tell us about it when we meet."

"But there's only four of us, and there's seven falls," Mikey Mo said.

"You're right, but have you got a better idea? We'll just have to do the best we can. If need be, we'll then explore the remaining falls together or make new assignments. Just remember, the Makapansgat pebble has been part of this equation up until now and could very well continue to be."

As the other people turned to head towards their assigned waterfall, Hardy noted that another man had his binoculars now trained on them. This man also turned away when Hardy looked in his direction. Hardy began to search the horizon. Within seconds, he saw the man he had seen earlier. This man still had binoculars trained in his direction. He again turned away. When Hardy looked up again, the men had their binoculars trained on each other.

*Odd! More security? I guess it's a sign of the times.*

Hardy glanced at both the men again. Each was on his cell phone calling someone while gesturing towards the other man.

*Really odd! Could they be talking to each other?*

The group reassembled thirty minutes later. No one had found anything even remotely resembling a clue as to what they were looking for.

Betsy made a suggestion. "You two each take one of the remaining smaller falls. Will and I together will take the largest fall we haven't examined yet. If we are still unsuccessful, we'll prioritize the falls and either visit each fall as group or assign a different person to revisit each one. Sometimes a different set of eyes will see something the first eyes missed."

As they turned to leave, Hardy noted, "Both those men have moved to different spots, but each still seems to be watching us through binoculars. They don't seem to be together. In fact, they seem to be watching each other as well as the park's guests. I need to make a note to find out if either of those guys works for YS when we get back to the entrance complex."

The second foray was equally unsuccessful. It was beginning to be frustrating.

"I haven't even seen what looks like a clue," Mikey Mo observed. Everyone was in complete agreement on that issue. They agreed with Betsy's prior suggestion for each person to revisit a waterfall different from the prior one he had visited.

"We've come too far now to quit," Hardy observed.

"Are those two men still here?" Will asked.

"Yes, they are, and they're still watching. But they're not standing out in the open any longer," Hardy said and pointed to where each of the men stood back in the shadows. "But right now I'm not worrying about them as much as I'm worrying running out of day before we accomplish our mission, forcing us to make a second trip here."

The group split up again, but Will and Betsy decided to stay together. As they threaded their way from one fall to another, Betsy stepped in a hole. Will caught her before she fell.

"You didn't twist your ankle, did you?"

"No, I'm fine."

"We both better watch out. I almost fell into a hole similar to it over here," Will said. "My hole is about the same size as yours was. It was the second one I've stepped into today."

Betsy took a few more steps before stepping down into an oblong trench. At first it appeared to have been hollowed out by the water flowing over the spot for a long period of time, but when she looked closer, it seemed to have more definition.

Suddenly she had an idea. When she drew a mental line between the three holes, it made a rough triangle with each hole being about equidistant from the other two.

"Will, let's climb to the top of this fall and look down. I just had a crazy thought."

"I'll take any thought right now, crazy or not. OK, follow me. What are you hoping to see?"

"I don't know yet, but I want to get up higher to get a panoramic view of things below us."

They climbed to the top, and both looked down.

"Will, what do you see?"

"I don't know. What am I supposed to be seeing?"

"Try imagining a face."

"Hmmm. You're right," Will said. "The three holes are like two eyes and a nose, and the trench you stepped down into looks like a big mouth. Maybe we've found the world's first happy face."

"And that big mouth looks to me like it's shaped like a banana — a Makapansgat face with a banana mouth," Betsy said. "This has got to be the waterfall the calabash was instructing us to find."

"By God, I think you're right! It does! The banana on the calabash is the key we've been looking for!"

"117 steps west of the banana, that is."

"I think you've done it! You've solved the riddle! Let's head back down there!"

"Do you think the treasure has been right here at YS all these years with tourists obliviously playing around it?"

"Anything's possible."

Will and Betsy almost ran to try to get back down the waterfall. When they reached the pool with the face, the Blacks picked a side point on the mouth to use as a starting point, and Will began to pace 117 steps. Nothing. They picked the middle point, and Will counted 117 paces once again. Still they saw nothing. He paced from the other end of the mouth, but again he came up empty.

"Let's think. What are we doing wrong? Is it the wrong number of paces? Or did Hardy translate the calabash wrong?"

Betsy thought for a second, "No, my dear. Don't think so. I'm going to guess it's the wrong length of paces. You're over six feet tall, and you take long steps. People were not as big 300 years ago."

"Once again, you're right," Will said. "I read Captain Cudjoe was only a little more than five feet tall."

"And barefooted on top of that."

"And the brush was most likely a lot thicker then."

"So let's cut our number of paces back by what – a third?" said Betsy.

"Or we'll keep the paces the same, and you do the walking instead of me since you're shorter than I am ... and then shorten your stride even more than usual. Try it the first time from the end of the mouth that is most westerly."

Betsy paced off the distance. She ended up before a wall fascia covered with vines and roots.

"Well, that didn't work. Let's try again from a different place," Will said.

"Not so fast. As long as we're here anyway, let's clip some of these vines off and see if there's more to this than it first appears. I'm not so sure this wall is natural."

"I'm sure glad we brought some garden tools."

After clipping some vines, Will looked at the fascia and commented, "I think you're right. This does seem to be man-made – crude but man-made, just like a lot of the stone walls we've seen all over Jamaica."

"Look at the places where those roots are growing through it. The outlines around them look vaguely round. And look at where that next root is growing below them. The area around it looks sort of round too. Do you think they look kind of eye and nose-ish?"

"Maybe," Will said. "I guess if you really stretch it. If that's the case, the root coming out of the nose-ish one looks like a big old booger."

"Only a man ... let me rephrase that ... only *you* would see that," Betsy said.

"But where's the mouth?"

"Notice where your booger root curves back in and grows back into the wall," Betsy said. "See this rock here." She pointed to a rock. "Looks kind of broken on one side, doesn't it?"

"OK, so what's your point?"

"See this rock down here?" She pointed to another rock. "Imagine it up where the other one is. What do you want to bet that at one time this was all one rock, and the root plus the erosion over 300 plus years pushed the broken-off piece down here where it is now?"

"We both know roots have been known to grow through solid concrete," Will said, "and it doesn't take 300 years for it to happen either."

"Now, put those two pieces together in your mind. Can you visualize a mouth?"

"I guess maybe if you're Salvador Dali," Will said as he pulled out the garden trowel he had packed. "Let's try to see it better."

A few minutes of digging loosened the stone, and he pried it out.

"Betsy, you were right. There is something on the back of this rock," Will said as he began to knock the dirt off the stone.

"We'd probably never get this out of the park without getting caught. Besides that would be stealing," she replied.

"That's all we need is to get arrested for stealing private property," Will agreed. "You snap some pictures of it. And take a couple of shots of the overall rock wall while you're at it as well."

"While I'm doing that, why don't you start digging and see if you can dislodge the other piece," Betsy said. "Let's hurry before someone comes along, and we get caught. I don't want to have a run-in with those security men who've been watching us all day."

Within minutes Will dislodged the other stone and began to clean it off. He compared the two stones. The jagged edge on each matched the other.

"Yep, this one's got something on the back of it as well. Are you finished taking pictures of the first stone?"

"Yes, but let me check the pics real fast and make sure the inscriptions are legible in them," Betsy said. "Then I'll snap some pictures of the second rock."

When Betsy had finished the second round of pictures and was satisfied that all of them were clear, she said, "Now, let's do our best to put both rocks back where we found them and cover them with brush. In this climate, it should only take a couple of rainstorms and this area will look completely undisturbed again. Then let's go find the rest of our group and get out of here while the getting's good. I'm positive we've found what we came for."

"Thanks to your good eye," Will said. "I knew there was a reason why I made you my queen other than your pinup-girl-bod and your cooking ability."

"As our good friend Henry Davis would say, 'One-eye woman a queen a blind country' (a one-eyed woman is queen in a blind country)," Betsy responded. Will smiled.

"I think your 'Jam' side is beginning to take over your 'Merican' side, my dear."

When they were satisfied they had covered up the rocks as well as was possible with what they had to work with, Will and Betsy returned to the picnic table. As Betsy waited there, Will began to scour the premises to round up Mikey Mo and Hardy.

"We're virtually positive we found what we came here to find."

"May I see it?" Hardy asked.

"Probably not a good idea. Rather not take a chance now since we photographed the rocks," Will told them, "I'll fill you in and show you the pictures after we leave here. If we have to come back another day for you to see the stones, we will, but I don't think it's going to be necessary."

When the jitney arrived back at the ticket office, Henry was waiting. Hardy asked him to wait for another second while he went into the office. The others waited in Henry's bus. When Hardy came back out, his face was screwed into a scowl.

"Anything wrong?" Henry asked.

"Maybe. Maybe not. We can talk about it later. Right now, let's get on down the road ASAP," Hardy said.

Will and Betsy did not know it at that moment, but their discovery had been observed by one of the men with binoculars. After they left, he climbed up to where the Blacks had found the face. He did not recognize the Makapansgat face, but he easily identified where Will had been digging and unearthed the "mouth" stones. He called someone on his cell phone who instructed him also to take photos. When he finished, he didn't bother to conceal the stones again. The second man, who had been watching him, waited until after the first one had left to see what everyone was finding so interesting. He too made a phone call as well and was told to take the stones with him. After he explained that he didn't think he could smuggle them out of YS without getting caught, he too was instructed to take pictures of the stones with his telephone.

Neither man understood what they were looking at or photographing. They didn't much care, since each was merely following orders.

J. T. SHAND

Tailor. Suits.

Made To Order

Beff Mutton

Sold Here

# Chapter 25

After they had left the YS property, Betsy said, "Hardy, do you mind now telling us what happened in the ticket office that seemed to upset you when you went back in as we were leaving?"

"Those two men with the binoculars – the ones who kept watching us – neither of them works for YS Falls."

"So they weren't security men after all?" Will asked. "Do you think they were members of the Shower Posse?"

"Maybe one was, but I don't think both of them were," Hardy said. "They seemed to be keeping tabs on each other as well as us. And each seemed to be reporting to someone periodically on a cell phone."

"I just thought they were just talking to each other," Mikey Mo said.

"I did at first myself," Hardy replied. "Now, ... I'm not so sure."

"My God, how many adversaries do we have?" Betsy asked.

"I really wish I knew," Hardy said. "But whoever they all are, they sure seem to know almost as much about our business as we do. You two are staying at Sundance in Discovery Bay, right? I'm going to suggest to The Colonel that our next meeting should be held there. Maybe if we change meeting locations, we can get one-ahead on whoever we're up against."

"And if that doesn't work, I'm going to end up being so paranoid that I'll put a rear-view mirror on my stationary exercise bike," Will said.

Everyone smiled.

The group had no way of knowing, but their comments were not confined to Henry's bus. Harry Dog was listening through a planted device. *Two alarms now went off instantly in his head.*

*How soon can I bug Sundance? And what fassy claffy (dickhead idiot) is watching my man? And who the hell does this fassy claffy work for?*

He looked quizzically at the photos of the YS stones his man had sent him.

*What the hell does the shit on these rocks mean? Well, at least whoever sent his man to watch my man doesn't know that the next meeting will be at Sundance. By the time it takes place, I'll arrange to be able to hear everything they're talking about. I won't need to be holding any Americans hostage. In retrospect, that wasn't such a great idea anyway.*

While Harry Dog was pondering the situation, Bunny Witter was making a phone call. He had been listening to the conversation in Henry's van as well.

"Garfield, you should have heard what I just heard," he said. "Colonel Winter's group saw your man and suspects something. They saw him watching them, but ... get this ... he wasn't the only person watching them."

"I know," Garfield said. "My man took a picture of the other jerk and sent it to me on his phone. One of Dudus' soldiers."

"So do you think Dudus' man recognized your guy?"

"My guess is that if my man recognized Dudus' man, Dudus' man recognized ours as well. ... Or if he didn't, he soon will."

"So Dudus will soon know we're meddling in his business?" Bunny observed.

"I'm sure if he hasn't figured that out already, he soon will."

"Rhatid! I hope this doesn't lead to more war with the Shower Posse."

Garfield said nothing.

"My man also sent me pictures of some damned rock The Colonel's people found at YS. I have no idea what it's saying," Bunny said. "I was just listening to the bug we put in Henry Davis' van. They're so scared they're going to start meeting at the white Americans' villa. It's in Discovery Bay and is called Sundance. You've got to get some men to plant some listening devices in there. I'm sure Dudus doesn't know about the venue change so at least we'll still be one step ahead of him."

"If Dudus got pictures of the YS rock, I'm sure he doesn't know what it means either," Garfield replied. "And I'm going to assume, like you did, that Dudus doesn't know about the meeting place change since we were the only ones smart enough to bug Mr. Davis's van. We'll still be one step ahead of him. We've just got to make sure we stay that way."

"I really want to get the best of that smirk batty hole (asshole) for a change. Get your men busy bugging Sundance immediately."

"Feel no way (don't worry), mi fren. Until, tek care a yuhself."

"Jah bless, mi bredda (God bless, my brother)."

RASSPBERRY JELLY
FOR SALE

## Chapter 26

E.J. heard a horn toot at Sundance's front gate and strolled out to see who it was.

"Greetings. How can mi help yu?" he asked the driver of a panel truck.

"Mi dehyah (I'm here) to do termite inspection," the man said.

"Wi no a dat wi tichi (we don't have a problem with insects)," E.J. said.

"Yu no undastan. De inspection free - part of yu termite policy. Mi hab to do it to keep yu policy in force."

"Cumon in den," E.J. said and opened the gate.

The panel truck drove up the driveway. The man got out and pretended to inspect the perimeter of the villa. As he walked around, E.J. followed him. Gina smelled something familiar she didn't like and began to growl and stalk him. Gina lunged. The man slipped on a wet spot, turning over a five gallon plastic bucket full of water on himself. When he stood, his pants were partially soaked. He was beginning to get angry.

Gina growled again.

The man looked panicked and became nervous.

# A Treasure Conspiracy

*Isn't dis the same dog mi poisoned? Mi tink (think) this mutt was dead. Does he remember mi? Dat why he growl?*

E.J. didn't understand what the problem was but knew he should immediately restrain Gina. The man had forgotten he had put some soft dog treats in his pocket in case the villa had a second patrol dog other than the one he thought he had poisoned a few nights earlier. They were turning to mush in his sweaty pocket. He kept anxiously looking over at the growling dog and in his nervousness, could not seem to think clearly enough to find a logical exterior location for a bug. Even if he had, it would have been impossible to plant it with E.J. standing there watching him as he continued to contain the periodically snarling Gina.

Harry Dog had provided him with two types of monitoring devices. One was a Voss-Mauser Bio-Trac GPS tracker. It was a small device which was implantable with a pain-free implant gun. It implanted a device about the size of a grain of rice under the skin with a sting not much more than a mosquito bite. His orders were to try to surreptitiously implant one in either Will or Betsy Black. He had brought a single device since he expected that he would only have one opportunity to do so. Harry had made it clear that he didn't care which of the two ended up as the carrier of the device since he assumed that the Blacks went virtually everywhere together anyway.

The man had also been instructed to plant Edictophone mini listening devices in the house. These wireless devices were not much bigger than the head of a screw and attached with adhesive. They would transmit conversations to recorders at Almond Hill, the villa next door on Sundance's eastern side. Harry would then monitor the Almond Hill recorders. So whether meetings were held at Colonel Winter's house or at Sundance, Harry expected that he would become the treasure hunters' undesired silent partner.

When the man entered the house, he once again explained his mission to Leva and convinced her to allow him to search the villa for signs of termites. As usual, Leva had left the front door and the back French doors open to take advantage of the breeze coming up from Discovery Bay. Betsy was in the kitchen with her. Leva was showing Betsy how to make a jerk chicken casserole. Leva had first put black beans into a casserole dish. A platter of chicken thighs sat to one side. She had gotten allspice, thyme and cayenne out of the cabinet which she planned to use as a rub on the chicken. Other ingredients for the recipe lined the counter. When the man entered, Leva was dicing a large peeled sweet potato to add to the bowl of beans, and Betsy was engrossed with watching her assemble what would prove to be a delicious dinner that evening.

*Perfect,* the man thought. *Neither dese gals paying mi the least bit of attention. A perfect time to shoot the backra* (white slave driver) *with mi mini tracker. She so engrossed with the cook, she'll never know de difference. She just think a mosquito bit her.*

Just as he aimed and prepared to release the GPS, Gina came running into the kitchen still recognizing the man's scent from Sundance's break-in. She growled but stopped when she smelled the soft bacon-flavored dog treats in the man's pocket. As she began to nuzzle him, Gina nipped at the now gooey, yummy treats, leaving dog slobber on the man's pocket. When he jerked away, it threw off his aim. Instead of hitting Betsy, the GPS flew into Leva's casserole dish of black beans. He was now so preoccupied with Gina that he didn't even know his tiny missile had missed its intended target. E.J. rushed over and once again restrained Gina, yelling "bad dawg, bad dawg".

"Hush (sorry). Mi apologize," E.J. said. "Mi duh know what got into her."

The upset man snapped, "Yu betta control yu dawg, or mi control it fi yu, house bwoy. Seen (understand)?" For emphasis, he then slashed his index finger across his own throat.

Thinking his first mission was accomplished, the man then began to look for what seemed to be a logical place to put the Edictaphone listening devices. He decided that Will's office would probably be the most likely place for a business meeting to occur, but he had to get Will out there long enough to plant it. While he was waiting for his opportunity, he took a second bug out of the pocket containing the dog treats. His pocket was coated with the wet, pulverized bacon-flavored treat.

*Damn dat dawg. If there weren't so many witnesses, mi tek care of he sorry ass - for gud dis time.*

The man wiped the device off and stuck it under the dinner table on the back porch and then secured a third moist bug to the underside of the coffee table in the living room. Gina followed him from one room of the house to another watching him.

The man became nervous and called for E.J. to come get Gina, but E.J. was cleaning debris from the swimming pool. Will responded instead.

"Here," Will said. "I'll hold the dog for a few minutes. I've been planning to take a break and stretch my legs anyway."

*Perfect,* the man thought. *This will get the damned American out of his office long enough for me to plant a bug there.*

Within moments, he pulled another bug from his pocket and stuck it underneath the top of Will's desk.

The man went back in the kitchen and approached Leva.

"Mi report yu termite problem OK," he said.

"Do mi need to sign anyting?" Leva asked.

"No problem. No paperwork," the man responded. "Bless up (have a nice day)."

The man called Dudus Coke from his panel truck and said "Mi dun."

"Dey believe yu story?"

"Dey suspect nuttin."

"Gud job."

After the man left, Gina went into Will's office and smelling the dog treat residue on the micro device began to lick it. When it came loose, Gina swallowed it. Liking the taste, she sought out the other ones and swallowed them as well before returning to the front yard to take a nap.

Shortly after the first man left, another truck pulled up to the front gate and honked. E.J. went to find out who he was, never suspecting the man was from the Spangler Posse. Garfield Williams had also dispatched one of his soldiers to plant listening devices in Sundance.

"Exterminator," the man announced.

"Wi do nuh need yu. Yu man just leff," E.J. said. "He say wi do nuh have termites."

This momentarily floored the Spangler Posse's would-be listening device installer.

*What de hell dis house bwoy talking about? Did Garfield send sumbody else?* he thought.

He had planned on posing as a termite inspector. He quickly recovered his poise as he thought of a "plan-b".

"Nuh, mon, mi nuh here to inspect for termites. Mi called because dey say yu have ants and roaches. Yu need to leh me in."

The thoroughly confused E.J. relented and opened the gate.

"Where yu bug sprayer?" E.J. asked when the man got out of his truck.

The man hadn't thought about this detail when he was forced to shift gears.

"Uh, noh," he quickly said. "Mi just inspect today. Mi send registered technician back to do spray anedda (another) time."

When E.J. gave him a disbelieving look, he said. "Mi can noh help (I can't help) damned Babylon system (government) regulations."

Before this man left, he too had successfully planted all the devices Garfield had sent him to install. After he left Sundance, the man went to Villa Brawta on Sundance's western property line to install the equipment and the relay and test them.

So now both the Shower Posse and the Spangler Posse were confident that each had regained control and were one step ahead of the other.

Each was only partially right.

```
CROW'S
TYRE
REPIARING
24 HOURS DAILY
SUNDAY TO SUN
```

# Chapter 27

"Do you mind if E.J. takes his day off tomorrow?" Leva asked Betsy.

"Of course not," Betsy said. "What's up?"

"E.J. is supposed to take his mother to a religious meeting."

"On a weekday?"

"It's a revival meeting."

At that moment, there was a horn-toot out at the gate. E.J. ran up the driveway to open it.

Leva smiled and said, "Great. I'll tell him. Henry and Rose are here. Now I can serve dinner."

Leva served the jerk chicken casserole she and Betsy had assembled that morning. They sat at the table, and E.J. asked the blessing.

"Tek (take) mi bady (body), Jesus, eyes, ears and tongue. Never let dem Jesus help to do dese wrong. Tek (take) mi heart and fill it full of love for dese all mi hab mi give yu (all I have I give to you). Give yuself to mi. And Lord, tank yu for de food we bout to receive for the nourishment of we bady sake (our bodies)."

Everyone said, "Amen."

"That casserole looks delish," Will said.

"There's plenty for seconds," Leva replied, pleased by Will's compliment.

Everyone took a serving. E.J. got the portion with the Voss-Mauser Bio-Trac GPS in it. He swallowed it never suspecting a thing and washed it down with a big swallow of tea.

"So what church does your mother attend?" Betsy asked.

"She's a Revivalist," E.J. said.

"I never heard of that," Betsy said.

"Some people call them Prayer Meeting Revivalists," Leva said.

"Tomorrow they be drilling," E.J. said.

"Drilling?" Will asked.

"Yes, you know, drilling and tramping," E. J. said.

The Blacks gave each other a puzzled look.

"What E.J. is trying to say," Henry interjected, "is marching and foot stomping. They chant and play drums to help the Holy Spirit become manifest and flow outward."

"Doesn't sound like any church we've ever attended," Will said.

"It's a Jamaican thing," Henry said.

"Is your mother Zion or Pocomania?" Rose asked E.J.

"She is a sister of Pocomania," E.J. answered. "Her shepherd is David Livingstone."

Since the Blacks kept looking confused, Henry decided to give them a quick history lesson.

"The Prayer Meeting Revival movement began in America in the 1850's, and in the '60's," he began, "it moved into Jamaica. Once here it divided into two groups - Zion and Pocomania. Zion is more Christian oriented while Pocomania is more African. The altar is covered with a white cloth and flowers, fruits, bibles, hymnals and candles are put on it in a stair-step fashion. Revivalists also always have a water pool since water is deemed to be the home of the functionaries like River Maid and Diver who protect the church members."

"The tramping E.J. was talking about occurs after the worshipers sing or read Bible verses. They stomp and beat on cymbals and other percussion instruments while they "drill" or march counterclockwise around a circle singing and playing drums or tambourines. It's kind of a peculiar march where they use forward stepping motions while they bend their bodies forward. They believe this singing and dancing opens their eyes to the presence of the spirits and opens their ears to the spirits' messages," Rose added.

"Sounds like some kind of holy-roller cult," Will said.

"Is your mother attending one of those quarterly revival meetings in Watt Town?" Henry asked E.J.

"The Watt Town in St. Ann?" Betsy asked.

E.J. nodded.

"The Watt Town meetings really showcase all facets of the Revivalists' religion," Rose continued. "You often have more than just the cymbals and the dancing. I'm told that sometimes you might see spiritual possessions, healings, and warnings from the spirit world."

"Yes, it should be an interesting day, E.J. Are you a believer?" Betsy asked.

"No, but my mother is. I told her I would pick her up and take her."

"Their services must certainly be interesting," Betsy added.

"They are not restricted to members," E.J. said. "I'll be glad to take you if you would like to attend."

"Well, we don't want to get in your way," Betsy said.

"No problem. Besides that, you've never met my mother, and she's never met you. I've told her so much about both of you."

"Well ...," Will and Betsy hesitated.

"Please come," E.J. said.

"You're sure ...."

"If the Blacks are going, I'll drive all of you in my bus. It's only fourteen miles. We'll go through Brown's Town to get there," Henry said to E.J. "I can keep an eye on Will and Betsy and keep them out of any awkward situations ... plus I'll answer any questions they have while you concentrate on taking care of your mother."

"This would be a good time of year to attend," Leva said, "since it's not so hot right now."

"I think it'll be fascinating," Betsy said. Henry and E.J. agreed on a departing time.

Harry Dog did not hear this exchange. All he could hear was the traffic out on the road. His listening devices by this time had passed through Gina's system and had been deposited in a pile of Gina's stool out by the front fence. Since E.J. had swallowed the GPS, Harry soon became aware of their trip the next morning, however, as soon as E.J. left Sundance. He began to track E.J.'s ingested GPS not knowing it would soon be leading him to a church service instead of Spanish treasure. Bunny Witter was also monitoring Sundance with the bugs he had planted. Harry quickly dispatched two of his men to follow as well. Bunny heard more than Harry did. He wasn't sure exactly what was about to transpire, but he didn't want to risk missing something important.

The following morning, Henry picked up E.J's mother, Gladys, in Orange Valley, and they headed into interior on Highway B3. Gladys was proudly wearing her pink and white uniform for the revival. The road became very steep as they approached Watt Town. An old car packed with worshipers was having trouble making it up a steep hill. The worshipers in white tunics and turbans got out and began to walk beside it. The old car remained under pressure. One woman led the group as they sang and circled the car, touching the car ceremoniously as they joyously sang and danced. They then changed drivers, and things improved slightly. Finally, with the people now pushing, the old car climbed to the top of the hill. Then the worshipers piled back inside, and their journey continued on the hill's downside as they continued to sing.

"Jeezam!" Henry said. "I thought that car was getting ready to break down, or that it might roll backwards into us."

They arrived in Watt Town without any further fanfare. Many vehicles were already parked, but more were arriving all the time. Henry had trouble finding a place to park. Lots of merchandise was for sale at the foot of the hillock. It was like a little market day.

Will and Betsy could sense the excitement when Henry pulled into town. The pilgrimage was well under way. There was singing on top of the hill, and people in colorful uniforms were lined up waiting to be formally received.

"Each church group is called a 'bans,' and its members can be identified by the uniform they're wearing. Before each bans can enter the church, they have to perform a certain ritual, and they all have to do it together, so if part of the group gets here before the rest, they just have to kill time and wait for the others to arrive," Henry said.

Newly arrived groups were on the "seal", as the consecration ground was called, each making their presence known in their own way. The inside of the church was packed, and Will and Betsy could see and hear singing, preaching and tramping going on.

Henry told them, "Let's go around all that," and led them up some jagged stones towards a revival tent. E.J. took his mom to try to find her bans.

The sun was high in the sky and colorful flags fluttered in the breeze. Inside the tent, food was being cooked in a makeshift kitchen. Different bans were scattered, each doing their own thing. Dedicated young and aged revivalists were in their element while other people were walking around nonchalantly, possibly not understanding the significance of the day, as they concentrated on all of the mouth-watering food present at this combination of a prodigious Pocomanian picnic and religious renaissance.

Betsy clicked away, taking pictures with her Smartphone. A woman in a multi-colored tunic and turban was dancing, singing and breathing heavily. She seemed to be working herself into a trance-like peak of exultation. Betsy was momentarily nervous when the woman seemed to be suddenly staring at her after Betsy snapped her picture. Then, just as Betsy's paranoia was taking hold, the woman shrieked, "Henry Davis?" and came over and started to hug Henry. He looked momentarily confused but then responded "Anne Lathem?" and began to hug her back. He introduced Anne to Betsy and Will and told them that he and Anne had grown up together. They talked about how the other person had changed in the decades since they had seen each other and exchanged phone numbers.

"This is quite a gathering, Anne," Will said.

"This is when we're delivered out of our darkness and our load … and we're free," Anne said. "We're free to speak, and we see the light, and our weight is gone. It's our moment of spiritual revelation."

"Yes, I can see that," Will said, not knowing what else to say. "The enthusiasm is certainly contagious."

"Our religion is spiritual, the old time religion of Christ of the apostolic age. We don't believe in sitting in church and letting the pastor do all the preaching and praying. The unity with God comes when the people themselves find the glory that's in religion and then show it.

"It makes us happy. There's a feeling that God is with us and is doing something good in the world. At a point, we break and enter a semiconscious state and shatter the barrier. We know that man is not alone - that God dwells in us and is moving in us. This is when we're inspired to speak in tongues. Even the uneducated are able to speak as if they were educated when that power is upon them, and it can tell about Christ and how to live," Anne said and began to hug them all and put flowers in their hair. "Glory be to Christ and the Holy Father!"

With that, Anne's focus appeared to dim as she seemed to enter a trance-like state and began to shout Hallelujah over and over. She began to stomp her feet and beat on a tambourine. As quickly as she had appeared and with no goodbyes, Anne was sucked into the boisterous crowd and joined a passing group of trampers.

By this time Bunny Witter's men had arrived and found a parking place. They silently watched Henry, Will and Betsy from a distance.

"Do you know who that woman was?" the first man asked his companion. "Did she give them something on a piece of paper?"

"Yes she did, and he gave her something back," the second man said. "I wonder what it was."

"Didn't you used to be a pickpocket?"

The man smiled and said, "They didn't come any better than me."

"Weeelll, do I have to spell it out?"

"No problem, mon. You will have both pieces of paper before we leave here."

If the two men had been more observant, they might have noticed Harry Dog's agents had arrived as well since LeVar and Gabriel were standing near them reading their lips as they talked. Each still had itching scabs on their faces as well as blurred vision from their accidental encounter with the caustic acid in Whistling Villa's swimming pool.

Gabriel motioned for LeVar to walk out of the earshot of Bunny's men.

"We gotta get those pieces of paper before they do," he said.

LeVar nodded in agreement and said "Or if we can't, at least make sure they don't leave here with the papers."

Will and Betsy saw a bearded, turbaned man and then heard his deep voice begin to talk in a sing-song manner.

"De shepherd shrieves in Egyptian light ... "

They could not hear what he said next so Henry motioned for them to try to get closer. People were elbow to elbow with them on all sides.

"Remorse of poverty, love of God
Leap as one fire; prepare the feast
Limp now is each divining rod,
Forgotten love, the double beast ..."

"What's he talking about?" asked Will.

"Don't look at me, white boy; I don't have a clue. I flunked Pocomania 101," Betsy said as the robed man began to speak something about a lamb bleeding on a Coptic cross followed by another statement about a Judah Lion.

"What does that make you, an educational slow poke?" Will said. "Were you in the bonehead class for laggards?"

"No. I just wasn't manic about manias," Betsy said to get in the last word.

Whatever it was about, it set off the crowd around them. Another robed participant began to beat a kettle drum; another one crashed some cymbals; still a third person began to madly shake a tambourine.

The group began to simultaneously sing a song that seemed to be titled *Evil, Evil.* This song competed with another group not far away who seemed to be singing about Zion and Armageddon.

The pickpocket slipped up behind Henry and prepared to make his move. LeVar readied himself as well. He had an ice pick in one hand and was prepared to use it if it became necessary, knowing there was very little chance he would be identified in the unrestrained, noisy crowd. The pickpocket reached for the note in Henry's shirt pocket. Just as he did, a stomper stamped LeVar's foot. He stumbled into the would-be thief, stabbing him in the back with the ice pick. The pickpocket gasped and jerked his hand. The flailing hand tore the pocket off of Henry's shirt as he grabbed the note with Anne Lathem's phone number between his index finger and his middle finger. LeVar fell face first into the dusty ground, still grasping the bloody ice pick for all to see. Bunny's man automatically pulled a pistol out of his waistband and aimed it at LeVar. Just as he did, a cymbal player and good Samaritan crashed his cymbals together, catching the would-be shooter's head between them. His ears felt like they would explode and his eyes clouded. LeVar threw the ice pick, but instead of stabbing the rival hoodlum, he only bounced the handle off of him. The ricocheting ice pick stuck in the calf of the man who was still enthusiastically reciting the religious poem.

"Have mercy on those furious lost

Whose life is praising death in life.

Lower the ..."

The man stopped in the middle of a sentence and screamed in the same breath, "Boxcova (damn you), yu bumboclaaat (wad of used toilet paper). I and Jah gon grab yu buddy (your privates) like a snapping turtle and nuh (not) turn loose till judgement day" as his leg gushed blood.

LeVar grabbed the note and began to run through the crowd with it. Henry stuck out his leg. LeVar tripped over it and went head first through a bass drum. The angry crowd converged on him and began to stone him. When they ran out of rocks, some began to kick LeVar. By the time Gabriel was able to intervene, LeVar was unconscious.

The note with the phone number floated away in the breeze.

```
┌─────────────────────────────┐
│  SUCK.LONGS                 │
│                             │
│  FOR SALE                   │
└─────────────────────────────┘
```

# Chapter 28

"Colonel, this is Hardy," Hardy Pushcart said into his cell phone, "I've had an opportunity to examine the latest clues concerning the Genovesa treasure and have come to some conclusions. Is this a good time for me to share them with you?"

"No," Colonel Winter said. "Since we have not solved our security problems here in Accompong, I would prefer that you assemble your team and share your thoughts with them directly. I'm also not sure this phone is secure. I'll have Mikey Mo get back to you with a time and a place."

"Do you wish to be present?"

"No. Not necessary since I'm not part of the ground force investigating the clues. Mikey will keep me abreast of what I need to know. Of course, this doesn't mean that I won't be involved on a need-be basis. I just think after the rash of undesirable incidents we've experienced that we need to be more security conscious than ever."

"I agree," Hardy said. "I'll wait to hear from Chicken. May I suggest we keep Mr. Davis in the loop and involved?"

"Of course! I have the utmost confidence in both Henry's perceptiveness and discretion. Our friendship goes back to childhood."

A meeting was arranged at Sundance. Leva, ever the perfect host, insisted on making some saltfish fritters with a honey jerk sauce and putting a big pitcher of tea in the middle of the table on the back porch. Henry arrived first; Mikey Mo brought Hardy with him and arrived shortly thereafter.

When he saw people arriving, Ruddy-Puss, the houseboy at Almond Hill, immediately made a call on his cell phone. He aspired to be a member of a gang – any gang. His brother Punkin-Puss was a Shower Posse member. Ruddy-Puss had become impatient since the Shower Posse didn't seem to be taking his ambitions seriously. The Spangler Posse's Garfield Williams answered Ruddy-Puss' call immediately.

"Mistah Williams, dis Ruddy-Puss at Almond Hill. Yu know, Punkin-Puss in Shower Posse brudda. De mon in de pikcha yu mon show mi is at Sundance right yah now (the man whose picture you showed me is at Sundance right now)."

"Him be deh lang (has he been there long)?"

"No, him just get deh. Yu wan mi to sup'm (he just arrived. Do you want me to do something)?"

"No, Ruddy-Puss. Yu criss. Mi tek care it. Jah bless (you did good. I'll take care of it May God bless you)."

"Will yu tell Mistuh Witter yu pleased with mi?"

"Yeh mon (of course)."

"Yu mek place for mi?"

"Yu canna big up yu chest (you can be proud of yourself). A foonu time will come (your time will come) if yu keep on prove yuself. Yu hab mi word (you have my word)."

Garfield Williams immediately turned on the relay in Villa Brawta so he could monitor the meeting taking place at Sundance.

After briefly enjoying Leva's fritters, the group got down to business.

Hardy spread the pictures Will and Betsy had taken at YS Falls out on the table.

"Notice the message on the back of these two broken pieces of stone when they are reassembled," he began. "They are inscribed,

'Kobina pili atá kúmaa yao ntonni.' This is Ashanti for a name and an honorary name."

Garfield Williams began to listen intently from his end. He would later repeat what he had heard, even though he hadn't understood it, to his fellow posse member, Bunny Witter. He did not know it, but when he did so, he would also be accidentally sharing this information with Harry Dog who was at that moment monitoring him.

"The Ashanti believe there is a bosom or subordinate spirit to God for each day of the week and this bosom acts as an intermediary between each bosom's human slaves and God," Hardy continued.

"What's a human slave?" Betsy asked.

"Persons who are born on that bosom's day," Hardy explained. "It is much like the Catholic's patron saint or angel. Each Ashanti child is given an African name for the day of the week in which he was born. This name is to honor their bosom. Is everyone up with me so far?"

The group nodded so Hardy continued. "'Kobina' means a male child born on a Tuesday. 'Pili' means second born. 'Atá kúmaa' means this child is the eldest or second born of twins. 'Yao' means his father was born on a Thursday. 'Ntonni' means that the father was considered to be a war hero. Have I lost you yet?"

"Almost," Will admitted, "but go on. I'm sure you'll pull it all together."

"There is also the word 'nyankopon' on one stone. This is an alternate Ashanti word for God. God to the Ashanti was 'nyame,' but he was sometimes called 'nyankopon'."

"So summarize all this for those like me who can't see the picture," Will said.

"I only wish I could," Hardy replied. "What we have here is the description of a person, but I don't know what the message is that the author is trying to convey."

"Let's brainstorm. Do any of these words designate a specific place in Jamaica?" Betsy asked.

"The closest place any word could be referring to *is* Accompong," Hardy said. "Accompong is the white man's bastardization of 'nyankopon'.

"So is this clue trying to lead us to an eighteenth century person in Accompong?" Henry asked. "Where would you find a record of an Accompong resident from this period?"

"The cemetery," Will said.

"If that's the case," Mikey Mo said, "there are three cemeteries to choose from since each tribe had its own."

"You're right, Chicken," Hardy said. "There is the Ashanti burial ground, the Coromantee burial ground, and the Congo burial ground. In each case, the graves traditionally are outlined with stones but do not have the customary western grave markers to identify the deceased."

"I know where each cemetery is," Mikey Mo said. "Each was placed in relation to the Kindah tree."

"And the graves are often marked with plantings like calabash, rose apple, crotons, or dragon's breath," Hardy said.

"So I guess we're going puttering in potter's field," Will said.

"Don't you mean groovin' in the graveyard?" Mikey Mo answered.

"I was thinking of it more as tomb tomfoolery," Betsy said.

"That's it," Will said. "Henceforth, we'll call ourselves by the code name of 'The Tomb-Fools'.

Betsy said, "How about 'The Raiders of the Tribal Tomb'?"

"Do you know what the acronym for that is?" Will said.

"ROTT?" Mikey Mo ventured.

"You got it. I can live with that. With a name like that, we're bound to have rotts of luck," Will said. "All in favor of our new name, say yah (yes)."

"The way you guys are going it's going to be the cataclysm in the crypt," Hardy said, refusing to be outdone by their alliterative descriptions.

"I know our new theme song," Will said. "Remember the hard rock band Oingo Boingo? They were in the Rodney Dangerfield movie *Back To School*.

*It's a dead man's party*
*who could ask for more,*

D.J. Mikey Mo took over singing.

*Everybody's comin', leave your body at the door*

*Leave your body at the door,* Will and Mikey Mo repeated, harmonizing somewhat with each other.

But Will wasn't ready to let the banter rest yet.

"It's in an area we call – the Twilight Zone …," Will said and then began to sing the notes to the intro to "The Twilight Zone" television show.

*Dum dum dum dum,*

*Dum dum dum dum*

Leva stood there watching and laughed.

"This whole bunch is dumb, dumb, dumb, dumb," she said as she circled her right ear with her pointed index finger.

Garfield Williams, who was listening on the other end, began shaking his head.

*A wah di rass (what the fuck)? Treasure hunters?* he mused. *Mi tink da cook tan right. (I think the cook's right). Dey just sick inna dey head (they're just sick people).*

Garfield then called Bunny to repeat what he had just heard.

```
NO ENTRANS

NO IDLEARS
```

# Chapter 29

Mikey Mo reported back to Colonel Winter. He repeated what he could remember about the Ashanti vocabulary lesson, Hardy's translation of the words, and the conclusion of the participants.

"This is going to be like looking for a needle in a haystack," he told Colonel Winter. "It's almost overwhelming. Where *do* we start?"

"Just remember, fill yu basket one item at a time," Colonel Winter replied. "I will call my LFMC contact Mr. Hong-Lowe. He is an anthropologist with the Local Forest Management Committee. He has a team which had a grant to study Maroon war strategies. I wrote one of his letters of recommendation when he tried to get in. They've done historical searches from available literature and have drawn up maps of the area inventorying and assessing the condition of historical Maroon sites. Don't know him well, but he seems to be a good guy. I'll just tell him you are doing genealogical research. I see no need for you to broadcast the true reason for your inquiry."

"I agree. Too many people know our business already. Should we all meet with him?" Mikey Mo asked.

"I don't see why not. I'll tell him to expect your entire group. His office is in the Jamaica National Building Society office building in the Catherine Hall section of Mo Bay."

"I know that part of town fairly well," Mikey Mo said. "I've worked Sumfest at the Catherine Hall Entertainment Centre before. That was when I got to introduce Barrington Levy."

The appointment was made, and Henry drove the group to Montego Bay. They went in on Creek Street to Humber Avenue. Harry Dog followed from a distance. Mikey acted as a tour guide, pointing out the Montego Bay Sports Complex and the Catherine Hall Entertainment Centre as they passed each. Soon they were approaching the JNBS building. It was a two-story beige building with yellow and blue accent trim going around the upper floor. LFMC rented unused space from JNBS. They had no problem locating LFMC's office where they found Hong-Lowe waiting for them. The man who came forward seemed to be partly Asian and partly Jamaican.

"Mr. Hong-Lowe?"

"Please call me Hu. Who do I have the privilege of addressing?"

Hardy noted the name plate on his desk – Dr. Hu Hong-Lowe.

Hardy introduced himself and said, "I am Dr. Hardy Pushcart and these are my assistants. I'm not sure what Col. Winter told you of my credentials. I am a consultant and researcher specializing in matters pertaining to ancient African history and African dialects, and my work often has a particular focus on topics relating to the Ashanti people. I am currently working on a project for a client who wishes to remain anonymous."

"How may I help you?" Hu asked.

"We are currently researching the genealogy of a family who we have reason to believe has forbears possibly buried in one of the cemeteries in or around Accompong. Have you made maps of the Accompong cemeteries and possibly identified some of the grave sites?"

"I take it that the family or families you are researching are of Maroon lineage."

"That is correct," Hardy said. "Have you been able to compile a list of the names of the Maroons who were living in and around

Accompong in the mid 1700's? If so, would it include which cemetery the person might be buried in?"

"No. As you know, record keeping was not as good three hundred years ago as it is now – especially for slaves or former slaves."

"We have reason to believe that this person might have been a war hero," Hardy said.

"Do you have a name?"

"An African name but not a slave name. Kobina Pili Atá Kúmaa Yao Ntonni."

"Hmmm! That name is possibly partially a derivation of Ashanti-Twi. With that possibility in mind, if I were in your shoes and had nothing more to go on than this name, I would probably first search the Coromantee graveyard. Many great Maroon warriors including Captain Cudjoe, Cuffy and Quamina were of Coromantee lineage. That graveyard is the one northwest of the Congo burial ground and just a few yards from the Kindah tree. I wish I could help you more."

"You have been very generous with your time this morning. We will take your advice under advisement."

"Good luck to you," Hong-Lowe said. "I would be interested in knowing about any success you may have. May Jah bless your efforts. I will draft a letter stating that you are not vandals but legitimate researchers and that this office is aware of your efforts."

"Thank you. Here's my email address," Hardy said and wrote it out for Hu. "Even though Col. Winter in Accompong will no doubt sanction us to be there, it never hurts to have our efforts validated by someone like you as well."

As soon as they left, Harry Dog visited Dr. Hu Hong-Lowe and demanded a recap of the items Hu had discussed with Hardy. He held a pistol to Hon-Lowe's head for emphasis. Before Harry Dog left Hu's office, he had the information he wanted.

As Harry drove back to his office, he had another thought about how Hu could be useful.

*I'll make the arrangement when I get there.*

```
LIVE FOUL'S
FOR SALE
```

# Chapter 30

Hu Wong-Lowe tapped on the steering wheel and sipped from an insulated cup full of high mountain coffee as he drove to his office. He was a doo-wop fan who sang along as he drove with Alton Ellis as Ellis sang his reggae interpretation of the old doo-wop favorite "Duke Of Earl."

"Duke, Duke, Duke, Duke of Earl, Duke, Duke, Duke of Earl."

He really enjoyed the old American songs and thought that they just didn't write tunes like that anymore. Traffic was light, and it looked like it would be a beautiful day. His car climbed a large hill. As he began to descend on the other side, he saw a roadblock. Two white Subaru patrol cars were parked angling into each other. Two men in patrolman's uniforms got out of each car as Hu approached. A green SUV that he had not noticed following behind him began to slow as well and came to a stop.

A patrolman approached Hu's car and tapped a black plastic baton on his window. Hu turned the music off.

"Will you please turn off the ignition and get out of your car, sir?"

Hu rolled down his window and said, "Officer, is there a problem?"

"Please exit your vehicle."

Hu rolled up his window and did as he was instructed.

"Have I violated any law?"

"Please walk back to the green car," The officer said and pointed his baton at the car behind Hu. Hu began walking obediently toward the SUV. He opened the back door and looked crestfallen. The Shower Posse member who had visited his office the previous day sat in the back seat. Hu gulped when he recognized Harry Dog.

*Why is Harry Dog detaining me now on the highway? I was cooperative yesterday.*

It suddenly hit him that these were probably not real law enforcement officers either, and if they were, they were on the Shower Posse payroll. Were Harry and his henchmen planning to kill him? He had told the gangster what he wanted to know the day before. .... And he had held nothing back. Hu felt weak suddenly.

Harry Dog noted Hu's discomfort and silently smiled to himself. He always got a sadistic enjoyment out of seeing fear in an adversary's eyes.

"It is good to see you again, Dr. Hong-Lowe. Please join me in the back seat so we can have a brief chat. At this time, I regard you as a friend to the Shower Posse. I try to get to know my friends. He held out a photo of Hu's daughter walking with some teenagers across Montego Bay High School's campus.

"You have a very attractive daughter. She favors your wife."

He then held out another snapshot of Hu's wife having lunch with some friends at the Pork Pit in Montego Bay.

"Do I understand correctly that your parents live in Chatham?"

He handed Hu a picture of his parents with their home in the background.

"Jamaica can at times be a dangerous place, but Shower Posse friends have very little to worry about. We look after our friends as a favor to them."

Hu's hands began to shake as he looked at the pictures.

*This gangster knows everything about my family.*

Harry Dog continued. "And our friends reciprocate when we ask an occasional favor of them in return."

Hu waited nervously for the next shoe to drop.

*What does this guy want of me now?*

He didn't have long to wait.

"You mentioned yesterday that Dr. Pushcart and his assistants are doing some research in the cemeteries surrounding Accompong. I am a bit of a genealogy buff myself. I want to be kept apprised of what they find. I want you to call Pushcart and tell him that you have a crew who will soon be trimming the weeds in the cemeteries there. I want one of my men to be on that crew."

"But I don't have such a crew, and I don't have the funding for one," Hu said.

"I will provide the funding and handle their pay. It won't even have to go on your books," Harry Dog said. "Day laborers are plentiful and easy to find. Grant me this favor, and in return I will see that your family continues to enjoy the protection of the Shower Posse, which will insure their safety."

Hu nodded his understanding. This was not a request for help; it was an order, and his compensation would be his family's safety.

Harry Dog nodded, and one of his men opened the SUV door.

"And of course, this whole affair will remain confidential," was Harry Dog's final statement as Hu exited the vehicle.

```
NOTICE
THIS PLACE IS LISCENED
TO SELL MOTO VEHICLE
PARTS
SHOES & CLOTING
IN ENVERNESS ST ANN
SIGN G. A. JARRETT
```

# Chapter 31

The newly self-named Raiders of the Tribal Tomb assembled at Col. Winter's house to plan their next move. Just as they were getting down to business, Hardy's cell phone rang. He immediately answered.

"Gud mawnin. Hu Hong-Lowe at the LFMC."

"An unexpected pleasure. Gud mawnin to yu as well," Hardy said. "What may I do to help you?"

"It is I who is calling to help you," Hu said. "As luck woulda (would have) it, I have just been informed that your search fortuitously coincides with a planned cemetery weed-cutting and cleanup in Accompong. I have the latitude to request the scheduling of the crew so that it can be present while you are doing your research. I have also secured permission for you to use their assistance to do some of the manual labor associated with your efforts. Just let me know which cemetery you plan to be in and on what day you plan to be there, and I'll schedule them accordingly."

"Will we be expected to share in their compensation?" Hardy asked.

"That's the best part. They have already been budgeted so it will cost you nothing. I would think this should help you immensely. Those cemeteries are old and pretty grown up, and the rocks in them can be pretty heavy to move around."

"Well, Dr. Hong-Lowe. It just so happens you called during a meeting in which we were just trying make some decisions and form a strategy on that very topic. May I get back to you? Your offer is very generous. Thank you for thinking of us."

"A (that's) fine. I'll be expecting to hear from you," Hu said. "Please get back to me as soon as possible since we do need to schedule the crew. Am I to assume you will be searching the Coramante burial ground first?"

"That is our tentative plan," Hardy said. "I'll be back to you as soon as possible. And tank yu (thank you) again."

Hardy ended the call and filled in the rest of the group.

"What a lucky coincidence," he commented after filling in the holes in the conversation for them. "Hu seems like a really nice and honorable man."

Mikey Mo looked at The Colonel and said, "Almost too much of a coincidence and maybe too considerate."

"I was thinking the same thing," Colonel Winter said. "As my grandfather used to say, 'Every man honest till de day him ketch'."

"Well - and I assume I'm speaking for the entire group - I welcome someone to do some of the heavy lifting. I was not looking forward to some of the machete and shovel work we could have in front of us. Especially in this Jamaican heat and humidity," Hardy said.

Will added, "Yes. After all, Betsy and I are only desk jockeys, not road-gang material." Betsy nodded in agreement.

"Then accept his offer, but still play your cards close to your vest. There's a lot at stake," Colonel Winter said. "Remember, some people clean a tap an' dutty underneath (some people who seem honest on the surface are dirty underneath)."

Hardy called Hu back, and they agreed on a time for Hu's crew to meet the ROTT gang at the Coramante burial ground. The following morning as Leva was pouring coffee for Will and Betsy, they heard a familiar car horn at the gate.

"Henry's here," Leva said. "E.J., go open the gate for him."

Within a minute, Henry joined them.

161

"Gud mawn unuh (good morning all). And how are my favorite people on this tun up (wonderful) day?" Henry said in his infectiously positive tone. "Mrs. Carter, that smell tells me you have once again outdone yourself."

"There's plenty to go around, Mr. Davis," Leva said. "Should I put out another plate so you can join us? Wi hab flittas (we have fritters). "

"Be (is) de Pope Catholic?" Henry answered. "From the looks of the sky, we have a fine day in front of us, and I can think of no better way to get it started than with your gourmet flittas (fritters)."

"Well, den slide yuself on over to de table before dey get cold," Leva said.

"Mrs. Carter, when dis jackass smell corn, 'im don slide, 'im gallop."

"Henry, I wish you worked for me at RST. Your positive attitude would be refreshing and stimulating for my entire office," Will said. "You remind me of the famous Key West treasure hunter, Mel Fisher. He discovered the Atocha Spanish galleon. He started every day telling his crew 'Today's the day'."

"Lily (little) axe can cut down big tree," Henry said.

Soon they finished breakfast, helped Leva to take the leftovers to the kitchen, and then hit the road. As they drove towards Brown's Town, Betsy commented, "Do you know what we're looking for?"

"Not really. I'm hoping I'll recognize it when I see it," Will said. "We didn't know what we were looking for at the Falls either, but we found it anyway. Let's hope Hardy has a better feel on all this than we do."

"One mysterious thing that seems to be recurring is that Makapansgat pebble," Betsy said.

"You're right. Let's keep that in mind as we are looking," Will said. "I'm sure glad that grounds-keeping crew's gonna be there. I wasn't looking forward to spending a whole day chopping with a machete. That was extremely considerate of Dr. Hong-Lowe to coordinate his efforts with ours. He didn't have to do that, you know."

Betsy said nothing, but The Colonel's wise observation from the previous day kept popping back into her mind.

# A Treasure Conspiracy

*Some people clean a tap (on top) an' dutty (dirty) underneath.*

Mikey Mo picked up Hardy. He and Henry coordinated with each other on their cell phones so that each arrived at the cemetery about the same time. Hu's men had not arrived yet.

"I don't know where to begin," Will admitted. "Kinda overwhelming."

"Why don't we just walk around and try to generally familiarize ourselves with the layout," Hardy suggested.

"Alone or together?" Betsy asked.

"Let's do it the first time together," Hardy suggested. "That way we will be more organized and make sure we've walked it in its entirety at least once. Also – who knows - one of us may see something another of one us has missed."

To a novice who did not know it was a burial ground, it probably would have just looked like just another poorly maintained clearing full of weeds and rocks. There were no monuments or concrete markers. There were no flowers on graves. It was simply a sloping barren patch of rugged ground which had been cleared a couple of centuries ago.

"I think the property may be sort of triangular in nature," Henry said and pointed at what he thought the perimeters of the property actually were.

A rusted, dented, pickup truck drove up, and parked. There were six rough looking men in the back. When it stopped, they jumped out. If Will and Betsy hadn't been expecting the men, they would have been frightened at their rough appearance. One had on an old football jersey with the number 85 on it. His unwashed-looking dreadlocks were contained in a dirty knit cap. The next man had on a tank top, cargo shorts and filthy looking sneakers which were held on to his feet by broken strings that had been tied back together. His dirty toes protruded through the shoes' worn-out ends. The next man wore a long-sleeve plaid shirt, a Florida Marlins baseball cap, and faded jeans with rubber boots. One of his eyes looked milky as if it had been damaged in the past. The next two laborers had dreads pulled back in pony tails and both wore t-shirts and shorts. Each was carrying a menacing-looking machete. A surly-looking, muscular driver got out of the truck. He reminded Betsy of a bulldog. He was skin-headed but had scraggly whiskers and had a scar that ran down the side of his forehead. He wore a sweat-stained straw hat. His dark eyes had no expression what-so-ever. Betsy shivered when she made eye contact with him and quickly looked away. He seemed to be the man in charge.

The driver spoke brusquely to Hardy, seeming to assume Hardy was the man in charge of their group. He didn't waste time on pleasantries or small talk or even introduce himself.

"Wi a go chop di grass. Where yu need wi fi start (we're here to cut the grass. Where do you want us to start)?"

"Wi jus get here too (we just arrived ourselves)," Hardy responded, "and we do a try (we are trying) to get the lay of the land. Wi also do a try (we are trying) to identify particular graves. Do yu hab any suggestions?"

"Nuh, mon. If yu dun (you don't) know, den wi start deh suh (then we'll start over there)," the man said and pointed. He turned around to one of his crew and ordered, "Gi mi muh cutlass (give me my machete)."

"Den wi look deh so (then we'll begin over there) as well," Hardy said, trying to be as non-confrontational as possible with the surly crew leader.

The men began to chop the weeds.

Hardy whispered to the ROTT crew, "Let's continue to familiarize ourselves with the entire property and stay out of their way until they get at least one area cleared. I don't want to accidentally rub this rough bunch the wrong way by getting in their path."

The rest of the group nodded in agreement. A half hour later enough weeds had been trimmed to allow the group to examine the newly-cleared ground underneath without risking getting in the cutting crew's path. The craggy, uneven land gave up no ready clues as to what they were looking for. It was hard to identify what was a grave and what wasn't. Nothing was identified, and each plot, if it was a plot, looked pretty much just alike. Some seemed to be slightly outlined in stones; other places there were no stones at all, or the rocks were jumbled in an irregular pattern.

They patiently waited for second area to be cleared. The morning continued to get hotter, and soon everyone was sweating. Still no discernible clues.

"I sure wish I knew what we are looking for," Will commented.

"That makes five of us," Henry said.

At the end of the day, they all felt like they had accomplished nothing and were beginning to get discouraged.

Mikey Mo commented, "Fellows, if it was easy, someone would have found it long before now. "There's always tomorrow.""

The following day was spent going through the same thing at the Ashanti burial ground. On day three they repeated the process at the Congo burial ground with the same results. The surly crew leader came each day but never became more loquacious with the ROTT crew than he had been on the first day. Hu never came to any of the cemeteries to check on his crew's progress and never even gave anyone a phone call.

"You talk about looking for a needle in a haystack," Will commented. "What do we do now?"

Mikey Mo suggested, "We still have some time today. Why don't we at least walk through the more modern Accompong Cemetery. Maybe it'll give us an idea. We're here anyway."

Hardy shrugged, "What the hell."

The walk-through proved to be another waste of time. They went by Ferron Winter's house to give him their non-report.

"I think we all agree that the Coromante burial ground that you searched the first day was the most likely place to find the clue we need. Would you invest one more morning of your time to indulge this old man? Now that the ground is freshly cleared and I can see things easier, may I accompany you to the Coromante cemetery tomorrow morning? My experienced old eyes may see something that you youngsters missed. After all, new broom sweep clean, but de ole broom know de corner."

Hardy said, "Colonel, tideh fi wi, tomorrow fi yu (today was for us, tomorrow will be for you)."

~ ~ ~

The following morning The Colonel accompanied the ROTT group to the Coromante burial ground, and they silently walked along beside him as he examined the grounds. Hardy started to say something, but Winter waved him off and said, "Just let me think."

Winter walked around poking at the brush with a walking stick.

"Didn't you guys encounter a banana shaped stone as a clue once before?" Winter finally asked.

"Yes," Mikey Mo said. "At YS Falls."

"Look at this stone here," Colonel Winter said, poking at an unusually even rock which was larger than those adjacent to it. "What does this look like to you?"

"Looks like it was shaped by a human being rather than mother nature. See how smooth it is," Hardy replied. "Kind of crescent shaped."

"Looks that way to me too, but I would have used the word banana-shaped," Colonel Winter said. He then paced about seven feet and smoothed the brush off another patch of ground.

"Here's another stone that looks quarried," he said.

"That one's curved too, and the way it's placed, it's almost like quotation marks enclosing something," Hardy said, "but it looks more like a curved calabash than a banana – the kind that's used to make curved smoking pipes to smoke ganja."

"My guess is that it's marking a grave site of some significance since I don't see any other plots with man-made stones," The Colonel said. He walked over a few feet and once again poked in the brush, but he didn't see a third artificial-looking stone.

"Nothing there?" Betsy asked. The Colonel shook his head.

Henry, who was standing a few feet away, unconsciously took the long-handled shovel he was tired of holding, put his foot on it, and shoved it into ground so it could stand up on its own. It clunked against a rock beneath the ground and fell over instead.

Will bent over, picked the shovel up, and attempted to force it in the ground again about a foot over. It clunked against another obstruction and fell over and this time hit Henry's foot.

"Excuse me, Henry," Will said and scooped up a shovelful of dirt before trying again. He hit the rock once more, and scooped up another shovelful. A smooth, round stone began to come into view.

"Keep digging, Will," Betsy said. "That doesn't look like natural limestone. I think it's man-made and almost perfectly round."

After a few more spadefuls, it was apparent Betsy was right. Eyes and a nose began to emerge. Finally, there was what could be a mouth.

"That's three stones," Hardy said. "One about right here," - he poked the ground - "would put the stones in a rectangle. He began to dig where he was standing. After a few spadefuls of dirt, he hit another smooth rock. They were now looking at a face.

"Another Makapansgat face," Betsy said. "Smiling, like it knows something."

"Of course, stones would get buried after all these years," Hardy said. "Just like you don't find sunken objects on top of the sand in the bottom of an ocean. They get covered over time – that's archaeology 101."

Henry stabbed his shovel around the banana-shaped stone and raised it up a few inches. "Someone grab this rock and pull," he said.

When they did the rock loosened itself from the surrounding soil and flipped over. Another Makapansget face had been carved in the back.

"Well, I'll be damned," Hardy said. "I think we've finally hit pay-dirt. Let's pry this one up," he said, pointing to the curved calabash shaped rock.

When they pried it up, there was a Makapansget face on the back of it as well. Exposing more of the round rocks exposed two more Makapansget faces on their bottom sides.

"I guess it's time we got back to work, my young friends," The Colonel said and looked at Mikey Mo.

"I was afraid you were getting ready to say that," Mikey Mo said as he wiped his brow, "but you mean *you* – not we. We could be digging for a long time. I wish there were an easier way."

"Pudden cyaa bake widout fiah (a pudding doesn't bake without fire)," Colonel Winter said. "The sooner you start …."

"I know – 'the sooner we finish'," said Mikey Mo. "I sure hope we're not doing all this work for nothing."

"No promises – ebery day a fishing-day, but no ebery day fe ketch fish (just because every day is a fishing day doesn't mean that on every day you'll catch fish)."

With those words of wisdom, the digging commenced with Mikey Mo and Henry initially manning the two shovels available. It wasn't long before each was panting, and Will and Hardy took over while the previous diggers cooled off and drank some bottled water. When Will and Hardy began to run out of steam, Mikey Mo and Henry resumed. An hour later they had dug five different holes about two feet deep each without finding anything.

"I sure wish we had that landscaping crew back here today," Mikey Mo said. "Every bone in my body is going to be sore tomorrow."

"I agree the strong backs would normally be welcome," Colonel Winter said, "but they would probably ask questions about things we don't want to discuss. I'm would not want to share our business with any outside parties unnecessarily. There's too much at stake."

The Colonel didn't know it, but the surly crew leader from the day before had been watching them search and dig from a distance. He was keeping Harry Dog apprised of their efforts with his cell phone.

At last, Henry hit an obstruction that gave in and partially shattered from his blow. In the dirt he brought back to the surface was a human bone.

"Look!" he called out and took another scoop of dirt. This time he came up with a shard of pottery.

You disturbed the occupant's grave," Mikey Mo said hesitantly. "I sure hope his duppy (ghost) isn't in there."

"Dat mek two of wi (that makes two of us)," Henry said nervously, inadvertently falling back into patois, "since dey say ever cave-hole have him own duppy (since they say every cave or hole has its own ghost)."

He began to stab around the object to loosen the dirt holding it secure. Soon they brought up a partially damaged. pottery crock and hauled it to one side. It had been sealed with wax. A chunk had been broken out of it where Henry's shovel had initially clipped it.

"That's an old Spanish olive jar," Hardy said.

"Let's break it open," Will said. "It's damaged anyway."

"Let's take it over to Colonel Winter's house and put it on a tarp or blanket first," Betsy suggested. "We don't want to risk losing part of whatever might be in it if the contents have been damaged."

"Good idea," Colonel Winter said. "Let's carefully get it over to Henry's van. It doesn't look that heavy. Quickly shovel some of that dirt back into the hole before we leave. We don't want to advertise any more than we have to or to leave a hazard for some unsuspecting person."

"I'll come back and do that later," Mikey Mo said. "Let's go see what we found."

As they carried the jug towards the van, their observer was calling Harry Dog.

"Dis Punkin-Puss. Dey find somethin," he said.

"What'd they find?"

"Mi dunno."

"Yu hab help? Sumady yu canna trust? Who wid yu?"

"Mi brudda. Mi can trust him. 'Im blud relation (my brother. I can trust him. He's a blood relative)."

"Den yu and yu brudda falla (follow) and fin' out."

While Punkin-Puss was preoccupied speaking to Harry Dog, Ruddy-Puss was also making a phone call to the Spangler Posse.

"Mistuh Williams, Ruddy-Puss – Punkin-Puss' brudda – remember mi? Mikey Mo fin' sumpin in Coromante burial ground. 'Im dig it up."

"Anything a anything (whatever happens), yu get hit (it) to mi todeh (today), and todeh might jus finally be yu day. Yu undastan wah mi a seh (do you understand what I'm saying)?"

"Yeh, mi undastan. Mi see yu hab no regrets, Mistah Williams. Tank yu for gi me dis bly (thank you for giving me this chance)."

```
we RePaIR
Beds ¢ scaℓes
heRe
```

# Chapter 32

"I can't wait to see what's in this olive jar," Betsy said as they stood around the concrete table in Colonel Winter's front yard.

"I sure hope whatever it is has survived over the centuries," Will replied.

"Well, the odds are really pretty good since it was sealed until a few minutes ago when we broke it open," Hardy said. "Well, we'll never find out just standing here staring at it."

"I just hope it turns out to be worth all the work it took to dig the thing up," Mikey Mo said.

"So do I," Henry said, "but in case it doesn't, remember no (not) all foot in a boot a good foot."

He got a laugh from the group.

Hardy began to tap on the jar around the broken area with a chisel and a hammer. As soon as the hole was big enough to reach his hand through, he said, "Keep your fingers crossed" and started to reach into the jar.

A voice behind him made him hesitate. They turned and saw a masked Punkin-Puss and Ruddy-Puss approaching. Punkin-Puss held a pistol.

"Tan back (stand back)," Punkin-Puss ordered and motioned them away from the table with the gun.

He smiled as he thought that this was a chance to show his authoritative side to his houseboy brother.

He reached into the cracked olive jar but quickly jerked his bleeding fingers back out, screaming "Rahtid! Madda-fuckin' batty crease (damn mother-fucking ass crack)!"

He ripped off his mask. Within seconds, saliva began to form around Punkin-Puss' teeth. Then drool formed and began to run down on his shirt. He suddenly bent over, wracked with pain. When he looked questioningly at Ruddy-Puss his eyes began to bulge. He grabbed the edge of the table as he sank to his knees and hit his head on the concrete bench as he fell. He hit the ground and his bowels let loose. A putrid smell enveloped him. His eyes now looked glassy. It was quite obvious the gangster was dead or close to it. Ruddy-Puss panicked and began to run back towards his brother's parked car, never even looking back. He jumped in the car that still had the key in the ignition and shot gravel as he floored it trying to distance himself from the horror he had just witnessed. Punkin-Puss' cell phone bounced off the seat onto the floor.

"What the hell?... ," Will cried out. "I never ... ."

"Something in the jar poisoned the creep," Colonel Winter said. "Thank God, Hardy, he reached in there instead of you."

"Don't thank God. God didn't plant the poison in the olive jar. Whoever buried it booby-trapped it," Betsy said.

"One more second and you'd be ... I don't even want to think about it ... What do we do with the body?" Will asked. "Call the police? Surely they can't blame us."

"Let's just put the corpse in that open hole we left over at the cemetery," Mikey Mo suggested. "I'm sure this creep is someone the world is better off without. Just don't touch him. I don't know what kind of residual may be left on him."

"Shouldn't we inform someone?" Betsy asked. "Don't we have a lot of explaining to do?"

"You forget the provisions of the Kindah treaty," Colonel Winter said, "and after all, I am *The* Maroon Colonel, and Accompong *is* my jurisdiction. If questions arise, I'll take care of them."

"Maybe you can handle the authorities, but whoever sent these guys doesn't give a diddly-damn about the Kindah treaty," Will said.

"Not to change the subject, but I've never seen a poison that lethal and fast-acting," Henry said. "I've got some visqueen in the van. Colonel, you stay here and make sure no one else touches that olive jar until we return. Come on guys, we got a little more digging to do."

"I guess I can dig that scene," Will said as he tried to lighten matters.

There was a collective groan before Betsy said, "Will, that was really not in good taste."

"Before you leave, give me his cell phone so I can destroy it," Colonel Winter said.

"He doesn't appear to have one on him," Henry said.

When they returned from the Coramante cemetery, the group stared at the olive jar waiting for someone to take the lead on what to do next.

"It's not going to open itself with an 'open sesame'. Let me break the whole side out of the jar so we can view what's inside of it," Hardy said.

He began chipping away at the olive jar until the hole was sufficiently enlarged. Then he took a stick and carefully pushed the shards away. There was broken glass vial inside with blood stains on it. He could see the residual of a green powder.

"That broken vial is what cut the gangster and poisoned him," Colonel Winter said. "We must have accidentally shattered it when we were trying to penetrate the jar."

"Or when we broke the jar at the cemetery when Henry hit it with his shovel," Will said.

"No, I'm sure it happened here. Otherwise it probably would have gotten on one of us when we moved it to transport it," Betsy said. "Thank God that didn't happen."

"Look lak there's a book in it," Hardy announced. "Let me chip away some more just to be sure things are safe."

He began to tap on the jar again. When the hole was large enough to see the entire interior, he saw a book wrapped in old, faded wall paper. He carefully lifted the broken vial with some tongs from The Colonel's kitchen and dropped it in an empty coffee can Colonel Winter gave him. The wrapping paper did not appear to have any green residue on it.

"Doesn't look like any of the poison got on the book," Hardy said. "Get a lid for that can and save it in case we need to prove something with it later."

The paper was extremely brittle and began to crack the moment Hardy tried to lift the book with the kitchen tongs. He carefully picked it up and laid it on the table on a garbage bag. He then got some scissors and began to cut the paper away. He used the tongs to stuff the paper into the can with the broken vial. When Hardy got the book unwrapped, it was apparent it was a family Bible.

"Is there anything left in the jar?" Betsy asked.

"Just another Makapansgat face," Henry said. "Hand me the tongs, and I'll take it out."

"If the jar contains a pebble, then we found what we were supposed to find," Betsy said.

"Have you got any rubber gloves, Colonel?" Hardy asked.

"My wife has some dish-washing gloves," Colonel Winter replied.

"Perfect. May I borrow them?" Hardy asked.

After he had pulled on the rubber gloves, Hardy carefully opened the cover on the Bible.

"It's a King James version," he said, "It shows a family tree."

He turned the page, "And there's a name written on the title page – 'Mary Hyde Tharp.' "

"Had to be part of that Tharp family which at one time was probably the richest family in Trelawny," Henry said.

"I'm going to need to study this and do more research," Hardy concluded. "Colonel, will you trust me with the book?"

"Of course," Colonel Winter said. "How long are you going to need it?"

"Hopefully I can report back by in the morning," Hardy said.

"Would you be offended if I sent Mikey Mo along to insure the safety of both you and this valuable book?" Colonel Winter asked.

"Not only would I not be offended, but it would ease my mind considerably."

"After all, there is one thug who got away," Henry said. "And I think we can be assured he reports to a pretty unsavory boss ... most likely at the Shower Posse."

"As much as I probably need a shower right now, I don't think I want the kind of bullet shower his boss might have in mind," Hardy said.

"Yeah," Will said. "You might get lead poisoning ... or worse."

# Chapter 33

Harry Dog honked his car horn at the gate to Almond Hill. Ruddy-Puss ran down to open the gate and let his visitor into the driveway. He swallowed hard when he saw who was driving the car. This was not someone he really wanted to see. Ruddy-Puss had been having second thoughts about his aspirations to become a gang member since witnessing Punkin-Puss's shocking death. Punkin-Puss's car was currently parked in Almond Hill's carport since Ruddy-Puss didn't know what else to do with it. Punkin-Puss's cell phone remained unnoticed and unmissed on the floor by the seat.

"Unno seet yu brudda (have you seen your brother)?" Harry Dog asked.

Nah, mon," Ruddy-Puss responded. "He nuh come bouh yah (he doesn't come around)."

"Shakey (strange). He phone GPS sey 'im here," Harry Dog said. "And ku paan lak him cyar (and that looks like his car)."

Since he was trapped in a lie, at that point the already nervous Ruddy-Puss began to confess to Harry Dog the shocking story on what had happened at the Coramante cemetery and how it had led to Punkin-Puss's demise. Once he began to talk, he rattled on and spilled the entire story, leaving few details out.

"So yuh no see what happen nex?" Harry Dog asked.

"Nah, mon. Mi got scared, and mi run weh (away)," Ruddy-Puss said.

"So yuh seh (say) yuh a cowad (you're a coward)," Harry Dog said accusingly. "Mi men tan up for they brudda (my men stand up for their brothers)."

"Nah, mon. Mi nuh a cowad (I'm not a coward). Mi tink (I thought) duppy (a ghost) got 'im. Mi nuh fight wid duppie (I don't fight with duppies). What yu wan mi do now?"

"Nuttin but keep yu mout (mouth) shut," Harry Dog. "Dis mi affair now."

~ ~ ~

The following morning Henry came by Sundance and picked up Will and Betsy for the trip back to Accompong. Hardy had relayed to them that he had now had adequate time to examine the Bible they had found the previous day and felt he could now initiate and lead a somewhat informed discussion on this most recent discovery. Once again the group would meet at Colonel Winter's home. Mikey Mo would pick up Hardy; Henry Davis would bring Will and Betsy. Harry Dog monitored Will's activities from Almond Hill and scheduled himself to be in Accompong at the appropriate time.

Colonel Winter's wife served the group some Jamaican coffee and fresh gizzadas at the front yard table when they arrived but then left them alone to conduct their business.

"First, let me say that Henry was correct yesterday about this Bible once belonging to the same Mary Hyde Tharp who was cited in Ruby Drain's diary – the same one who was once a member of the wealthy Trelawny Tharps. Let me give you a brief reminder of the Tharp family history. In the 1700's and 1800's this family had thousands of acres of sugar fields and also thousands of slaves. John Tharp II's father owned two estates in Hanover Parish. His mother was a Frost. John II was educated at Eton and Trinity in Cambridge and then returned to Jamaica. He married Elizabeth Partridge and through her, acquired Potosi Estate in St. James Parish. He chose to invest in the newly formed Trelawny Parish and eventually owned ten estates there."

"Congratulations, Henry, on your memory of local history. You weren't present when Colonel Winter here told this story initially," Betsy said. Henry smiled.

"Elizabeth died and left John with five surviving children," Hardy continued. "After Elizabeth's death, John had an illegitimate daughter by a slave named Hannah Phillips who he named Mary Hyde Tharp. She became over time his favorite child, and he sent her to England to be educated. John remarried a widow named Ann Gallimore who was considerably younger than himself … her maiden name by the way was Virgo …, and as a result, he received Lansquinet and Cheshire Estates along with all their slaves. Their marriage ended with a scandal when Ann got pregnant and subsequently had an illegitimate child following an affair with one of John's son-in-laws who was at the time married to his daughter, Eliza."

"Shoot, Hardy, you make it sound like Peyton Place Parish," Will said.

"Jacqueline Susann or D.H. Lawrence would have had a ball with this subject matter," Betsy agreed. "So continue and refresh our memories as to what happened to Tharp's fortune."

"As John grew older, he became estranged from his children and ended up leaving the whole shebang to his baby grandson who turned out to be mentally ill. Before it was all over, the fortune was lost in a horrendous litigation."

"This is all very interesting," Mikey Mo said, "but where does this leave us – at a dead end?"

"Maybe not," Hardy said as he carefully opened the Bible. "There are two bookmarks in Mary Hyde's Bible, both in the Old Testament."

He opened Mary Hyde Tharp's Bible to the first bookmark. It marked Ecclesiastes 12: 1-7."

"What does it say?" Colonel Winter asked.

"I read it, but nothing jumped out at me," Hardy admitted.

"Well, please read it again. This time out loud for all of us to hear," Colonel Winter asked.

"Betsy, why don't you read it?" Will suggested. "You have a good reading voice, and Hardy will have the luxury of just listening this time."

Betsy began to read, "Ecclesiastes: 1 – 'Remember now thy Creator in the days of my youth, while the evil days come not, nor the years draw nigh, when thou shalt say, I have no pleasure in them'."

"That didn't tell me anything. Ring any bells with y'all?" Will said and looked around.

Heads shook.

"Then please continue."

Betsy read Ecclesiastes: 2 and then paused. Nothing. Only shrugs. Then she read Ecclesiastes: 3 through 5. Still nothing.

"Ecclesiastes: 6. 'Or ever the silver cord be loosed or the golden branches be broken, or the pitcher be broken at the fountain, or the wheel broken at the cistern'."

Everyone shrugged again.

"I'll read one more verse," Betsy said. "Ecclesiastes: 7 – 'Then shall the dust return to the earth as it was: and the spirit shall return unto God who gave it'."

"Nothing's jumping off the page at me," Will said. "Turn to the next bookmark."

Betsy turned to Jeremiah and began to read. After she read Jeremiah 17: 3, The Colonel said, "Stop, Betsy. Read that passage again."

"'O mountain of Mine in the countryside. I will give over your wealth and all your treasure for booty, your high places for sin throughout your borders'."

"Stop right there," Colonel Winter said, "and let's take stock on what we currently know."

"Or don't know," Hardy said.

"That's equally important," Winter added and began to summarize the facts about the Tharp family.

"Have you compiled a list of John Tharp's plantation holdings?" Will asked.

"Besides Potosi and Bachelor's Hall in Hanover, he owned Bunker Hill, Covey, Merrywood, Pantrepant, Unity, and Windsor in

Trelawny Parish. He also owned Dean's Valley Estate in Westmoreland, plus the Good Hope Great House, and Chippenham Park in St. Ann. He was living at Good Hope when he died. I think he had other holdings as well."

"Jeezam! That's a lot of places to look for our next clue," Henry said.

"Then we've got to narrow down the search area," Betsy said.

"How in hell do we do that?" Will asked.

"Probably with the Bible," Betsy said. " It seems apparent she preserved it and hid it for a reason. And I don't think she marked those Bible verses just because she liked them. Let's face it, those are not the passages most people derive inspiration from."

"They sure aren't Psalms," Will agreed. "Let's read them again, and this time put our thinking caps on."

"Betsy's right," The Colonel said. "Listen for key words or phrases."

Betsy read the passages again.

"Can I assume the silver cord, the golden bowl and the pitcher refer to the hidden Spanish treasure?" Hardy asked.

"And returning to the earth is talking about it being hidden?" Mikey Mo asked.

"And mountain of mine in the countryside might refer to one of the Tharp estates?" Henry said.

"So what?" Will said. "You named eleven of them … and you said there may be more."

"What about the reference to a cistern or a broken wheel?" Betsy asked.

"Potosi once had a major sugar mill It's now in ruins. Tharp constructed it there to harness the water from the Martha Brae River to turn the rollers to crush the cane. He diverted water to the site with an aqueduct and used this water to turn the water-wheel that had gears to rotate the rollers. There was a cane chute built from dressed, smooth stone. Ox carts delivered the cane to the top. Workers then pushed it into the chute, and it was delivered to the mill in the valley about 100 feet below.

"Cane juice was then extracted from the rollers and fed through gutters into the boiling house where it was stored in large cisterns. After it was purified with lime, the juice was then boiled in a series of copper cauldrons. The scum was used to make rum. After the final boiling, they had barrels that were a combination of sugar and molasses. The final step was draining the molasses out through a weep-hole in the barrel and then exporting the sugar to Europe. Potosi was considered to be very innovative in its day. They now call the property River Bumpkin Farm and grow mostly bananas on it," Hardy said.

"No wonder Tharp was rich man. He was obviously very intelligent," Will said.

"It was very efficient – there was virtually no waste since the crushed cane was dried out and then used to fire the furnace in the boiling house," Hardy added.

"Stop! This is more than just an interesting story," Betsy said. "I think you may have hit a key word that leads to the clue we need. Potosi had cisterns – Ecclesiastes refers to cisterns."

"You said it's in ruins. Does that mean that the wheel is broken?" Henry asked.

Hardy nodded.

"Yes. Definitely beyond repair. You might say it's merely a nonfunctional period piece," he said.

"Hardy, you have accidentally given us the clue to the clue," Will said.

"Well, accident or no accident, without Hardy's knowledge about sugar refining, we still wouldn't have a clue," Betsy said.

"Because we weren't listening the first time around. Just goes to show you why God gave you two ears and one mouth," Colonel Winter said. "To encourage man to listen more than he speaks."

"Well, Potosi, here we come," Mikey Mo said.

"Is there a great house?" Betsy asked.

"Oh, no," Hardy said. "It was destroyed years ago. Nowadays there's only ruins."

"Then we'll just have to plan to have a wheel good time," Will said.

"One more pun like that and I think I'm about to throw up wheel soon," Betsy replied.

```
                     MENUE
                          CHIPS
          BREAKFAST    CHICKEN
             COFFEE       ROAST-
                            PORK
                           FISH
      MACKRIEL AND BANANA FLITTERS
      BOIL EGGS           JUICES
      FRY DUMPLINGS      SOUP
      VEG. ETC.
```

# Chapter 34

Hardy made sure that there would not be any trespassing issues by calling the current owner of River Bumpkin Farm and getting his permission for the ROTT group to come on the property. He told the owner that the group was doing research on historic 18th century sugar processing. Since Potosi was open for public tours, he arranged a day and time that a tour would not be on the property.

Will and Betsy went on Google and found some pictures of the old Potosi Estate. The Makapansgat pebble that they had found with the Bible was sitting next to the computer. As they were studying the pictures, Leva came into the room.

"Just made some fresh tea," Leva said. "What are you looking at?"

"Pictures of the old Potosi sugar plantation in Trelawny," Betsy replied.

"I remember my grandmother talking about that place," Leva said. "In fact I think some of my people were slaves on it at one point."

They flipped through some of the photos on the computer.

Leva picked up the Makapansgat pebble and laughed as she said, "Where'd you get the happy face? Did know notice there was one kind of like it on that stone wall we just looked at in those Potosi pictures? I didn't know they had happy faces in the 1700's."

Will looked at Betsy and said, "Do you think Leva's right? Could the stonework on one of the archways at the bottom of the cane chute be linked to the Makapansgat pebble on the desk? Is that the clue we're looking for? Will, page back a couple of pictures, and let's look again."

Will paged back and immediately now saw what Leva was talking about.

Betsy jumped up and began to hug Leva. "Leva, I love you. I think you just showed us what we're supposed to be looking for. I don't know why we didn't see it ourselves. Honey-pye, I'm going to rename you Eagle-eye."

Leva looked puzzled that this likeness so apparent to her had escaped both Will and Betsy's recognition and said, "That's the first thing I noticed. I must be a happier person than you are. Why's it important?"

"I can't tell you now," Betsy said, "but I'll tell you what I can when we get back from Potosi. You're wonderful, Honey-pye."

"I've been trying to tell you that," Leva said. "Now suddenly I'm wonderful just because I know a smiley face when I see one? Does this mean I get a raise? Now that I know how much you like them and how happy they make you, I'll have to show you a happy face *every* day."

The following morning the ROTT group headed out for Potosi, unaware that they were being followed by Harry Dog and one of his men, Champagnie Peter. When Henry arrived, Mikey Mo and Hardy were sipping coffee and waiting for them. They each parked their vehicles and walked down a gentle path which wound along the Martha Brae River. It was shaded by verdant foliage, and they could see various types of bananas from both sides of the trail.

Mikey Mo pointed out a prickled lala thorn tree to them.

"There's a Jamaican legend about that tree," Mikey Mo said. "The story goes that if a young man wants to find out if his girl is true to him, he will climb the thorn tree. If she's truly the one for him, she will then pull out the thorns."

"Is that's what's called affixing a horny relationship with a 't'?" Will asked.

Betsy elbowed him and said, "My guess is they had a thorny relationship from the get-go."

"Well, that tree certainly illustrates the Jamaican proverb that marriage hab (has) teeth and it bite hard," Henry added.

"Right you are, Henry," Hardy said. "And I bet the lala thorn's duppy has a prickly personality."

Soon they arrived at their destination. The terrain was extremely rough and had stones and random boulders strewn precariously virtually everywhere. There were the remains of a series of arched columns side by side outlining what looked like what had once been an elevated road or bridge above them.

"Reminds me of the supports for the Long Key viaduct on Flagler's old overseas railroad," Will observed.

Betsy agreed.

The hill above the structure was extremely steep with the remains of the old stone cane chute descending down to it. Thick, wild, native vegetation had retaken much of the hill on both sides of the chute and was covering and obscuring many of the stones. Unruly plants grew in most of the mortar spaces between the stones. Under the arches was another set of larger arches set perpendicular to those above them forming a tunnel under the ones above. Just like the remains of the boiling house and the other buildings that they had also passed along the way, everything was rubble and in ruins.

"Mi raah (oh, my God). This looks overwhelming," Mikey Mo said.

"So did the cemetery and the falls," Hardy reminded him, "but we solved those riddles. I'm sure we can do the same thing again."

"Just remember," Henry reminded Mikey Mo, "unless wi tek it, wi neva hab it. (unless we take it, we'll never have it). Nobady gon hand it to wi (no one's going to hand it to us), so wi might as well stop wi belly-ache and get busy."

"Amen, Mr. Davis. OK, guys. Gather around," Will said. "Here's the picture I told you about - the one that Betsy and I printed off of Google – the one that Leva, our cook, thought had impressions in it that resembled the Makapansgat pebble. Let's make it a priority to look especially for this formation, but don't make the mistake of focusing only on that. And we're probably going to have to chop away brush with our machetes to be able to see anything anywhere."

"Do we know how current this internet photo is?" Henry asked.

"No idea," Betsy said. "I'm pretty sure it's a vintage photograph. The terrain may or may not still resemble what it was when it was taken."

"If this Makapansgat pebble idea turns out to be erroneous, I'm not sure what we should do next," Mikey Mo commented. "We could stay out here looking forever since we have no idea what we're really looking for."

"And be sure to wear out our welcome with the property owner," Will said. "You can be sure he's not going to stand for us making a strip mine out of his historical site which he also uses as a tourist attraction."

"Will's right. Don't hack more than you have to," Hardy said. "I really don't want to have a run-in with the property owner and force Colonel Winter to have to intervene."

The group began to explore the rubble with the picture in hand to try to identify the particular stone arch in it. Many arches were hard to see because the forest had largely reclaimed them. No arch appeared on the surface to be an obvious candidate. They began to chop away the vines with their machetes to try to expose the stone beneath. Gradually they began to eliminate the arches that held little likelihood of being the one they were looking for. Soon everyone had worked up a good sweat, and the group voted to take a water break. After catching their breath, they resumed thinning vines.

Will approached an arch that was in an advanced state of decay. Roots had pushed part of the wall over, and he had to pick his way through rubble to approach it. A vine was growing through two holes about a foot apart in the stone. Several stones beneath had fallen out completely. The holes reminded him of something out of Indiana Jones, and he could visualize snakes coming out of them.

He turned to Betsy and said, "Isn't it amazing that vines can penetrate these entire pieces of solid rock?"

"Anything's possible, but it does seem implausible. And on this one, there must have been man-made holes here originally. Look how level the two holes are horizontally. Too level not to be man-made."

"Like someone was hanging something from the wall," Will said.

"Possibly," Betsy agreed.

As she turned, a rock in the debris slipped and rolled down the slope a few feet. Betsy almost lost her balance. Will caught her arm before she fell.

"Careful," Will said. "You don't need a broken ankle."

When the stone that had almost caused Betsy to fall had tumbled over and had rolled, it flipped, exposing a different side.

"Look, Will," Betsy said tentatively. "Is it my imagination, or is that a carved groove in that rock?"

"I think you're right," Will said. "I wonder if that's the stone that was originally beneath those two that had the round holes. I think I can maybe pick it up and carry it back up there. Let's find out."

He filled part of the void in the gap with another stone and then retrieved the one with the indention. When he shoved the rock having the groove into the remaining space above it, it fit perfectly and made what looked like a mouth.

"Well, I'll be damned," Will said. "Now it does look like two eyes and a mouth."

He chopped the vines coming out to the eyes with his machete. Another slightly sloping horizontal groove appeared over the eyes where a forehead should be.

"Do you see what I see?" Will asked.

"That line above the eyes definitely makes this resemble the features of our Makapansgat pebble," Betsy said.

"With no head-like outline surrounding it," Will added. "If you hadn't stumbled over the mouth-rock, we never would have found this."

"You know what they say about how it's sometimes better to be lucky than smart," Betsy said.

"My darling, I can assure you – you're both," Will said. "You got me to fall for you, didn't you?"

"We'll analyze my youthful wisdom later," Betsy said.

They called the rest of the group over. Everyone agreed that the reassembled formation reminded them somewhat of the face on their Makapansgat pebble. Will removed the two stones he had temporarily put back in place and then began to pry the eye-stones loose with his shovel. Behind the eyes was a dirt void full of roots and loose dirt.

"Anyone want to reach in?" Hardy asked.

"Not me. Not after what happened with that Spanish olive jar at Colonel Winter's house," Mikey Mo said. "Who knows what might be living in there."

"Or what might have been planted as a booby-trap," Henry said.

Everyone else agreed.

"Yeah! And we wouldn't want the Potosi duppy to get you," Will said as he turned with his arms raised over his head, curling his fingers into claws. He began to walk in an exaggerated manner.

"Slowly it turned. Step by step …."

"You've met my husband," Betsy said. "He's part of Dumbo and Costello. I'll let y'all guess which one he is."

"OK, Dumbo. You'll just have to make the cavity bigger by removing a few more stones," Hardy said, "and then we'll cut some of the roots away. I'm sure glad I brought my tree-limb lopper."

"And my gloves," Henry said.

"Let's not forget to put the stones back in place when we're done whether we find anything or not," Betsy said. "After all, this is not our property."

Soon a couple of small boulders fell away, giving Hardy room to flex the loppers enough to begin cutting roots. Henry put on this gloves and began pulling and removing the cut roots after they were severed. Then Will loosened the remaining dirt with the butt-end of his shovel. Henry began to rake the loose dirt and other debris out with a trowel. Will reinserted the butt-end of the shovel. This time he felt it poking something hard. He punched again at a different place and felt something solid again. He continued to probe. The solid object appeared to be about two feet long and about a foot or so high. Outside of that area his shovel continued to hit softer dirt.

"I'm pretty sure there's something lodged in there," Will said. "Let me see if the blades on Hardy's loppers will loosen it up some more."

He jabbed and cut, pried, and then continued to jab and cut. The object finally moved. Henry reached in with his gloved hands and grabbed what seemed to be a handle. When he pulled, the handle broke. He reached back in with both hands and grabbed the object on each side. It began to slide out of the hole. As it got to the edge, Henry lost his hold on it, and it fell. It tumbled end over end down the slope until Mikey Mo stopped it with his foot.

"It's a metal strong box!" Mikey Mo yelled.

"Did it break open?" Will asked.

"No," Mikey Mo said. "Just got dented up a little. Let's open it."

"No, not here," Betsy cautioned. "Let's wait until we get back to The Colonel's house. Someone may come along."

"Betsy's right," Will said. "Mikey Mo, can you lift it? Is it heavy?"

Mikey Mo bent over and lifted the box slightly before saying, "It's not that heavy I can pick it up easily by myself."

"Then get the box back to Henry's van," Will said. "Henry, you go with Mikey and clear out a place for it. Hardy, you and I will start filling this hole back in. It'll go faster if we put some stones in it first. Betsy, take these loppers and cut some brush to lay over the hole so we can hide where we've been working. I'll drag the branches back and lay them over the opening. I don't want some tour guide reporting our digging to the property owner and then have the property owner to start asking what we stole out of his wall."

```
┌─────────────────────┐
│                     │
│   DENTAL            │
│                     │
│   SERVICES          │
│                     │
│   SUNDAYS           │
│                     │
│   2:30 PM           │
│                     │
└─────────────────────┘
```

# Chapter 35

Harry Dog watched through his binoculars as Hardy and Will picked up each stone to begin disguising where the ROTT gang had been digging.

*I'm not sure what's in that strong box, but I gotta find out. I'll waylay them on the road. I've got surprise on my side. It'll be a few minutes until they're ready to depart. I should be able to set up an ambush site by then.*

"Cum on, Champagnie. Hurry," he said. "Wi cyaan get di box dehyah. Wi haffi to fin di place to stop dey on di road (we can't get the box here. We'll have to find a place to stop them on the road)."

Harry Dog and Champagnie ran for the car so they could get far enough ahead of Henry to choose a place to wait for the ambush. He found a place up the road where it was wide enough on one side for him to pull over. Just beyond his car was a steep slope where the land had at one time been strip-mined for bauxite. The steep slope went straight down twenty feet or more. Harry Dog looked for something to use for a roadblock, but the only tree branch he could find light enough for him and Champagnie Peter to drag out onto the road only blocked one lane. He told Champagnie that the strategy would be that he would flag down Henry's van as if he needed road assistance, and when Henry slowed, Champagnie would rush in from the side with his pistol drawn. Once Henry's van stopped, Harry would then draw his own pistol, and immediately they would be in control. It should then be a simple matter for them to force everyone out and steal the strongbox. Nothing fancy. It would be just a simple straight-forward holdup.

Within minutes, they heard Henry's van approach. Mikey Mo and Hardy were following in Mikey Mo's car. Harry Dog pulled his hat down to disguise himself and held out his arm. He let his left wrist flap limply up and down like Jamaicans do when they are trying to thumb a ride As he expected, Henry began to slow. Champagnie Peter, however, came out from behind Harry Dog's car prematurely with his pistol drawn. Mikey Mo was following, He recognized the twosome and blew his horn to warn Henry of danger. He immediately jerked his car wheel to the right and headed right for Champagnie Peter. Peter dived to get out of Mikey Mo's way, but Mikey's bumper caught him anyway. There was a crunch as Mikey ran over Champagnie's foot, crushing all the bones. He then turned back to the left in front of Henry and aimed his car for the stunned Harry Dog. Harry Dog dodged, but Hardy who was riding shotgun had by now gotten out his machete and extended it out the window as Mikey veered back. The machete sliced Harry Dog across the rib-cage, and he tumbled down the slope. The blow wasn't fatal, but the panicking Harry Dog was bleeding profusely and lost his pistol in.

Mikey then backed up and pushed Harry Dog's car over the edge. It rolled down the steep hill and then began to tumble after it struck a tree and a large boulder almost simultaneously. The gas tank ruptured, and the car exploded. They could hear Champagnie Peter screaming about his mangled foot. He was no longer a threat.

Mikey Mo pulled up beside Henry and yelled across to him, "Coo yah, Mr. Davis. Falla mi. Yu gotta get yu passengers bloodclaat outa dehyah ya now (look here, Mr. Davis. Follow me. You've got to get your passengers the fuck out of here right now)."

"Where to?" Henry asked.

"Detour to Sundance," Betsy yelled. "I'm sure they expected us to go to Accompong."

BEWRAY OF
BAD DOG

# Chapter 36

Ruddy-Puss was trimming some coconut palms at Almond Hill when he heard Henry's van drive down Sundance's driveway. Curious, he ran back upstairs in the villa so he could peek over the fence unobserved. There seemed to be a lot of excitement and chatter going on as the group unloaded the strongbox from the van. Betsy asked Leva if the table had already been set for a meal and asked her to clear it if that was the case. They then carried the box out onto Sundance's back porch and placed it on the round resin table. Mikey Mo stayed out in the driveway for a few moments checking the bumpers of his van for possible damage before joining them. Ruddy-Puss wondered just what was causing all the commotion. Mikey Mo called Colonel Winter on his cell phone to update him on their latest acquisition. Colonel Winter said he would dispatch a couple of armed Maroons immediately for Sundance. Ruddy-Puss could see Mikey Moe pacing back and forth on the porch as he talked on the cell phone and wondered who he was talking to. The others chattered excitedly to Leva as she quizzed them on just what they had brought home. This only increased Ruddy-Puss's curiosity.

In the meantime, while Henry had been driving the ROTTers to Sundance, Harry Dog was checking to see what kind of condition that he and Champagnie Peter was in. Champagnie was still screaming unintelligibly about his mangled foot but did not seem in imminent danger of dying. Harry Dog dialed Dudus Coke. He told Dudus that the ROTT group had dug up some kind of old-looking strongbox at Potosi and briefly related the confrontation that had occurred when he had attempted to steal it from them. He expected Dudus to rake him over the coals for failing, but Dudus only said through gritted teeth that he would dispatch a car immediately to pick Harry and Champagnie up and get them both medical attention. Harry asked Dudus if there were any Shower Posse members close to Accompong that morning. When Dudus responded affirmatively that Razor-Sharp could be near, Harry Dog immediately called Razor-Sharp and dispatched him to The Colonel's house with orders to call him back if he spotted Henry's van in Accompong. As soon as he had made arrangements to have Harry Dog and Champagnie Peter picked up, Dudus checked the tracking device Harry Dog had attached to Henry's van. By now, he was getting disgusted with Harry Dog's seeming inability to handle matters. Once he determined that the van's probable location was Sundance, he called Almond Hill and asked to speak to Ruddy-Puss. Ruddy-Puss confirmed that his assessment was correct. Henry's van had just arrived at Sundance, and he told Dudus that something curious seemed to be occurring.

In the meantime, Bunny Witter of the Spangler Posse continued to monitor Dudus Coke's transmissions. He called his associate, Garfield Williams, put him on notice that it appeared something was beginning to break with the Genovesa treasure situation, and told Garfield to dispatch a man to Villa Brawta in Discovery Bay.

"You better get someone over to that villa in Discovery Bay," Garfield said. "I don't know what those people found, but I want it. We're not going to let either Ferron Winter or Dudus Coke beat us now that we're this close."

Back at Sundance, as they examined the strongbox and were trying to decide how best to get into it, the ROTT crew was totally unaware that both of their adversaries had already located them and were closing in on Sundance.

Mikey Mo tested the strongbox lock by tapping on it tentatively with a hammer. This produced no results.

"Chicken, let's see what a screwdriver will do," Hardy suggested. Mikey stuck a small slot-head screwdriver in the lock-hole and wiggled it around.

Nothing happened.

"Try tapping on the screwdriver with a hammer," Henry suggested.

This too produced no results.

"I think we're just going to have to drill the lock," Will said.

"E.J. keeps some metal drill bits here at the villa."

"Oh, I hate to see us destroy a valuable relic," Betsy said.

"There's other boxes," Will reminded her, "but there's only one Genovesa treasure."

"Will's right," Mikey Mo said. "If we find five or six hundred million in Spanish gold, I'll get The Colonel to buy you a new box as a memento and even get him to engrave your name on it."

E.J. fetched his drill and an extension cord. It didn't take long to drill out the rusted lock, but the lid still stuck tight.

"Something's sealing this thing," Henry said and began to pry again with the screwdriver. The lid began to loosen. Dried wax crumbled onto the table. The brittle wax gave way, and there was a slight pop as the last of the wax released its hold on the strongbox top. The lid grudgingly opened on corroded hinges.

"I think it's either another diary or a journal," Hardy said.

He tried to remove the fragile book, but the cover was stuck to the bottom of the metal box.

"Careful. Don't tear it up," Betsy said.

"I'll give you one of my spatulas to slide under it and loosen it up," Leva said. "Let me go get one out of the kitchen drawer."

The spatula loosened the book sufficiently to detach one end from the box. Hardy gingerly held one end of the book up with his fingernails while Henry loosened the other end with the spatula until it also came loose. Then they carefully grabbed the book while Mikey

Mo moved the box out of the way so they could set their find on the table. Hardy opened the front cover.

"This also says Mary Hyde Tharp ... This must be her personal diary," Hardy said. "We won't be able to read this whole thing in a few minutes. You're going to need to give me some time to concentrate on it undisturbed and then give you a report."

"Then you should plan on spending the night here," Betsy said. "Sundance has a guest bedroom downstairs by the TV room. It has its own bathroom and shower. You can work in it to your heart's content. I'll get Will to put the ping-pong top over the pool table, and if you want to spread any papers out on a larger surface, you you'll have that to use. One word of caution, the room can be accessed from the outside using the French doors leading to the backyard. So always keep the door locked and remember to put the chain on it. The only other access to that room is using the main staircase inside the house. I don't think we want to risk trying to take the book anywhere else and maybe have another run-in with the Shower Posse in route. We can all alternate serving as security here while you're studying it."

"Colonel Winter is also sending some Maroons to Sundance for added security," Mikey Mo said. "Between all of us and them, we should be able to adequately protect you and the book. But our most important security is that we should be the only people who know we even have it here."

Hardy excused himself, retreated to the lower level of the house, and began to peruse the diary. He took a legal pad to take notes and some Post-its to mark pages of interest. He also took his cell phone in case he wanted to photograph any specific pages. Leva occasionally checked in on him to see if he needed something to drink or snack on, but other than that, he was left to himself so he could concentrate. He read the diary all afternoon long.

In the meantime, The Colonel's three men arrived, and Will showed them around the grounds. The leader had features that were slightly Asian. He introduced himself as Cooley Man and his associates as Bo-Bo Banana and Bigga. Will could readily understand the street name Bigga since the man was at least six foot five, but he wondered how Bo-Bo Banana got his name.

The Colonel sent Mary Hyde Tharp's Bible down with Cooley Man in case Hardy might need to refer to it as a reference guide. Will and the ROTT men decided two Maroons would patrol the yard, and one man would patrol Sundance's interior. Since they didn't know how long it would take for Hardy to study the diary, they made contingent nighttime plans. Leva checked her cabinets and told Betsy she had enough groceries to feed everyone for several days if necessary without going to the market. Colonel Winter's men would patrol in shifts with one man sleeping and two men patrolling at all times. The sleeping man would sleep in the extra bed in E.J.'s room. The ROTT gang would use the guest bedroom on Sundance's main level, and if necessary, someone could sleep on the couch.

Despite his injury, Harry Dog pleaded with Dudus to remain involved. Since Champagnie Peter was out of action, he arrived at Almond Hill with a Shower Posse member known as Tivoli Tommy. Tivoli Tommy's street name, originally was Tivoli Tommy-Gun, came from his fondness for automatic weapons. It had gradually been shortened over time to Tivoli Tommy. Tommy was driving the car since Harry's side still severely ached from the 20 plus stitches he had received after Hardy had slashed him with his machete. Harry's movements were stiff from the tight bandage encircling his rib cage to keep him from pulling the stitches loose. He had refused the pain killer the doctor tried to give to him, deciding instead to smoke ganja all the way to Sundance. He willingly shared his joints with Tommy. When Ruddy-Puss asked Harry about why he was moving so stiffly, the grouchy Harry growled back, "Hit none of yu business, ediat (idiot) house bwoy (boy). Hole yuh cahna, and leh mi mind mi (mind your own business, and let me mind mine). Since yu dun have a guest in de villa now, mi and Tommy stay ya."

"How lang?"

"Until mi say different," Harry Dog said. "Undastan?"

Harry and Tommy's arrival did not go unnoticed. Bigga was peering over the wall and saw the car drive up. He recognized Harry Dog immediately and reported Harry's presence to Cooley Man. Cooley Man told him to give Bo-Bo Banana a heads up but not to alarm the residents of Sundance yet about Harry's presence.

# A Treasure Conspiracy

The Maroons were not the only ones who were aware of Harry Dog and Tivoli Tommy's presence. Rainy and Apple J, the men who had been dispatched by Bunny Witter had arrived at Villa Brawta. As they rode by Almond Hill, they saw Tivoli Tommy standing next to his car finishing a joint. Both men recognized Tommy immediately. They didn't stop but sped up before Tommy could see them and drove into Villa Brawta on the opposite side of Sundance. They set up a stakeout position there.

Hardy stayed holed up in the downstairs, and no one saw him again for the rest of the afternoon. Henry went the short distance up Primrose Hill to Club View to check on Rose and to get in a brief nap before going back. As the dinner hour approached, Betsy knocked on the downstairs door and asked Hardy if he would be joining them for dinner. He responded that she should ask Leva to give him another thirty minutes, and he'd be out. He said he was in the final stages of compiling some notes that he would share with the group that evening.

Before Hardy emerged thirty minutes later, he locked Mary Hyde Tharp's diary and Bible locked in his briefcase. He didn't want to risk letting either item out of his sight. He also carried a legal pad of notes in his other hand.

"Well, my friend?" Will asked. "What do you have to report?"

"I'm famished and brain-dead. Let's have dinner first. I need a break before my eyes start to cross," Hardy said. "And then after we eat, we'll discuss it in private."

His eyes darted in the direction of Cooley Man who was standing across the porch.

Will nodded his understanding.

*After all we've been through, you can't be too careful.*

Betsy walked over to Cooley Man and said, "Would you join us for dinner? And if Bigga is awake, invite him as well. Since Bo-Bo Banana is patrolling the yard, we'll make him a plate."

Leva announced, "Dinner is served."

"Smells wonderful," Hardy said.

"Nothing fancy. Just some peas and rice, some curried goat and a salad," Leva said.

"You don't know how good that sounds," Hardy said.

When they had finished and helped Leva and E.J. carry the dishes back to the kitchen, Hardy suggested that they call Henry so he could share his notes with everyone at the same time.

"Why don't you bring Rose down?" he said when Henry came to the phone. "She can visit with Leva while we're talking."

When Henry arrived, the group excused themselves from Cooley Man and Bigga and went downstairs to sit on the sectional sofas by the TV in the first floor room.

"This diary was very enlightening," Hardy began.

"Enlightening good or enlightening bad," Will asked.

"Both," Hardy said. "The beginning of the story agrees with the original stories that were told in Spanish galleon Captain Francisco Guiral's diary and Ruby Drain's family journal, but then the tale deviates and ultimately takes a totally unexpected direction.

"Before I get to the part of the story filled in by Mary Hyde Tharp's diary, I'm going to briefly recap what we already knew before we found it. In 1740 during the War of Jenkin's Ear, the Genovesa was taking several tons of gold and silver back to Spain, but Captain Guiral became nervous because British Royal Navy's Vice Admiral Vernon had scored some recent major successes against the Spanish. Rather than risk a confrontation with Vernon, he offloaded much or all of his cargo and hid it in the Cockpit Country using kidnapped slaves from Trelawny's Potosi Estate. He planned to kill the slaves to protect the treasure's location, but three of them escaped and recorded the location of the treasure's hiding place by putting part of a rough map on each of three calabashes. The Genovesa did not get captured by the British but instead sank a few days later in a hurricane. For three hundred years the world has erroneously thought the treasure went down with the ship. Using these calabashes as a starting point followed by some astute detective work, we've managed to get to the point where we are now."

"Which may be a dead end," Mikey Mo said. "Is this what you're trying to let us down easy with?"

"Chicken, no, this is where you're wrong," Hardy said. "Thanks to Mary Hyde Tharp's journal our search is still alive and well."

"You mean you now know where the treasure is?" Mikey Mo asked anxiously.

"I didn't say that, my friend. I just said we're not dead in the water. Bear with me, and you'll see how in the next few minutes. As you remember, Mary Hyde Tharp was John Tharp's illegitimate daughter by the slave Hannah Phillips. Hannah became close to one of the slaves who witnessed the Spanish hiding the treasure, and he gave her complete instructions showing the treasure's location. Before Hannah died, she passed this map on to her daughter, Mary. Mary befriended Major John Jarrett, a participant in Tacky's Rebellion as well as a future leader in the Second Maroon War."

"Would you refresh my memory on Tacky's Rebellion?" Betsy asked.

"An unsuccessful slave revolt that occurred in 1760."

"And before the Second Maroon War?" Will asked.

"I'm coming to that. Jarrett was convinced that there would never be a lasting peace between the Maroons and the British. He dreamed that the Maroons would someday have their own homeland. He shared his dreams with Mary on many occasions. When Mary went to England, she traveled to France on holiday and used that trip to contact the Spanish ambassador. He put her in touch with Manuel de Godoy, the Spanish prime minister under Charles IV.

"Through Godoy, she negotiated with the Spanish crown to help recover the Genovesa treasure in return for unspecified concessions for the Maroons. They worked out a deal that was not disclosed in her diary, but before her plan could be put into action, the Second Maroon War broke out."

He paused and waited for questions.

"So tell me about the Second Maroon War," Will said.

"The Second Maroon War was very short – less than a year – and this time the British were prepared and were victorious. It began when two Maroons were flogged by a black slave for stealing two pigs. The Maroons took their grievances to the British, and the British made the complainants prisoners. The Maroons declared war but were outnumbered by the British troops ten to one. Defeat was inevitable this time. The British general, George Walpole, forced the Maroons to beg on their knees for the King's forgiveness, return all runaway slaves, and agree to be relocated to another location in Jamaica. Jamaica was not what the devious British had in mind, however. They rounded up the Maroons and shipped them off to Nova Scotia."

"Holy crap," Will said. "And then what happened?"

"Some of them ended up going back to Africa. Some of them eventually found their way back to Jamaica. Many died in Nova Scotia."

"And Major Jarrett?"

"He and his family ended up in Freetown in Sierra Leone."

"So what happened to the treasure? Did the Spanish end up with it?" Mikey Mo asked.

"Could be, but I can't tell for sure," Hardy said, "but Mary keeps referring to some sort of agreement, so something had to have happened."

"But she doesn't tell what the agreement was?" Betsy asked. "So we're no better off than we were."

"I wouldn't agree with that. She says the agreement with the Spanish was hidden because they didn't want it to get into British hands. She said it was rolled up and concealed in a piece of artwork."

"What kind of art work?" Mikey Mo asked.

"A wall-hanging, a wood carving – I think."

"Oh, gud grief," Mikey Mo exclaimed lapsing into patois. "Do yuh know how many millions of carvings deh got in Jamaica and de chance of finding one tree-hundred year old?"

"Yep, I know it seems daunting on the surface," Hardy said, "but the calabashes did manage to survive all those years, so a wood carving might have as well ... and Mary did draw a picture of the artwork in her diary. So if the calabashes could survive, why couldn't the artwork have made it as well?"

Hardy got the diary out of his briefcase and paged through it to a page he had previously marked. The group looked at a very unusual collection of figures done in relief. At the bottom were three men's heads arranged in a circle looking at each other. They were obviously either African slaves or natives of some sort. The heads were surrounded by and seemed to be looking at a calabash with what appeared to be a crude face carved in its center. Above this was a cluster of bananas on the left with a cat and a parrot facing them. At the top was an elephant with an upturned trunk. Astride the elephant was a large round pot or urn being held in place by the elephant's trunk.

"My friends, believe it or not, I have seen this piece of art. It's about three feet high and is carved out of mahogany," Betsy said.

"No shit? Where is it?" Hardy blurted out.

"Will, don't you remember this piece? It was hanging in Madame Erzube Blanton's office on Bourbon Street," Betsy said.

Will looked at the drawing again and said, "Hmmm! Yeah ... I guess you're right. When we were there, I remember you were making small talk with her about a wood carving while I was going through my briefcase looking for our introduction letter from Colonel Winter."

"Who is Madame Erzube?" Hardy asked.

"She's a direct descendant of Ben, one of the three slaves who escaped and survived when Captain Guiral hid his precious cargo. Ben was the one who was sold to the Marquis de Vaudreuil in New Orleans to be a house servant. Madame Erzube owns a voodoo shop called Voodoo Blues on Bourbon Street in New Orleans. The calabash had been passed down through her family. Colonel Winter negotiated with her to buy it and dispatched us there during Jazz Fest to pay her and retrieve it."

"OK, so *she's* the one he mentioned. I know who you're talking about now. He never told me her name," Hardy said. "Isn't that when you first ran into problems with the Shower Posse?"

"That depends on if you're only referring to our most recent series of run-ins," Betsy said. "Our first run-in was when I was trying to protect the bank's loan portfolio during the Highway 2000 construction project."

Both Henry and Mikey Mo said at the same time, "Boy, do we ever remember."

Will said, "Does this mean someone's got to go back to N'awlins? I volunteer."

"Only if I'm there to protect you," Betsy said and laughed. "It's too easy for you to get in trouble in the Big Easy by yourself."

"My bodyguard!," Will said to Hardy as he hugged Betsy. "Everybody needs one."

"I've got too much time and money invested in that body of yours not to look after my own interests," Betsy said.

WARNING
NO URINATE
ALLOWED

# Chapter 37

While Hardy was conducting his briefing with the rest of the ROTT gang, Cooley Man was having his own brief low-key meeting with Bigga and Bo-Bo Banana. Each man shared his observations with Cooley Man about their concerns that the villa might be subject to attack from both Almond Hill and Villa Brawta.

"Mi tell Chicken, but tell he to hol it dung (keep it a secret) for now," Cooley Man said. "We dunna wan he be acksidental blabba mout to de rest of de group and vex dem (we don't want him to accidentally tell the other members of our group and upset them). Mi aks (ask) The Colonel what to do."

He dialed Colonel Winter on his cell phone and told him that he and his men suspected they were not being watched by just one gang but possibly two – sandwiched in by the Spangler Posse on one side and the Shower Posse on the other.

"Are the posses aware of each other's presence?" Colonel Winter asked.

"Mi dunna tink so," Cooley Man answered.

Colonel Winter told Cooley Man to give him a few minutes to devise a scheme to combat the situation and said he'd call back with instructions. Colonel Winter was true to his word and called back within minutes.

"Here's my plan," The Colonel began. "I have dispatched a couple of reinforcements for you. They are bringing props with them that will enable us to try to turn the two posses on each other and keep your men out of a firefight with either of them. I don't want any of our people hurt or killed if it can be avoided. Here's how it is going to work. We are going to conduct a furtive mock raid simultaneously on both Almond Hill and Villa Brawta in the wee hours of the morning while their occupants are sleeping. We will make each raid appear to be unsuccessful but will leave clues that will make each posse think they are being attacked by the other one and will lead them to conduct their own counter attack on their supposed aggressor. Then we'll sit back and watch them fight it out with each other."

"What de clues you chat about?" Cooley Man asked.

"As you know even though posses don't have a uniform per se, they are partial to yellow, green, and red. One of our raiding parties will leave a baseball cap with these colors at each villa in a place where it is sure to be found and where it will look like it might have been lost in the invader's attempt to run from the botched invasion attempt. I am sending two soiled, used looking caps for that purpose."

"How dey know which posse axxidentally dropped de cap?" Cooley Man asked.

"Have you ever heard of Demon Devon and Stinky Finger?"

"Yeh, Demon Devon belong to Shower Posse, and Stinky Finger a known Spangler."

"If you know those names, you can be sure our adversaries do. Demon Devon's name will be written in one cap with an ink pen, and Stinky Finger's in the other. Just make sure you leave Demon Devon's name on Spangler's doorstep and Stinky Finger's on the Shower Posse's and not vice versa otherwise de nancy rope tie de nancy (otherwise the spider's web will trap himself)."

"But wi haven't seen either Stinky Finger or Demon Devon."

"You know that and I know that, but they don't know that. I just chose two names each of them would easily associate with the other posse."

"But how will dey know where to find each odda (other)?"

"Because on separate occasions each will *accidentally* overhear your men talking to each other earlier that evening in the yard about our concerns that we are being watched from the other villa and how we think our observers are gang members. Now do you understand?"

"Mi unnastan but me hab one more question."

"Fire away," The Colonel said.

"Won't dey see yu men arrive at Sundance and wonder?"

"No, because they will park their car at Henry Davis's house and he will bring them to Sundance in his van. I'll call Henry and tell him he has some guests arriving shortly and what to do with them."

"OK. Sounds like it might work."

"If you put on a good performance, it will. Just make sure the guests are inside our villa and are kept safe. Now brief Mikey Mo and put him in charge of caring for them. I want to avoid having anyone at Sundance injured, and I want to minimize the chance of retaliation when all is said and done. Any questions? I will leave the details of the fake raid up to you. Just be careful not to get caught or hurt. May Jah bless, my brother."

Cooley Man called Mikey Mo aside and told him they were being watched from both sides of the yard by two different posses, but that he and Colonel Winter were in agreement that they should not unnecessarily alarm the rest of the Sundance's occupants at this time by giving them too many details since the situation would be handled discreetly using a devious plan devised by The Colonel. Mikey Mo concurred.

"De main ting is to keep dey safe in de villa and to keep dey from complicating tings by axxidental calling de Constabulary (deputies) when the paati (party) begins," he explained to Mikey Mo.

Mikey Mo said he would meet with the other guests and tell them that he did not want them outdoors for any reason for the remainder of the evening, and that he would fill them in completely at a more appropriate time.

Five reinforcements arrived. Henry parked in the carport, and they quickly scooted unobserved into E.J.'s quarters. It was decided that the mock home invasion would occur one hour after all lights in both villas had been extinguished for the evening. Bo-Bo Banana would go with one of Colonel Winter's men to Villa Brawta while Bigga would simultaneously go with the other man to Almond Hill. Cooley Man and the other three Maroons would stay at Sundance to open and close Sundance's gate, patrol the wall and be present in case a man was needed on that front for some unexpected development such as Sundance coming under attack. A baseball cap with the name implicating the other posse would be left in a bush just off of each front porch. Once the caps had been planted and the raiders had had time to retreat to a safe place near the property line, they would leave both Villa Brawta and Almond Hill's gates ajar to give the appearance of a hasty retreat. They would wake each villa's residents by setting off a small firebomb in each yard containing fire crackers. Each would be placed far enough away from the villa so as not to start a fire and in a place where one villa couldn't see what was occurring at the other. The goal was only to get the occupants' attention, not to burn down the villas and attract the fire department or Constabulary. Then the mischief-makers would sit back at Sundance and watch as the battle between the two rival posses was sure to begin.

While it was twilight, Cooley Man had Bo-Bo and Bigga patrol the wall next to Almond Hill while talking to each other to begin setting the stage for what was to come. He could see Tivoli Tommy on the other side of the wall.

"Mi tink mi know guest at Villa Brawta. Mi tink mi see him before at de rum bar (I think I've seen him at the rum bar) wid Garfield Williams," Bigga said.

"Shhh! Dunn be blabba mout or sumady hear wi a chat (don't be a blabbermouth or somebody's going to hear us talking.)," Bo-Bo said, playing out the script they'd rehearsed.

"Yu right. Mi hope nobody hear."

Tivoli Tommy's radar went up, and he headed back for the villa to tell Harry Dog what he had heard. Bigga winked slightly at Bo-Bo, and they walked around to the other side of Sundance to continue the ruse with the residents of Villa Brawta.

As luck would have it, both Apple J and Rainy were checking the lawn at Villa Brawta when they got there.

A Treasure Conspiracy

"Mi tink mi know guest at Almond Hill," Bigga said. "Mi tink mi see him before at de rum bar wid Tivoli Tommy."

"Shhh!" Bo-Bo said. "Dunn be blabba mout. Sumady hear wi a chat."

"Yu right. Mi hope nobody hear."

Apple J and Rainy stopped walking and looked at each other.

Bo-Bo and Bigga casually strode back to Sundance to report to Cooley Man "missions accomplished."

Mikey Mo encouraged the occupants at Sundance to have an early evening, reasoning that the sooner all lights were extinguished at Sundance, the earlier those watching Sundance's activities would feel that they could call it a day. He also reminded everyone not to be alarmed if they heard any unusual noises later in the night and not to call for help. By ten o'clock, everyone at Sundance had retired to their bedrooms as Mikey Mo had requested. By ten thirty, all lights were out. Cooley Man and his crew patiently waited. About midnight, the last light was extinguished at Villa Brawta.

"One down, one to go," Cooley Man told Bigga. "Shouldn't be too long now until lights-out at Almond Hill. Forty-five minutes later, Tivoli Tommy finished his last patrol of Almond Hill's grounds for the day. He then extinguished the yard and house lights and went to bed himself.

"Wi give it annuda hour and if everting still quiet," Cooley Man said, "wi mash up da place (we'll take the place by storm)."

When he was satisfied that everyone in both villas was asleep, Cooley Man dispatched the two teams to plant the baseball caps where they would easily be found. When his men had returned safely, he heaved the firebombs over the wall on both sides and watched them roll under or near some shrubbery. Both went off almost simultaneously, setting off the firecrackers they contained. The dark night lit up as the firecrackers began to pop and shatter the firebomb bottles.

Lights went on at both villas and the armed thugs ran out in their underwear, weapons in hand. Cooley Man and part of his crew watched from the shadows at Sundance. Bigga and Bo-Bo Banana and the other men listened from the fence surrounding the opposite side yard. They could hear cursing as the confused gangsters darted back and forth trying to find their late-night invaders.

Cooley Man made a fist and held two thumbs up.

"So fur, so gud," he said as he smiled.

He heard Tivoli Tommy call out to Harry Dog. "Coo yah (look here)."

Tivoli Tommy held up the baseball cap one team had planted. "Where yu find that?"

"Inna de thorn bush on de front porch. It hab a name in it."

"Leggo and mek mi see."

Harry Dog grabbed the cap and read "Stinky Finger" out loud.

"Mi know him. Him a Spanger Posse," Tivoli Tommy said. "He dehyah (is he here)?"

"Yu said di bloodclaat (fucking) guest at Villa Brawta maybe is a posse memba," Harry Dog said. "Hit muss (it must) be Shower Posse. Now mi vex (now I'm pissed). If di bloodclaat (fucking) Spangler Posse wan bruk in (wants to break in) Almond Hill, dey muss wan war (a fight). If dey wan war, mi give dem war. Get dressed and get yu tool (gun)."

A similar scene was occurring at Villa Brawta. Rainy and Apple J both recognized the name in the cap they found as well. Demon Devon was a longstanding Shower Posse member, and everyone knew it. Now revenge was their only option.

As Apple J put it, "If wi leh (let) dat pum cheese (vaginal discharge) get away with dis, wi no betta than pussywool batty boy (wimpy queers). Wi show dem who bowcyat (sucks private parts). When mi finish with Demon Devon, he suck *mi* buddy (penis)."

The two groups met in the street, and the name-calling began. The fight escalated when Rainy took a swing at Harry Dog with a chain, only to wrap it around his baseball bat. The fight abruptly ended when Tivoli Tommy produced a CZ 75 automatic pistol and prepared to fire. Just as he aimed his weapon, Rainy's chain jerked Harry Dog's bat out of his hands, snapping the bone in his wrist. The bat flew into Tivoli Tommy's gun almost jerking it from his hands and sending his barrage of bullets straight into the air. Before he could get his weapon back under control, Apple J's thrown knife penetrated his right arm.

Tivoli Tommy screamed and dropped his pistol. Still on automatic, bullets sprayed Sundance's front wall. Apple J and Rainy ran back for Villa Brawta before another volley of gunfire could erupt. Harry Dog and Tivoli Tommy retreated to the safety of Almond Hill.

From the relative safety of Sundance's front yard, Cooley Man smiled.

He thought about something his mother used to say years ago, "When rat like fi romp 'roun' puss jaw, one day 'im gwine en up inna puss craw (if a rat keeps playing too close to a cat's mouth, one day he's finally going to end up in the cat's belly)."

# Chapter 38

Bunny Witter sat in his office in Kingston trying to evaluate the panic-stricken report he had received from Rainy and Apple J about the fracas they had had with members of the Shower Posse at Sundance. He asked himself - what would cause them to attack his men unprovoked at Villa Brawta when they were on a stake-out? He didn't want to go to war with the Shower Posse if it could be avoided, but he wouldn't avoid a confrontation if it meant he would lose face with his men. He also certainly didn't want word circulating among the posses that he and the Spangler Posse were pussies who were afraid to fight. A rumor like that would cause him to experience defections among his men at best and at worst some brash up-and-comer in the Spangler Posse might challenge him for his leadership role. But he also knew a war with the Shower Posse was most likely a losing proposition since they were the strongest posse in Jamaica. He really didn't want to be on Dudus Coke's shit-list if it could be avoided. Well, at least at this skirmish, his men had escaped more or less unharmed and had instead harmed their assailants – a small miracle considering Demon Devon's reputation. But why would Dudus risk sending one of his best men to lead this low-level assault when he had so many unimportant young bucks who would relish the chance to show "The Pres" what they were made of?

He decided that the smart thing to do was not to just duck the matter and hope it went away, but to try to talk to Dudus one leader to another before irrational, hot-headed emotions caused the situation to escalate further.

Dudus Coke sat in his office trying to evaluate the events of the previous evening as well. He had had two men wounded for what seemed to be an inexplicable reason. Well, at least he had the name of one of the perpetrators, Stinky Finger. But Stinky Finger had to be answering to someone. Was it Bunny Witter or maybe Garfield Williams? There had been some bad blood between him and Garfield Williams in the past, but surely Garfield wasn't stupid enough to take on the Shower Posse. Whatever the facts were, this could not be ignored, but an overt retaliation would bring unwelcome attention from law enforcement as well as making captive politicians reticent about granting Dudus favors.

Bunny Witter sighed and dialed Dudus' private number. He might as well get this over with.

"Dudus, Bunny Witter. A matter has come up that I wish to discuss with you. I'd rather talk to you in person if it's convenient today. Why don't you let me treat you to lunch? South Avenue Grill has an excellent lunch. You tell me what time is convenient for you. Bring some of your men if you wish, but I would like our discussion to remain confidential. I believe South Avenue is open for lunch at noon."

He waited nervously for Dudus to respond. Dudus remained guardedly cordial and named a time.

"12:30?" Bunny said. "I'll see you then. I'll be out back by the pool. I'll make sure the table we get has privacy. And I'll pick up the tab for your men as well. May Jah bless."

Bunny arrived early to make sure of the arrangements. He wanted no snafus. He walked through the rustic, one-story building to the lushly landscaped patio out back. A walking-bridge led across the pool past the bar. He stood and glanced around him. He could choose to be under the building with its open, arched rough-wood ceiling where ceiling fans kept the air circulating or he could choose a table at the head of the pool. There was a high-top table area as well and a corner section. There were more tables back by the far wall under green awnings. Yes, these would be best. This was no time to go cheap. He gave the hostess J$10,000 to reserve the three tables he wanted. When she hesitated, he added another J$5,000 to her tip. She smiled and readily complied with his wishes. He would have one table for Dudus and him, another table for Dudus' men, and a third for his own men. He did not want to risk sitting the two groups at the same table.

Dudus walked in with two bodyguards. Bunny had brought two men himself. The hostess seated the three groups. Bunny opened the conversation with small talk and asked Dudus about his family as he waited for the waitress to take their orders. The waitress recommended the steamed coconut snapper fillet. They both agreed that sounded excellent and both ordered tea in lieu of a rum drink. Bunny asked if they should speak in English or patois. Dudus agreed English would be fine.

"My men reported to me that there was an unfortunate misunderstanding in Discovery Bay," Bunny began. "Apparently your men misinterpreted my men's presence and thought they were a threat. This misunderstanding caused my men to retaliate."

"Strange," Dudus said. "My men reported that your men first became aggressive with them, forcing them to defend themselves. Your men tried to invade the villa housing my men."

"My men reported that your men invaded their villa, and that this set the stage for the subsequent confrontation."

"Your man, Stinky Finger, lost his cap in the bushes at Almond Hill. I know it was him. His name was in the sweatband," Dudus said.

"Impossible," Bunny replied. "Stinky Finger wasn't even there. My men Rainy and Apple J were conducting that stakeout. And they weren't staking your men out. I sent them to watch the occupants at Sundance. Your man Demon Devon tried to break into Villa Brawta. I have a cap with his name in it."

"No way," Dudus said. "Demon Devon was back in Tivoli Gardens. Harry Dog and Tivoli Tommy were staying at Almond Hill on a mission totally unrelated to you."

"It appears someone wants to pit the Shower Posse against the Spangler Posse."

"And almost succeeded."

"You didn't want to start a territorial war, did you?" Bunny said.

"Of course not. That's always a last resort. Wars are not good for business."

"I wonder whose business would benefit if we went at each other."

*Surely Bunny's not that naive,* Dudus thought. *Is he trying to play me?*

"I can answer that. Ferron Winter. That sly old dog is up to no good again," Dudus said.

"He's been a pain in my ass for a long time. But Winter nuh dog. Him be Anasi (Ashanti spider in African folklore). Anasi aginnal, him eva deh trick people fi get di upper hand (Anasi is a trickster. He's always tricking people to get the upper hand)."

"It appears we have a mutual enemy with an unknown agenda," Bunny said, "and it would be in our best interest to work together."

"I agree."

*Unknown agenda, mi ras (my ass),* Dudus thought. *Is it possible that Bunny doesn't know about the Genovesa treasure?*

As Bunny smiled back agreeably, he thought, *Is it possible that Dudus doesn't know that my sole motivation is trying to get that treasure for myself? I'm sure glad I didn't accidentally tip my hand. We'll work together all right – until I learn where that gold is. After that, fuck him and the Shower Posse both. Dudus can do anything he wants with Colonel Winter. That's his feud; I just want the gold.*

Out loud, Bunny said, "I'm glad we cleared the air and found we have a mutual adversary, even if we don't know why. Yes, it's time we worked together for our common good."

Dudus smiled and thought. *You may not know why, but I know why that old bastard is stirring up the pepper-pot soup, and yes, we'll work together ... Unless I find de bumba ras clot miself, and den it ever man fo hm self (unless I find the ass-wipe myself, and then it'll be every man for himself).*

Bunny mirrored Dudus' thoughts.

~ ~ ~

While Dudus was having lunch with Bunny Witter and declaring a truce, Harry Dog had returned to Almond Hill alone and was smoking a joint and drinking Wray & Nephew rum as he looked at the hard cast now immobilizing his wrist. He still couldn't believe he and Tivoli Tommy had failed to take out two members of the Spangler Posse. Unbelievable! He and Tommy hadn't managed to wound either of them. He didn't want that getting around since Spangler Posse member Stinky Finger was not supposed to be that good. And who was the other man Stinky Finger had with him? Disgusted with himself, Harry threw the baseball cap across the room.

*How could this have happened? Mi be bad bad bad, and everybady know Tivoli Tommy is a psycho especially when he have his tool (gun).*

Harry's plan to solidify his future in the Shower Posse was now in danger. And unfortunately there was no way for him to lay off the blame on anyone else; Dudus had made it clear from the get-go that this was Harry Dog's operation. Harry had never admitted it to anyone, but he secretly harbored hopes of succeeding or deposing Dudus Coke one day. Now he just knew he had lost face with Dudus and felt he had better regain Dudus' respect in a hurry before he lost face with other Shower Posse members as well.

*Real men follow sumbaddy dey respeck.*

Harry took another swig of rum, and inadvertently slammed the bottle on the table. A sharp pain ran through his injured wrist. He began to recap all the things that had thus far gone wrong since this operation had begun. First, he had caught flack because the New Orleans Shower Posse had lost, for all intents and purposes, a valuable man who had never recovered from the broken ear drum or the slashed arm. Also the man's speech had been permanently altered by the blow he had taken to his Adams apple from Will Blacks' kubatan. Then there was Knuckles Biddle. His body had never been recovered to this day and probably never would be. No telling where the Maroons had buried him. And then there was LeVar and Gabriel. LeVar had been killed at the Pocomania revival, and Gabriel was almost legally blind from the caustic soda bath he had taken in Whistling Villa's swimming pool. Champagnie Peter was lost. Gangrene had set in on his mangled foot, and it had been amputated. Tivoli Tommy would be out of action for who knows how long. And Punkin-Puss had been killed. And then there were his own injuries. His rib cage was being held together by stitches and a tight bandage that made it almost impossible for him to get a decent night's sleep, and now his goddamned wrist was broken. He let go a string of expletives. How could these amateurs have gotten that lucky that many times?

*I've got to get things back under control. The best way to regain everyone's respect is to get for Dudus what he wants – that strongbox at Sundance and its contents. ... And I better do it in a hurry. Then everyone will forget about these unfortunate setbacks. ... But for now I need an idea and a plan.*

He called out to Ruddy-Puss.

"C'mere, house bwoy," Harry said. "Tell me everyting yu know about de guests at Sundance."

Ruddy-Puss began to tell what he knew about each of Sundance's occupants. Before the conversation had concluded Harry learned that Leva Carter had a teenage daughter named Emma Lois who attended Ocho Rios High School. Harry suddenly had a plan. He decided the Carters would be his next target. He'd kidnap Leva's daughter and threaten to kill the girl unless the Blacks gave him the strongbox and its contents. He smoked another joint but then began to doubt himself when he thought of all the ways this operation could go wrong – just like when he had kidnapped the Blacks. If this operation went south, and the law got drawn into it, giving Dudus some public black eye, he'd be finished for sure. No. He had to do something that, if it failed, he could have a hope of keeping from Dudus. ... And if it succeeded he would take sole credit for. But if it failed ... he could blame on someone else like the houseboy.

*Mi complicating dis too much. K-I-S-S – keep 'hit simple stupid. What have mi done best all mi life – and can continue to do even in mi condition? Fight! Mi just take what mi want like mi always has. And if those bloodclyaat (fucking) people get in mi way, mi just kill they asses. Mi wait for 'em to leave, and mi just go over de fence and take what mi want.*

Harry called Ruddy-Puss over again.

He took a final drag on his reefer and said, "Yu still tink yu Shower Posse material like yu brudda, Punkin-Puss was? If yu do good, mi put in good word for you with The President. Mi want yu to

213

watch Sundance and let mi know if anybuddy comes or goes. Yu unnastan?"

With that, Harry Dog poured himself another glass of rum and water, rolled another reefer and turned on the radio. Soon Kashief Lindo's soft reggae version of "Killing Me Softly" came on and not long after that, Harry dozed off into a hazy sleep. The next thing he remembered was Ruddy-Puss shaking him.

"Sir, Mr. Davis's van left Sundance a few minutes ago, and he took some passengers with him. Colonel Winter's men left shortly after that."

"Did you see who was in the Mr. Davis's bus?"

"No. It was pulled in the driveway so they loaded from the other side."

"Did de house bwoy go wid dem?"

"Mi tink so."

Harry grabbed the binoculars and peered over the wall. All seemed quiet.

*Bet nobuddy home. If sumbuddy home, The Colonel's men would still be there. Dis mi opportunity just to go get dat strongbox while dey gone.*

He watched Sundance for about ten minutes more. He saw no sign of activity, and the dogs didn't seem to be out. Most of the lights in the house extinguished. It probably wasn't going to get any safer than this. He'd find that strongbox and be long gone before anyone returned.

What Harry had no way of knowing was that Leva Carter had stayed behind and was taking a nap in her bedroom.

Harry's side was still tightly bound. If he tried to do too much he was sure to tear some of the stitches loose. He'd already done that once. And then there was the matter of that damned wrist in the cast. Hard to climb a wall with one arm. He sure wished he had Tivoli Tommy with him, but Tivoli Tommy was in as bad a shape as he was in.

*Mi guess mi have to depend on de house bwoy.*

He called Ruddy-Puss over and said, "Yu did good watching de house. Now mi give you opportunity to really prove yuself. Yu going to help mi search for sumthin while de folks gone."

He then explained to Ruddy-Puss just what they were looking for. Ruddy-Puss climbed over the wall and unlatched the gate so Harry could join him. The front door was unlocked. Within minutes, they were inside Sundance searching for the elusive strongbox. Harry was looking in a closet in the guest bedroom while Ruddy-Puss looked under a bed.

Suddenly there was a clang, and Harry blacked out. He staggered backwards and fell on one the single beds in the guest bedroom. There was a second clang, and suddenly Ruddy-Puss was stretched out on the other bed. Leva Carter was standing there with an iron skillet in her hand. She had caught Harry in the back of his head with her forward swing, and with the back-swing she had decked Ruddy-Puss.

When both men regained consciousness, each tried to rise. Harry was on his back tied down with the butcher's twine Leva used to tie up roasts in the kitchen. His good arm was tied to the headboard. Another piece of twine began with the headboard, was then wrapped around his neck before it wrapped several time around the arm in the cast, and returned to the other bedpost. If Harry tried to pull, he only choked himself. His feet were secured to the foot board. He had a splitting headache. He had a hard time focusing on Leva. It looked like she was standing there holding a long handled spatula.

Ruddy-Puss had fallen on the other bed face first. Leva had tied him to the bed spread-eagle in the same position he had fallen. Both men jerked on the bonds before realizing that their efforts were futile.

"What are you two doing in my house?" Leva demanded. "You think you can rob my house, houseboy?"

"No, Miz Leva," Ruddy-Puss gasped. "Mi no thief. It just mi, Ruddy-Puss from Almond Hill."

"I know who you are, Nakomis McCauley. I know your people," Leva said. "And it's Mrs. Carter to you, young man. I didn't tell you that you could call me by my given name. You young people today have no respect for your elders. Now what are you doing in my house, and who's this hoodlum with you?"

Without waiting for Ruddy-Puss to reply she reached into Harry Dog's pocket and extracted his wallet. The driver's license said Harry McLeon. The scrap of paper with his notes about Leva's daughter,

Emma Lois, fell out. She read the name, the age, and Ocho Rios High School.

"Why have you got my daughter's name?" Leva demanded. "Are you some kind of pervert? You hurt my daughter, and you'll find out what real trouble is."

"It mean nothing," Ruddy-Puss managed to say. "Mi promise."

Leva slapped him between the legs with the spatula. Ruddy-Puss gasped.

"Don't you lie to me, Nakomis. You won't have any buddies (balls) to hurt anyone with by the time I'm through with you."

She swatted Harry Dog between the legs as well just for emphasis.

"I always had you pegged as a rude boy (hoodlum). And I knew your mama, Emily. She should have raised you better than that."

She looked at Ruddy-Puss again and raised the spatula like she was going to strike.

"Mi no pervert. He made me tell him about Emma Lois," Ruddy-Puss said. "Mi save her. Mi keep he from kidnapping her."

Harry Dog gave Ruddy-Puss a murderous look.

"Don't you lie to me bwoy," Leva said and swatted both men between the legs another time. "Why would he kidnap my Emma Lois unless he's a pervert. I don't have any money."

She raised the spatula again and swatted Ruddy-Puss on his exposed ass.

"Wi come to get dat metal box Mr. Davis brought back dehyah (here)," Ruddy-Puss said.

"Mi talk Harry out of dat kidnap plan. Wi search for de box here instead. Mi bring Harry here to protect yu daughter, so he not harm her."

"Bloodclaayt liar. Ediat (idiot)," Harry Dog blurted out. "Mi see yu never in de Shower Posse now. Yu allas be nothing more dan a pogay (gay) house bwoy."

"Such language." Leva said and slapped Harry between the legs again with the spatula. Harry gritted his teeth and groaned.

"Is that what this is all about?" Leva then asked. "You want to be one of those thugs. Your mama be shamed you be wanting to follow after that no-good older bruddah of yours. You better be glad I knew your mama, or I'd make a girl out of you, right now."

"Yu batty-gal, batty-crease pumm-pumm (you lesbian, asshole pussy). Yu don know who you deal wid," Harry screamed.

Leva slapped him between the legs again with the spatula and said, "I told you about such language. You keep this up, and I'll be turning you from Harry to Harriet."

"Are yu gwaan let wi go?" Ruddy-Puss. "Yu do, wi don come back. Mi promise."

"No, I'm going to let you lie there and repent some more. I'm not going to let you loose while I'm here alone with you. Will and Betsy will be back here soon, and I'll let them decide if we should call the Constabulary. They may have some more questions for you. In the meantime, I'm going to put on some gospel music for you to listen to, and I want you to think about your sinful lives. And remember God is a forgiving God ... even to ... God, please excuse my own language ... low-lifes like you. Glory hallelujah! Praise the Lord! "

As he lay there, Harry Dog's thoughts did not revert to God. They reverted to Dudus Coke's reaction if he ever found out about this latest debacle with a domestic. Total embarrassment. He also thought about how he would never be respected again by the members of the Shower Posse if they ever found out that the great Harry Dog had gotten taken down by a middle aged cook and cleaning lady. His new name would probably revert from Harry Dog to something like Fuzz Nuts. Lastly, he thought about how he was going to be walking bowlegged for the next week.

Ruddy-Puss's thoughts were not religious either. He thought about what would happen to his job at Almond Hill if Leva told the owner about this incident. Then he thought he probably ought to quit anyway and find someplace to live where Harry Dog couldn't find him later. He also worried about having to defend himself from a big, dark, hairy tif-tif boy (fag) if he got sent to jail. He would willingly repent, as Leva had suggested, but at this juncture it would do him no good anyway.

```
┌─────────────────────────────────────────┐
│                                           │
│   GROVE MOUNT FURNISHING                  │
│   COME  AND  SEE  THE                     │
│   LATEST  STYLE  IN                       │
│   ANTIQUE  BUILD  AND                     │
│            REPAIR                         │
│        CHECK B. ATKINGS                   │
│                                           │
└─────────────────────────────────────────┘
```

# Chapter 39

Leva heard Henry's van pull back into Sundance's driveway, and she met them at the front door.

"Kingtoo," Leva said smiling. "You forgot to take the garbage out of the guest bedroom, and it's beginning to smell.

"Yes, ma'am," E.J. said obediently and went to take care of things.

He quickly came back out stuttering, "Th .. th ...there ... there's two men tied up on the beds."

"Well, I'll be," Leva said. "No wonder the beds are mussed."

The rest of the ROTT gang came running to see what E.J. and Leva were talking about. Both Harry and Ruddy-Puss were still securely tied just as Leva had left them – one facing down, the other facing up. Harry began screaming intimidating threats when they walked in. He tugged on the butcher cord, but all it did was cut into his wrists.

"I had two visitors while you were gone," Leva said. "Two wannabe thieves, but I took care of them."

Harry yelled, "Bitch witch!"

"I know that one," said Mikey Mo as he pointed towards Harry. "He's in the Shower Posse.

"And that's Ruddy-Puss from Almond Hill with him," E.J. added.

"I know who they both are," Leva said. "And now they know who Leva Carter is as well."

She held up her skillet proudly and waved it in the air. "I cooked their goose with this frying pan."

"I guess they were trying to steal the strongbox," Hardy said. "Well, boys, hate to tell you, but even if you'd gotten it, it wouldn't have done you much good."

Mikey Mo was already calling The Colonel for instructions. When he got off his cell phone, he said, "The Colonel says to bring them to Accompong but to be careful. That one in the Shower Posse is a dangerous man."

"And I'm a dangerous woman," Leva said. "I'm a skillet-toting, Bible-thumping mama."

There was another horn toot. It was Cooley Man returning. Mikey Mo went out to get Cooley Man to hold a gun on the twosome while he and E.J. untied them and rebound them with duct tape. Bo-Bo Banana and Bigga stayed outside to patrol the yard. Once the two men were rebound, they immediately loaded them into Henry's van. Cooley Man and Bigga decided they would follow behind in case the Shower Posse tried to waylay Henry on the highway and rescue the two hostages. Harry Dog continued to scream that each and every one was soon to be dead.

"Are you going to be back by dinner?" Leva asked. "Mr. Davis, you and Mrs. Davis are invited to dine if you want to come. And by the way, would you pick up some lettuce and tomatoes while you're out?"

The drive to Accompong was free of any incidents. Harry continued to try to intimidate them along the way until Mikey Mo tired of listening to him and put some duct tape over his mouth.

Colonel Winter decided that he did not want to resolve this matter at his home in front of his wife. He walked over to Flashy's Place. Locals were huddled around a flickering TV set watching a replay of a classic soccer match. Despite everyone knowing the outcome of the match, the rum and beer drinking men were cheering on their favorite team like they were seeing the game for the first time and had put bets on the line. Functioning as a quasi Accompong community center, Flashy's provided an ideal place for locals to relax, play dominoes, and conduct Rastafarian philosophy "reasoning" sessions.

The shop-come-bar is no more than four meters square, with mostly empty shelves providing little more than a few bottles of Guinness and some canned vegetables. Set back from the rest of the town on a hilltop, its glassless windows are open to the clear Jamaican sky.

Despite his gold tooth, the owner, Flashy, does not personify pretentiousness or the image of a typical money-motivated small town business person. "Pay me later. No problem, mon." are sentences a visitor hears over and over again. At different times, Flashy will invite friends or patrons to mind the business while he accompanies someone for a leisurely walk around town. Flashy calls it "circling." Any person accompanying Flashy on a such a stroll will pass other shop or business owners similar to Flashy chatting with one or two of their own patrons over their counters or will possibly encounter them out on their own circling jaunts. It's not uncommon for Flashy to stop and join in others' discussions to offer his own insight or add his two cents worth to their gossip.

When Henry drove up to Flashy's, Colonel Winter had already arrived. Winter was "holding court" with some locals while he waited. He had instructed Henry by cell phone to drive around behind the building to more discreetly unload his cargo. Cooley Man and Bigga locked Harry Dog and Ruddy-Puss in Flashy's storage room until The Colonel was ready to deal with them. Winter had decided he wanted to meet with the ROTT group first.

Will asked why they were meeting at Flashy's. Colonel Winter then explained to them that he had decided that there was less risk meeting at Flashy's since he was surer it would not be bugged and there was less of a possibility that the Shower Posse would start a scene in this public place. Hardy showed Colonel Winter a photocopy of Mary Hyde Tharp's diary page containing the sketch of the unusual relief-art wooden wall hanging cited in it and explained his impression of the carving's significance.

"Colonel," Betsy began after Winter had briefly examined the drawing, "as we told Hardy, Will and I have seen this exact woodcarving. It was hanging on Madame Erzube Blanton's office wall in New Orleans. See that pot or urn being balanced on the elephant's trunk at the top of the carving. It could possibly make a good place to conceal paperwork. Depending on how much someone hollowed it out, it could easily be made large enough to hide documents and then plugged back up. I haven't cleared this with Will, but if you want us to return to New Orleans to try to find out if I'm right, we'll gladly volunteer to do so."

"Absolutely. It's good by me," Will said. "Count us both in."

"You don't know how much I appreciate your offer," The Colonel said. "You're the logical ones to go. You know the city, and Madame Blanton knows you and is more likely to trust you than she would a stranger."

"Colonel," Henry said. "If I may put my two cents in, send the Blacks unannounced. If Madame Blanton knows ahead of time there is something valuable hidden in her family heirloom, she might just retrieve it before they get there and try to keep it for herself."

"Yeah," Hardy agreed. "That's all we need is for her to take it to some greedy lawyer in New Orleans who might then complicate things greatly legally or might urge her to make outrageous demands."

"Or bring Dudus Coke back into the picture after we may have finally gotten him out of our hair," E.J. said.

"Both of you are right," Will said. "If we are going to have to negotiate, I'd rather be there to do it in person and not give her time to overthink things before our arrival."

"Good points, but let me make this clear," The Colonel said. "We are not low-lifes there to gyp Madame Blanton out of property she rightfully owns. That's not the way we do things."

"But she wouldn't even know that she owns this property if it weren't for us," Mikey Mo said. "We deserve to be partners in whatever this turns out to be."

"Or at least get a finder's fee," Hardy said.

"OK, it's decided," Colonel Winter said. "Will and Betsy will be going to New Orleans as soon as it can be arranged. And it goes without saying that no one outside of this core group is to know a thing about their mission – including your brave cook, Mrs. Carter."

He laughed and added, "I still can't believe your cook took down the great Harry Dog. Henry, take the Blacks back to Discovery Bay so they can begin to make travel arrangements."

"What about Harry Dog and Ruddy-Puss?" Mikey Mo asked.

"Just leave them to me," The Colonel said. "Chicken, go tell Cooley Man that I want to talk to Harry alone after Henry leaves. And Henry, take Bigga with you. I don't want Bo-Bo Banana to have to protect Sundance by himself twenty-four/seven. Cooley Man can handle our prisoners here now by himself. Now, Will … Betsy, may Jah go with you. And thank you again."

After Henry left, Colonel Winter told Cooley Man to separate the two prisoners so he could talk to each separately and that he wanted to talk to Harry Dog first. At The Colonel's instructions, Cooley Man put Ruddy-Puss in the back seat of his own car to wait his turn.

Colonel Winter pulled a folding chair into the storage room where Harry was sequestered. Harry was still bound and was sitting on a stack of cases of Red Stripe. He was sweating from the lack of air circulation in the hot storage room.

At first Colonel Winter just sat absentmindedly looking at Harry as he stroked his chin and pretended he was thinking. Harry squirmed and gave him hateful looks in return.

After a pregnant pause, Colonel Winter finally slowly shook his head and said, "Harry McLeon, what am I going to do with you? You have caused me some measure of inconvenience, but the best I can gather, we have caused you more trouble than you've caused me. Didn't you lose a man in New Orleans? And then there was Knuckles Biddle. I'm sure you don't believe me, but I'm sorry Knuckles got killed. And then there were those two men injured at Whistling Villa and then one of them got killed at the Pocomania revival. Aren't they called LeVar and Gabriel? I did not mastermind those incidents – some of my people had the imagination and initiative to orchestrate those affairs on their own. And I'm truly sorry you got hurt as well as some of your other men. Just for the record, those injuries were caused by the Spangler Posse not us. Knock-on-wood, we haven't lost anyone yet, and I'll repeat, I'm sorry you have. But you know the old saying 'when crab walk too much, 'im lose 'im claw'."

Harry said nothing. He just sat and stared hatefully.

"Let me ask you a question, Harry?" Colonel Winter continued. "Is this initiative something you have instituted on your own, or was it something you were ordered to do by President Dudus?"

Harry finally broke his silence. "I don't have to answer any of your questions."

"Harry, Harry, Harry. Just what am I going to do with you?" The Colonel said in measured tones. "I've been giving this some thought. As you well know, for all intents and purposes I am both judge and jury in Accompong. ... And we Maroons were at one time a very warlike people. ... After all, how many years did the British try to defeat us before signing the Kindah Treaty? Yes, even today no one knows the mostly uncharted Cockpit Country like we Maroons do. And it's still very wild, and there are no written maps. In case you're wondering, I doubt if Knuckles Biddle will ever be found. We probably couldn't even find him again ourselves now. Anyway, one of my options is to have you disappear somewhere in the hills."

Harry was beginning to fidget. The hateful look in his eyes was gradually being replaced by fear and dread. He knew that if Colonel Winter deemed this to be the best alternative, there was nothing he could do to prevent it.

The Colonel sighed and continued. "Yes, that's one option, but I would rather not extend the hostilities with Dudus Coke. He and I have had our moments in the past, and it would be good if we could resolve these matters with a less extreme option. This could easily be done if you could convince him to concentrate on his own affairs and not meddle in mine. You never did answer my question of whether this is a Shower Posse project or an affair you are doing on the side. And I also wonder why it has taken on such importance. The posse, after all, has plenty of money and more coming in all the time."

Harry began to think of the ramifications of telling Dudus that he had failed once and for all. Dudus did not take failure well. He certainly wasn't going to tell Colonel Winter that he and Weasely Lineitem had planned this operation to become a major thrust in the Shower Posse's money laundering initiative or that the two of them were planning to make personal fortunes on the side at Dudus' expense. He cringed when he thought of the ramifications of his entrepreneurship getting back to Dudus. It would not only mean his death but a slow, painful death for his family as well.

Colonel Winter sat silently and stared at Harry before speaking again. "Just for the record, Harry, even if you had been successful in stealing that strongbox from Sundance, it would have done you little good. The clues are encrypted in such a way that if a person does not have accompanying information they are meaningless. Therefore, future initiatives on your part are only going to accomplish more casualties, and I certainly don't want any of my friends or fellow Maroons to be hurt or injured for no reason.

"Yes, making you and your friend disappear would be the simplest option except for one extenuating circumstance – your mother. Olivia Jones once meant a lot to me. We came very close to building a life together. Both of our families were intent on not letting that happen so she ended up marrying Otis McLeon. But here's my dilemma. Otis is not your true father. I am. And I would hate to have to destroy the only thing remaining from your mother's and my relationship.

"I am the duly elected Colonel of the Accompong Maroons. I was elected with a duty to represent them and to do the best I can for them. They are my people. I was attempting to do my duty when you thrust yourself into my affairs recently. This duty is still my responsibility, and I take it seriously. As bad as I would hate to, if I must, I will sacrifice you and your companion for the better good of the Maroon people. But as a father, I would prefer not to have to make that decision. It would sadden me greatly and would be a burden I would have to carry for the rest of my life."

Harry did not know what to say. If he had made a list of every possible outcome from this confrontation with Colonel Winter, he would never have imagined this disclosure.

"Son, you have no chance of success. None. Even if you were to steal the clues you know about, you wouldn't be able to put the puzzle together. Your only hope would be to steal the treasure from us after the fact. You have an equally slim chance of making that happen. Only because you are my son am I willing to let you live and only then, if you pledge to me that neither you or the Shower Posse will interfere in this matter going forward.

"Just remember, if you choose not to take my advice, I will be forced to regard you as a threatening stranger and treat you accordingly … and I have a long memory. You will be looking over your shoulder for the rest of your life, and when you least expect it, my men will track you down and dispose of your body in one of the numerous limestone caves here in the Cockpit Country. And remember, if you become a liability to Dudus, his loyalties will probably wane as well.

"I'll leave you with a proverb. 'When your own funeral is approaching, you will not be able to choose your grave diggers'.

"The fact that I'm your father will be a secondary consideration to my responsibilities as Maroon Colonel. I sincerely hope that a choice does not become necessary, my son. And by the way, my belated condolences over the death of your mother. I wish I could have attended her service. She was one terrific lady. With that said, I'm going to leave you now to think about what I've just said."

With his comments concluded, Colonel Winter got up walked out of the storage room and left Harry Dog alone to think.

"Cooley Man, please tell me what you know about our other guest before I meet with him," Colonel Winter said.

Cooley Man filled The Colonel in on the fact that their prisoner went by the street name of Ruddy-Puss and that he was the houseboy at Almond Hill, the villa adjacent to Sundance. He also filled him in on the fact that Ruddy-Puss' brother, Punkin-Puss, until recently was a member of the Shower Posse, and that he suspected that Ruddy-Puss hoped to be asked to join in the future as well. He reminded Colonel Winter that with Ruddy-Puss' assistance, Almond Hill had been used recently for nefarious purposes by the Shower Posse as their observation and listening post to monitor the goings-ons at Sundance while Villa Brawta on the other side of Sundance had been used for a similar purpose by the Spangler Posse. The Colonel clarified a few more things with Cooley Man and then told him he was ready to meet with Ruddy-Puss.

"I'd prefer not to sit in your hot car," Colonel Winter said, "but I do want to keep those two separated for the time being. Please retrieve one of the lawn chairs in Sharpy's storage room. Please indulge an old man and get one and set it up under that almond tree over there. Then we'll get the houseboy out of the car so I can talk to him. Let the houseboy sit on the ground and lean against the tree."

When everything was set up Colonel Winter sat for a couple of minutes and stared down at Ruddy-Puss like he had done Harry before saying, "What's your name, son?"

"Call mi Ruddy-Puss."

"I don't mean what your rude boy friends call you, what does your mama and the good Lord call you?"

"Nakomis Kyle."

"Nakomis Kyle what?"

"Nakomis Kyle McCauley."

"Now we're getting somewhere. Where were you raised?"

"Falmouth."

"I'm pretty sure I know your people. Are you Emily's boy?"

"Yes."

"Yessir to you. Your mama taught you better than that."

"Yessir."

"I remember you had a brother. Didn't they call him Abeku?"

"Dey called him Punkin-Puss."

"There you go with those rude boy names again. I heard he went bad. You wanta go bad like him?"

"Punkin-Puss was a sumbaddy. He were connected."

"If you mean the Shower Posse, I don't call that connected. It just means he took up with some low-life company. It's a miracle he lasted as long as he did. And now he's dead … I think I'm beginning recognize you ... weren't you with him the day he got killed trying to rob me?"

Ruddy-Puss began to fidget and stare at his feet.

"Of course. I do believe you were the other masked man – the one who was fortunate enough to live. You should have learned your lesson that day, but obviously you didn't. Is that what you want, son – to be dead like your brother or would you rather go to prison?"

"Punkin-Puss was a big man."

"And don't you ever forget. It only takes a little pepper to burn a big man's mouth."

"At least dey dunna call he house bwoy. He allas had money in he pocket. He had respeck."

"Not by decent folks he didn't. And that respect isn't doing him much good in the ground. Though he's now sleeping better than when he was alive. Hard to sleep when you don't have a good conscience, and your brother didn't have a good conscience. Son, a good conscience is better than a big wage. I'm glad your mama's not here listening to you. She'd be ashamed to hear your greedy talk. A greedy mek fly coffin go a hole (a greedy fly follows the coffin into the ground). What am I going to do with you?"

Ruddy-Puss only stared.

"I could cut my losses with you, son, and bury you up here in the hills in an unmarked grave alongside your sorry brother. I can do that, you know. You're in my town, and I make the rules. No one would ever know the difference – and the way you've been conducting yourself, very few people probably would care. If I could see a sign that you should be saved, it'd be foolish for me to resort to that. Waste of a human life. ... But if you're dead set on being a low-life like your brother, I'd probably be doing society a favor. Yes, I'd be saving future victims and also the taxpayers a lot of money. What would *you* do if you were in my shoes?"

Ruddy-Puss was beginning to perspire heavily. Winter could begin to see the fear in his eyes.

"You still haven't given me a reason why I shouldn't just end everyone's misery right now. You know what they say, sometimes it's better just to take your losses."

"Mi do betta; mi promise," Ruddy-Puss said desperately.

"Son, you come from good stock. You don't have to always be a houseboy all your life. Think of that job as only beginning not an end until itself. Work is how you will get ahead and have the things you want, not by being a rude boy. Remember wanti can't get it, getti no want it (have-nots covet what haves take for granted). I'm going to give this matter some more thought, and I want you to do so as well. I know you're tired of listening to this old man's platitudes, but I'm going to leave you with one more – you lie wit dawg, you rise wit fleas (if you lie down with the dogs, you *will* get up with fleas)."

```
STOVE
SPECILIAST
73. RED HILLS
RD. PH 59118
WE BUY SELL
AND REPAIR
GAS  KERRO GAS
```

# Chapter 40

"Return my friend Nakomis to the hot back-seat of your car and leave the windows up. Then let's you and I have a cold Red Stripe," Colonel Winter told Cooley Man. "And we'll leave Harry Dog in that hot shed a little longer. A little more discomfort might help clear his thinking before I continue our discussion about his future."

After The Colonel slowly enjoyed a cold beer with Cooley Man and watched some of the soccer match with the other men, he returned to the storage room. Harry Dog was soaking wet with sweat and very uncomfortable. Part of his distress was from the heat, but part of it came from his nerves. He now not only had not just Dudus Coke to worry about but Colonel Winter as well. This sure wasn't working out like he had envisioned it when Weasely Lineitem had helped formulate the plan to not only solve the Shower Posse's money laundering problems but to create a personal annuity for the two of them … and make him heir apparent to Dudus Coke. This should have been a grand-slam home run for "The Dog". Maybe it had never been a complete lay-up since it had been partially contingent on finding the Genovesa motherlode, but he had sure never envisioned the spin-off problems that had occurred since then or the harm to life and limb that those problems had brought about.

He had made one decision for sure today. He wasn't ready to die. Harry wasn't sure if Colonel Winter had meant what he said about killing him, but he wasn't ready to risk his life to find out. He would say whatever The Colonel wanted to hear to buy time until he could find a better solution and a better way out of this mess. Crossing Dudus Coke was not and had never been an option that Harry relished however, but having a bullet put in his head and having his body dumped in a remote limestone cave was an even worse fate.

Harry Dog wasn't the only person thinking of options and strategies. Ferron Winter was doing so as well. He fully anticipated that Harry would say anything if he thought it would keep him out of further trouble. After all, Harry was a habitual, amoral liar. The Colonel couldn't believe the two of them shared the same genes.

Colonel Winter took his lawn chair back into the storage room and sat down again. Harry was still sitting uncomfortably on the stack of Red Stripe cases.

"Well, my son, do you see how hopeless it is to continue on the path you're on? Unlike you who is motivated by personal greed, I am trying to find this Spanish treasure for the good of my people. Let me remind you again, even if you and your men had been successful in stealing every clue we have thus far assembled, you were still doomed to failure since you would not have had the knowledge to interpret what you had."

He pointed to his own head and continued. "That knowledge is up here. You could not have even abducted part of my team and succeeded since our knowledge is partially housed within the brains of multiple team members. And even they have not unraveled the mystery entirely. It is an ongoing process of discovery. Do you understand the futility of your actions? It has gained you nothing but only served to inconvenience and delay my people from concluding this investigation. Are you ready to come clean with me yet? I don't want to hurt you, son, but I will if I have to."

He paused and waited for Harry to speak. Harry said nothing. Winter continued.

"You may be able to lie your way out of here, but your lie will be exposed if you continue to meddle in my affairs. And then you will never be safe. Some of your fellow posse members in reality have their allegiance to me, and only I know who those people are," Winter bluffed. "You will forever be wondering. And if I find out that you have crossed me, there will be *no* further warnings."

Winter slashed his index finger across his own throat. "You will be the late, fondly remembered Harry McLeon. Is that how you want to live? I wouldn't."

Harry still said nothing but was noticeably rattled. His eyes looked less defiant and more concerned.

"Tell me, Harry," Colonel Winter said. "I'm going to ask you again. Is this an individual initiative, or is it an assignment from Dudus Coke?"

"Yu know if mi ansah, mi bloodclyaat dead (you know if I answer, I'm fucking dead)."

"You just answered my question," Colonel Winter said. "I'm going to leave it up to you how you handle the President, but what I said, still goes. I don't want any more interference from either of you. Otherwise … ."

He let the rest of the sentence go unfinished.

"I normally don't give second chances. You can thank your mother for your chance. Olivia Jones was an amazing woman. It's too bad you didn't pick up more of her good traits instead of the bad ones from your stepfather, Otis. If you'd done so, I would have proudly found a place for you in my organization. Now, do I have your word, that you will no longer involve yourself in my affairs? If so, later today I will have Cooley Man drive you to a neutral location, and let you out there. You can tell Dudus as much or as little as you wish, but I don't want to see either of you again. Agreed? If so, you can go with Jah."

"Yah, mon."

"That is *yes, sir*. I am still your elder and your father, and I expect the respect I deserve."

"Yes, sir."

"And I'll remind you one last time. There will be no second chances. I believe in the proverb – 'Sorry for mawga (skinny) dog, mawga dog turn round bite yu'."

With his meeting concluded, Colonel Winter got up and prepared to meet again with Ruddy-Puss. One thing Harry Dog immediately decided - he was not going to share this conversation with Dudus Coke. Dudus definitely would not give a mawga dog a second chance. His only out with this situation was to pretend it was business as usual when around Dudus and procrastinate, therefore accomplishing nothing, thereby secretly dooming his mission to failure. He could then blame his failure on someone else. He would rather fail due to circumstances beyond his control rather than being viewed as a disloyal liability to the Shower Posse. An occasional failure might be forgotten; disloyalty would be remembered forever.

Cooley Man led the sweating Ruddy-Puss back out to the almond tree and sat him on the ground again. Colonel Winter sat in the lawn chair a few feet away and looked down at him.

"I hope I'm not making a mistake, but I've tentatively decided to let you live – for the time being. I hope I don't regret my decision. If I do, I won't repeat my mistake. I *will* cut my losses at that point. But you still are going to have to pay. I do not want you living next door to Sundance. I will have Mikey Mo take you back to Almond Hill to pack your belongings. You can either tender your resignation or you can just leave with no notice. It's up to you. I'm banning you from accepting any positions in Discovery Bay going forward. Other than that, I don't care where you live or work. It's up to you. I'll tell no one of your past involvement with the Shower Posse or that ethical decisions can sometimes be problematic for you. I hope this will serve as a wake-up call, and you'll associate with more reputable people going forward. If I hear that you have associated yourself with the Shower Posse or any other gang, there'll be no second chances. I don't want to see you go down the same road as your brother. You are still a young man capable of choosing the road that you wish to travel through life. I hope you will take the high road and find the way that's best for you. Remember, 'every hoe have it tick a bush' (there is something for everyone in the world). Now, go with Jah."

FURNITURE AND COFFIN

# Chapter 41

"I'd hoped to make it a one-day trip to New Orleans, but it looks like we're going to have to spend the night whether we want to or not," Will told Betsy. "If I try to push everything into one day, there's only two hours between the flight up there and the one back to Jamaica."

"That might not be enough time to conclude our business," Betsy agreed.

"That's what I thought. Certainly doesn't leave any room for anything to go wrong," Will said. "Spirit has a nonstop that gets into N'awlins at 10:59 PM local time, and the return flight isn't until 1:19 the following afternoon."

"That should be enough time to do what we have to do," Betsy said, "unless Madame Blanton says 'hell no,' and then no time is going to be long enough."

"I agree. I'll book it."

"By the way, where are we staying?"

"Hilton on St. Charles Avenue."

"You mean the Hilton on the river?'

"No. I picked this hotel because it's one we've never stayed in before, and it's a place no one would expect us to stay in. Plus, it's less than a ten minute walk from Madame Blanton's shop on Bourbon, and it's big enough for us to remain anonymous."

"Is that the old St. Charles Hotel?"

"No, it's on the 100 block of St. Charles; the Hilton is in the 300 block. The Hilton was actually built back in the '20's as a Masonic temple and at one time was one of the tallest buildings in New Orleans. Hilton took over the property after it got wiped out in Hurricane Katrina."

"Sounds like an interesting adventure. Well, let me tell Leva we're leaving for a few days," Betsy said, "while you call Henry and give him our flight schedule."

"We'll be back in a couple of days, Leva," Betsy said, walking into the kitchen. "Hold the fort down until we get back."

"Going back to Key West?" Leva asked. "I hope nothing is wrong. Lexie's OK isn't she?"

"Things are fine there. Lexie's doing great," Betsy said. "It's just that we've got some unfinished business to attend to."

"Is there a phone number in case I need you," Leva asked.

"I'll check in with you," Betsy said.

Leva looked like she expected more of an explanation or at least some clarification so Betsy said, "I can't talk about the trip now. We were sworn to secrecy for the time being by Colonel Winter. Just take my word for it though, it may result in a good thing. Henry's going to take us the Montego Bay airport later today and pick us up when we get back."

"By the way, I was talking over the fence to Monique, the cook at Almond Hill," Leva said. "She said she lost her houseboy, Ruddy-Puss. He just suddenly up and quit."

"Oh yeah," Betsy said feigning surprise. "Did he get a better job?"

"She said he wouldn't say. Didn't want to talk about it. She said a man just brought Ruddy-Puss over to get his stuff, and he left. No notice; no nothing. Didn't even ask for a reference."

"I guess you just never know with young people. I'm sure she won't have any trouble finding a replacement though," Betsy said, letting the matter drop.

After dinner, Henry drove the Blacks to Sangster International Airport. They packed light, each only taking an overnight bag. Will took his briefcase. The flight actually ran a little ahead of schedule. Will and Betsy were able to easily catch a cab to St. Charles Avenue, checked into room 640 at the Hilton, and were in bed a little after midnight.

They got up the following morning, and Will told Betsy to take a shower first so she could then "put on her face" while he took his shower. He turned on the early morning news while he waited his turn. Suddenly he heard a shriek and ran to the bathroom.

"Now I know why you wanted me to shower first – so I could be the guinea pig. This ancient shower turns from hot to cold and back with no warning. I'm lucky I didn't get scalded."

"It's just old, like everything else in downtown New Orleans. Thanks for running interference and giving me a heads up though."

Their next experience was better. They ate breakfast in the hotel's executive lounge. It had a pool table and lounge areas with many places to sit. Some people were using their laptops and cell phones; others were reading the morning paper as they sipped their coffee. Betsy Googled Voodoo Blues to see what time it opened.

"Opens at ten. Let's time ourselves to get there about the time Madame Blanton opens," Betsy suggested. "I hope she opens the shop herself and doesn't come in later."

"I'm pretty sure she will. She didn't appear to have that many employees or to be the trusting type who often delegates."

It was a couple of blocks walk to Canal Street, and then even strolling at a leisurely pace, they were at Bourbon in less than ten minutes. Another seven blocks and Will and Betsy saw the now familiar Voodoo Blues neon sign featuring the sunglasses bespectacled skeleton peering from beneath his pork pie hat. The two-sided plastic "open/closed" sign on the door had been flipped to the "open" side. They heard Dr. John suddenly begin to sing as if someone had apparently just turned on the sound system in the store. As they walked under the skeletal Elvis, they saw Madame Erzube setting up the cash register for the day. She seemed to be the only person other than them in the store.

The bell on the front door dinged as they opened it, and Madame Erzube looked up. They couldn't tell if she smiled or frowned when she saw the Blacks, but it was obvious she remembered them. She was still wearing the same style head wrap she'd worn the first time they had met her. Now she seemed even taller than they remembered her being.

Madame Erzube cleared her throat, peered over half-glasses, and said, "Didn't think I'd be seeing you two again. I guess you came all this way to tell me the Maroon museum with my artifacts is now open? And if you did, I don't have any more calabashes to contribute."

"Good to see you again, Madame Blanton," Will said. "No, the museum isn't open yet, but it's still being organized. If you can spare us a few minutes, we have another matter to discuss with you."

"Something I can make money on?" Madame Erzube asked.

"Possibly, ma'am," Betsy said. "We won't know until we talk. May we speak to you in private in your office?"

"When my girl, Willie Sue, gets here to watch the front of the store. She should be walking in any second."

"We'll just look around the shop while we wait for her to arrive," Will said.

When Willie Sue arrived, Madame Erzube took the Blacks back into her office and closed the door.

"If your Colonel Winter wants his money back, there are no refunds. All sales are final," Madame Erzube said.

"No, he is very satisfied with his last transaction with you. The item he sent us here to discuss with you is the wood carving hanging behind your desk."

"Well, you can just tell The Colonel it's not for sale."

"He doesn't wish to purchase it. He's asking that you let us examine it. The carving may have another dimension that you're not aware of."

"I'm not going to let you cut it up," Madame Blanton said, "and I'm certainly not going to let it out of my sight."

"Ma'am, we don't wish to take it anywhere, and we do not plan to destroy it. We can conduct our examination right here in your office."

"So what you lookin' for?"

"We won't know until we examine it, but I think you know The Colonel would not have sent us all this distance if he didn't believe it could be important to the Maroon people. You can watch us while we inspect it," Betsy said.

"And if The Colonel's suspicions are confirmed, it might lead to a profitable opportunity for you," Will added.

"Or it might just fill in a hole in Jamaican history. We won't know until we look," Betsy said.

"Well, I guess it can't hurt for you to look at it."

Will offered to take the carving off the wall, and then they laid it out on Madame Erzube's desk. Will and Betsy turned it over and examined both sides. The wood appeared to be solid. It was truly a work of art, and the wood had a patina that only age could give it. Betsy pulled out her copy of the drawing from Mary Hyde Tharp's diary and placed it on the desk next to the carving. The two were identical – the same slave heads, same cat and parrot, same bananas, and the same elephant holding a round pot or water jar with his trunk.

"Where did you get that drawing?" Madame Erzube asked.

"From the diary of one of your ancestor's," Will replied.

Betsy began to examine the carving with a handheld magnifying glass. She looked at the front. There wasn't even a crack in the mahogany. Will flipped it over. The back was rough-hewn and unsanded. There were a few small random age cracks where the wood had dried. Betsy next looked more closely at the calabash in the center – nothing. The interior of the top of the water jar had been hollowed out. When she looked down in it with her magnifying glass, it almost appeared that some of the wood grains ran in different directions from each other.

"Look at this, Will," Betsy said and gave him the magnifying glass.

"I think there may be a wooden plug inside the water jar," he said. "Do you mind, Madame Erzube, if I try to remove it?"

"As long as you don't destroy my family heirloom," she said.

"Do you have a wine corkscrew?' he asked. "If I can screw it into the plug, I might be able to just pull it out without further damaging it. I doubt if someone in the seventeen hundreds would have glued a plug in. I'm sure it was probably just carved to fit the hole tightly and then sanded."

"I wouldn't be a true New Orleanian if I weren't prepared at all times to have a drink," Madame Erzube said and laughed. "Wait a second."

She returned with two wine bottle cork pullers. One had a T-handle; the other had ears to use for prying leverage on a wine bottle.

Will took the one with the T-handle, and pushed with all his strength as he twisted it clockwise. Fortunately the wood was a wood softer than mahogany surrounding it. When the screw seemed to have taken hold, he began to pull. The plug started to move. He screwed it in a bit further and pulled again. The plug moved some more and suddenly popped loose. It was only about half an inch deep. A long round cavity appeared in the wood that seemed to possibly run the length of the entire piece. Something was rolled up in the hole and had been tied. He held the carving upside down, and a paper began to slip out. He shook the carving a couple of times until there was enough paper showing for him to grab an edge. Then he carefully pulled the paper the remaining way out.

"Do you have some scissors?" Will asked Madame Blanton.

"In the drawer," she replied.

He found the scissors and carefully cut the rotten leather string with very little effort. He put one edge of the paper under Madame Blanton's stapler and slowly began to unroll the rest.

"It's some kind of document," Betsy said. "It appears to be written in Spanish."

"And there's a second page," Will said.

"What is it?" Madame Erzube asked.

"I really don't know," Betsy said. "And I don't even know modern Spanish much less, seventeen century Spanish."

"But it must have some importance. Someone went to a hell of a lot of trouble hiding it to insure that it survived," Will said. "We're going to need to get someone to translate it for us."

"There's a lady professor in Jamaica who The Colonel has relied on in the past – a Dr. Halliburton-James. She's a professor at the University of the West Indies," Betsy said. "We need to get hold of Colonel Winter and find out what he wants us to do next."

"Madame Blanton, will you trust us with this document?" Will asked.

"I'm not so sure," she said. "I barely know you."

"Would you allow us to photograph it?" Will asked.

Madame Erzube hesitated.

"Madame, Colonel Winter is one of the most trustworthy men I have ever met," Betsy said. "And he sent us on this mission because he trusts us implicitly to do the right thing. None of us has any idea what we have here. It may only be more of Mary Hyde Tharp's family history for all we know, or it may be something far more valuable. We do know that it was valuable in Mary Hyde Tharp's eyes, or she wouldn't have gone to all this trouble to preserve it. Whatever it is, you have my word that we will always be 100% honest with you and return the document to you with a full translation after it has been examined by an expert. Would you be willing to discuss the matter with Colonel Winter? If so, I'll get him on the phone."

Madame Blanton agreed to talk with Colonel Winter. After a lengthy conversation, Madame Blanton hung up and told the Blacks, "He wishes for you to call him back."

When they dialed The Colonel, he told them that he and Madame Blanton had come to an agreement. He would set up an escrow account and deposit US$25,000 in it to insure the safe return of the document. Once it was translated, Madame Blanton would be entitled to a full translation. In the meantime, she would allow the Blacks to photograph as well as photocopy the pages and send the photos to him. He said he had leveled with her that the document might be the key to finding some gold that was rumored to have been hidden in Jamaica, and that he had agreed to having a formal contract drawn up splitting anything found with her. The contract would be emailed to Will and Betsy that morning and would already be signed by him. They were then to get Madame Blanton to sign and to witness her signing. After scanning both the contract and the document and sending the scans to him, they were then to return to Jamaica with the original.

With their business in New Orleans concluded, the Blacks were on time to get to the New Orleans airport to catch the 1:19 Spirit flight back to Montego Bay.

```
CONTACT
              D.A. McLAUGHLIN
    F    SIGNS & HOUSE and HOUSE PAINTING
    O         TOMBSTONE MAKING ETC
    R         THE PUBLIC'S FAMOUS
              ARTIST
         NOMRIEL, PRATVILLE P.O.
```

# Chapter 42

Cooley Man drove Harry Dog back to Kingston and released him there. He didn't risk going near Tivoli Gardens and running into Shower Posse members. He dropped Harry off at the Hi-Lo Food Store at Manor Park Plaza assuming Harry would be able to make arrangements to get home from there. After that, Cooley Man drove Ruddy-Puss back to Discovery Bay to get the few things he owned and then dropped him in Falmouth reminding him again that Colonel Winter had banned him from working in Discovery Bay going forward and of the consequences of non-compliance. By this time Ruddy-Puss had decided that there was more to being a posse member than the seemingly false glamour on the surface and had decided that maybe he was not cut out for that kind of life after all.

Harry had resigned himself to the fact that he had little chance to beat Colonel Winter and that the potential cost was too high. He now had to take what was left now of his original plan and make it into a workable "plan B" that, while it might bring him fewer benefits than the original would have, would still not be a total loss. And to do so in a manner in which Dudus Coke's knowledge of his failure would be minimized. Anything else would be a loss of face he would never recover from. Now it would be all about the spin. He could still see where he and Weasely Lineitem could use drug money to buy scrap gold and use the gold resales for a money laundering mechanism. This should pacify Dudus somewhat. And Weasely could still make money from melting the gold down and siphoning some off for the two of them. He still would make side money. It just wouldn't involve the monetary windfall that would have come if he had been able to throw the Genovesa treasure into the equation. But Dudus didn't need to know this yet. In the meantime, he would pretend to continue to chase the Genovesa gold and he would just keep kicking the can down the road until he could find a final resolution. This would keep him from risking another run-in with Colonel Winter and his men. He sighed when he thought of the cost that these run-ins had incurred to date.

~ ~ ~

In the meantime not knowing this, Dudus Coke was still trying to figure out how to use Harry to steal the strongbox that he assumed was still at Sundance and was scheming how to keep Bunny Witter from finding out that he had no plans to cooperate with him or share any future profits with the Spangler Posse. Bunny had a similar dilemma in reverse regarding Dudus. Neither of them knew that the strongbox was now nothing more than a historical artifact since Will and Betsy were in New Orleans obtaining and bringing back the document that would hopefully answer the riddle.

~ ~ ~

Will and Betsy landed at Sangster International Airport in Montego Bay at 2:05 local time. Henry was there to pick them up for the hour-long drive back to Sundance. Will had decided that the document would be temporarily stored in his locked filing cabinet in his Sundance office in a purposely mislabeled file folder until The Colonel instructed him what to do with it next. If worst came to worst, they would still have the photocopies and the pictures they had made in New Orleans. On the way back, Henry informed them they had an appointment the following morning with Dr. Halliburton-James at the

University of West Indies in Mona.

"Has The Colonel made any security provisions for us for the trip?" Will asked.

"Only me," Henry said. "No one else knows yet about your mission or what you brought back. But as a precaution I don't want you to call anyone, including Colonel Winter, between now and tomorrow. The phones may be bugged."

"I agree."

"I don't think we'll have to worry about our old nemesis, Harry Dog," Henry said. "I'm pretty sure Colonel Winter put the fear of God in that rude boy. I'll pick you up at 8:30."

Henry arrived promptly at 8:30 and joined Will and Betsy for breakfast. Leva made soft-boiled eggs with plantains, ackee, and hard dough bread.

"Jeezam!" Henry commented. "Did I lose track of what day it is, Mrs. Carter? Is it Sunday?"

"I just thought I'd give our travelers a special breakfast to welcome them home, Mr. Davis," Leva replied. "After all, you do have a long ride today if you're going to Kingston."

Henry decided to take the new toll road across the mountains to the south coast to Mona to meet with Dr. Halliburton-James. At The Colonel's instructions, Mikey Mo had emailed a copy of the document to her while the Blacks were still in route back from New Orleans. They carried the original with them in case it might be needed. The Colonel told Mikey Mo to pick up Hardy and to meet the Blacks at Halliburton-James' office.

The two groups assembled at the university and walked together to Halliburton-James' office. After brief pleasantries, they got down to business. She asked if she might see the actual document. Will got it out of his briefcase and passed it over to her. She examined it briefly and handed it back, commenting on its excellent condition.

"What you have here, folks," Dr. Halliburton-James began, giving them the report she had already secretly given to Dudus Coke, "is a Spanish land grant. It's dated 1795, and it's signed by the governor of Cuba, Luis de las Casas y Aragorri, and Spanish Prime Minister Manuel de Godoy. It's conveying property with the coordinates of 24.551

north and 81.7800 west to one John Jarrett of Maroon Town, Jamaica. I looked up those coordinates. They are the coordinates of Key West, Florida. I really don't know if this document is still valid and enforceable or if it's now just another historical curiosity."

She looked at Will and Betsy before continuing.

"Mr. and Mrs. Black, the name John Jarrett may be meaningless to you since you're Americans, but as Mr. Hardy will no doubt fill you in later, it's a name well known to Jamaicans. Major Jarrett was an important Maroon leader in the late 1700's during the Second Maroon War. The British expelled him from Jamaica along with others they considered to be trouble makers. He died in Freetown, Sierra Leone."

Will and Betsy patiently listened and let her talk but did not disclose their own knowledge of this Jamaican history. The disclosure would have served no purpose. Hardy looked at them and slowly shook his head as a sign for them to save any analysis or discussion on the Spanish land grant until after they had all left Halliburton-James' office. They concluded their meeting, thanked Dr. Halliburton-James for her time and bade her farewell.

When they got back onto the sidewalk, Hardy said, "There is a café called Pages in the student bookstore here on campus. I'll treat you to some coffee, and we can talk there."

They chose a table in the back corner and ordered coffee.

"This document certainly dovetails nicely into the information we got from Mary Hyde Tharp's diary," Hardy said. "I'm glad you picked up on my hint that I didn't want to discuss everything we know in front of the good doctor. Now we know what the mysterious deal was that Tharp mentioned in the diary. It must have been an exchange of the Genovesa gold for the real estate he wanted to use as a Maroon homeland. Now let me fill you in on some remaining bits of Spanish history from that period that will complete the picture.

"In 1788, King Charles III died and left the Spanish throne to his son Charles IV. Charles IV kept up an appearance of running the country, but in actuality he was a very passive ruler. His passion was not governing but hunting. His wife, Maria Luisa, became the de facto monarch and ran Spain through her prime minister with Charles rubber-stamping their actions. About 1790 Maria Luisa began to cut costs by decentralizing control of the Spanish empire. She did this partially by issuing Spanish land grants in the new world. This was in part brought about by a need to bolster the national treasury because of an ill-advised war against France. After some dissension brought about by the French war, her prime minister was replaced by the queen's lover, Manuel de Godoy, who was a very shrewd, and able politician. He was able to cozy up to Charles IV as well as Maria Luisa since Charles had no idea de Godoy was having an affair with his wife."

"So you're saying de Godoy was in a sense porking both the king and the queen?" Will asked.

"Is that what you call an eighteen century switch-hitter?" Betsy added.

"No, early Eurotrash," Mikey Mo threw in.

"They called shysters the same thing then that we call them now," Henry said, "politicians practicing what we Jamaicans call 'politricks.' The main thing that has changed is now instead of screwing the queen, they now screw their constituents."

"Anyway, clowns, if you're through, I'll get back to my story," Hardy said. "De Godoy's policies wishy-washyed back and forth between alliances between Spain, Portugal and Great Britain gradually devaluing Charles credibility with all sides. When it was convenient, he also aligned himself with Napoleon. Finally with economic pressures worsening, with rumors of Maria Luisa's affair leaking out, and with gossip about the king's overall ineptitude leaking out, Charles IV was forced to abdicate in 1807, and the Spanish throne was turned over to his son Ferdinand VII. Ferdinand was the last of the Bourbon dynasty since he was later forced out by Napoleon."

"I'm starting to understand," Betsy said. "Let me interrupt and fill in the history after that from the American perspective. I'm pretty sure Ferdinand was the king who sold Key West to the United States."

"I guess not knowing or maybe not caring that it had been previously deeded by land grant over to Major Jarrett," Will observed, "an action that probably would have had racial overtones."

"The governor of Cuba was the one who later deeded the property to an officer in the Spanish Navy, and then it was later transferred to the United States," Betsy said.

"And matters still stay murky after that," Will added. "If you'll remember, the Spanish naval officer then sold the same property to two different Americans, and one of those, John Simonton, had to get President Andrew Jackson to pull political strings to finally get him clear ownership to the property."

"I'm sure none of these people realized the claim John Jarrett had on the island since he was never actually able to present the land grant and take possession of it since he and his people were exiled to Nova Scotia in 1796 and he was never able to return to Jamaica again," Hardy said.

"And because he was a former slave," Henry threw in. "All Jamaicans know Jarrett ended up in Africa and got buried there."

"What a mess," Mikey Mo said. "Wait'll The Colonel finds out about this."

"Wow!" Will said. "So the mother-lode of a treasure the world has been seeking since the 1750's was actually secretly found and transferred back to the Spanish crown in the 1790's."

"So it seems," Hardy said. "Now, do you understand why I didn't want to have this discussion in front of Dr. Halliburton-James.?"

"And this is what we've agreed to share with Madame Erzube Blanton – a world class mess?" Will said.

"Looks that way," Betsy said. "Look at it this way. She's no poorer than she was yesterday."

"Hope she doesn't put some bad voodoo curse on us," Will said and laughed.

Mikey Mo then said, "I'm going to take Hardy back to Accompong with me to explain all this to Colonel Winter. Henry, you take the Blacks back to Sundance."

FOR THE BEST IN

WELDING

BUGULAR BARS

GATES GRILL ETC.

# Chapter 43

For the next two days Will and Betsy waited impatiently at Sundance for some kind of update or feedback about the Spanish land grant. Finally on the third day, their phone rang. It was Mikey Mo calling E.J. He asked if it would be convenient for Colonel Winter to pay the Blacks a visit. E.J. suggested that Leva prepare a special lunch for the occasion and that the Davis's be invited.

Mikey Mo drove Colonel Winter up from Accompong, and they arrived in the late morning. Hardy Pushcart was with them. The Colonel immediately hugged Leva and complimented her for her decisive and effective handling of the Harry Dog and Ruddy-Puss break-in as well as the cooking smells emanating from her kitchen. Leva glowed at the unexpected accolades being showered on her by this VIP she truly respected.

Will laughed and teased her. "Are you blushing, Leva?"

"Does it show?" she replied.

"I brought you all together today for a reason," Colonel Winter said. "Why don't we move to the living room, where everyone can be comfortable on the couches. And yes, Leva and Kingtoo … my assistant tells me you go by Honey-Pye which very aptly names you, my dear lady ... I want you to join us as well."

When everyone was seated, The Colonel continued.

"When I assembled this diverse group, I had no idea that before matters were concluded I would regard you not as my agents but as my extended family and myself as your surrogate father, but I do. ... Except in your case, Henry. You and I have been cousins since childhood. Henry, would it embarrass you for me to reminisce?"

Henry smiled, knowing what The Colonel was about to say.

"Henry Davis and I have known each other since childhood. We both lived back up in the hills. Leva and E.J., I too had a street name in those days. I was called Ferret, after the rat, since I could be somewhat elusive to adults. We called Henry Hang-To. Well, one day when we were nine when Hang-To and I were playing, we accidentally came up on a ganja field. The owner mistook us for government agents and took a shot at us. The bullet hit a tree near me, and a splinter ricocheted off and stuck in my shoulder. Hang-To carried me back to the village on his back. The doctor said this probably saved my life since otherwise I could possibly have bled to death. We have been de facto cousins since that day. Did I get the story right, Henry?"

Henry nodded, and said, "Cuz, you'd have done the same for me."

Colonel Winter nodded and continued.

"As you know, I'm prone to use what non-perceptive people may regard as trite sayings, but many an intelligent point can be made with these tried and true folk adages. 'Ebery (every) day debil (devil) help tief (thief), but one day God help watchman'. Well, Jah was looking over my shoulder the day I assembled this group, and I want to say thank you to each and every one of you.

"After one of our Maroon faithful, Ruby Drain, died after a long and productive life and gave us the initial clues that a veritable fortune might have been hidden in our Jamaican hills, I knew that finding it would be a long shot, but a long shot worth trying for. After all, it had eluded some of the best historians and treasure hunters in the world for over 300 years. Well, it appears that there was a reason for this elusiveness – it probably was secretly found and returned to its rightful owners many, many years ago, and another asset was substituted in it place. Your highly intelligent team unearthed this fact, something that some of the most accomplished and best-funded treasure hunters in the world had failed to be able to do.

"The asset we now all know I'm referring to is the Spanish land grant for the island of Key West in Florida. Is this a valid document? I don't know. Is it enforceable? Once again, I don't know. But I've turned the matter over to attorneys experienced in these matters. If they were to decide to pursue the claim, it will probably be years before there is a resolution, and that resolution may be reparations or maybe nothing at all. I won't be surprised if the matter is still pending after I die. I was hoping the discovery of the Genovesa treasure would bring a windfall to the Maroon nation, but that will most likely not be the case for many, many years if ever."

"Have you consulted Madame Erzube about her rights?" Betsy asked.

"She has been apprised of the situation, and the attorneys have been informed of her vested interest in the whole affair."

"Sounds like you've accomplished about as much as can be expected in this short time-frame," Will said. "No wonder it's been several days since we last heard from you. I'm sorry our mission couldn't have been an outright success."

"I assume by your statement that you're wondering if I consider our mission a failure and you failures as well. I'll tell you right now — no, no, no. Would I engage in this hunt all over again? Absolutely, and despite the near-term outcome, I want to reward you in a modest way for your tenaciousness and loyalty. I realize these rewards are inadequate, but I do want to show my appreciation for your efforts.

"Dear people, I have rented a four bedroom villa at Strawberry Hill, the five-star resort 3,000 feet above Kingston, for you, Henry and Rose Davis, and the Carter family. Charge whatever you desire at the resort, and the bills will be sent back to me. And you will meet a special guest. I've made arrangements with my good friend, Strawberry Hill's owner, Chris Blackwell to have the seminal reggae pioneer Jimmy Cliff join you for a private party. Enjoy. Thank you again for all your efforts."

"So we'll be trading gold coins for reggae gold," Will said. "Works for me. Will we get to meet Mr. Blackwell?"

"I'll see what I can do," Colonel Winter said.

Will looked at Henry and Rose and gave a thumbs up. Leva's smile went from ear to ear she was so pleased that she and her husband and children were being rewarded as well as the rest of the team and would get to meet the legendary Jimmy Cliff.

"Aren't the rest of the ROTT team going to join us?" Betsy said. "They deserve to be rewarded as much as we do, and it would make it complete if you and your wife would join us as well."

"No. It's your holiday. You earned it, and you shouldn't feel obligated to entertain me. I'll be very satisfied just hearing about your weekend there. Dr. Pushcart, who I talked to earlier, opted for a different reward," Colonel Winter said. "These serious academicians like Hardy sometimes march to a different drummer. He wants to take a special upcoming seminar being offered at the University of Havana on the War of Jenkins' Ear. Our recent activities have opened his thirst for knowledge to know more about it, and I've agreed to sponsor him. Hardy, thank you for your contribution to this adventure. Your knowledge was invaluable, and now you will be taking it to a whole new level."

"You've still forgotten E.J. and Mikey Mo!" Henry said.

"No, I haven't," Colonel Winter said. "They still have one more job to do for me to wrap up the loose ends on this affair. When that is done, they have opted to take a cruise."

"Royal Caribbean has a cruise called 'Sail with the King'," E.J. said. "It's a seven-day Elvis cruise on their ship the Allure of the Seas. Mi never been on a cruise ship before."

"I should have known that this would be irresistible to both a D.J. and an Elvis fanatic," Betsy said. "I can just see Kingtoo and Chicken singing 'Good Luck Charm' for the whole ship."

"It's certainly not going to be 'Return To Sender'," E.J. said.

"Well, my reflections on this cruise says 'It's Now or Never'," Mikey Mo added. "Mi never been on a cruise ship either."

"E.J., I'll feed the dogs while you're gone," Leva said.

"You won't have to," The Colonel replied. "I'll send one of my people down to do Kingtoo's chores while he's gone."

"May I ask the nature of E.J and Mikey Mo's wrap-up assignment?" Will asked. "Maybe we could be of assistance and help them get it done sooner."

"I'd rather not comment on specifics since it is somewhat sensitive," Colonel Winter replied. "Now, let's have lunch. I can't stand just smelling it any longer."

Leva served a lunch consisting of pumpkin soup, snapper steamed in coconut milk, butter beans and a salad. After relaxing on the porch after lunch, Colonel Winter excused himself for the drive back to Accompong.

Once The Colonel had left and the kitchen had been cleaned up, Will took E.J. off to one side.

"What's this mysterious mission that Colonel Winter didn't want to talk about?"

E.J. grinned and started to speak but then stopped, "Mi betta not say."

"E.J., you know you can't keep secrets from me," Will said. "Now, come on, give, or I'm going to hide your Elvis jumpsuit so you won't have it to take on the cruise."

As Will and Betsy sat on the back porch, E.J. finally admitted what their assignment was.

"The Colonel decided to get even with the Shower and the Spangler posses for meddling in Maroon affairs," he finally said.

"And how is he going to do that?" Betsy asked.

"Using what I think you in America call a scavenger hunt," E.J. said. "Please don't tell anyone I told you. Did mi use the right term?"

"We know what a scavenger hunt is," Will said. "I'm just trying to imagine … ."

"He's got Mikey Mo and me hiding things in the hills for them to find which they think will lead them to the treasure," E.J. said, "you know, fake clues for them to find it. He's going to make them think the treasure really does still exist and sucker both of them into looking for it."

"So what?" Will said. "I'm not sure I understand what he's trying to accomplish."

"He's leaking the exact same clues to both posses, but they don't know that. He's thinking that as greedy as they both are, each group will do anything to beat out the other group."

"So he's going to try to start a gang war between the two factions by pitting them against each other as they both look for a fortune that doesn't even exist," Betsy said.

"That old sly dog," Will said. "So he figures they won't be able to overcome their greedy natures, and he won't have to pay them back directly for their sins by risking the Maroons since their sinful ways will make them punish themselves."

"Or to paraphrase Colonel Winter, 'chip neber (never) fly far from de block'," Betsy said.

"I think that's sort of what he meant," E.J. said, "His exact words were 'Noh care how boar hog try fi hide under sheep wool, 'im grunt always betray 'im' (no matter how hard a boar hog tries to pretend he's a sheep, his grunt is going to always betray him)."

"E.J., let me tell you what Will Black says, 'you mess with the bull and you get the horn'. Betsy, I can't wait to hear how this turns out."

Thank you for reading.
Please review this book. Reviews
help others find Absolutely Amazing eBooks and
inspire us to keep providing these marvelous tales.
If you would like to be put on our email list
to receive updates on new releases,
contests, and promotions, please go to
AbsolutelyAmazingEbooks.com and sign up.

About the Author


David Beckwith is a three-generation native of Greenville, Mississippi, with a BBA and an MBA from Ole Miss. His parents owned an independent cash commodity trading firm which also cleared securities trades through Goodbody & Co. David spent 40 years in the securities business, the first half of his career with Bache & Co. and its successors, the second half with Morgan Stanley. He retired as a Senior Vice President with approximately $500 million in responsibilities. For 25 years he has served as an adjunct professor at five different universities.

His first book was a narrative nonfiction work published by the University of Alabama Press in 2009 entitled *A New Day In The Delta*. The Mississippi Institute of Arts and Letters chose it as the runner-up for nonfiction book of the year. The book is often compared to Pat Conroy's *The Water Is Wide*. David started writing the Will and Betsy Black Adventure Series in 2010.

Moving to Key West, David Beckwith was tapped to write a book review column for the Key West *Citizen*, which David continues to produce on a weekly basis.

www.ingramcontent.com/pod-product-compliance
Lightning Source LLC
Chambersburg PA
CBHW051147030726
47504CB00004B/1080